Praise for *The Refusal* ... *Series*

**Shortlisted for twenty-one romance book awards**

**Winner of EIGHT book awards:**

Winner of the Global Book Award, The Pinnacle Book Achievement Award, The Los Angeles Book Festival, The NYC Big Book Award, the 16th National Indie Excellence Awards, and The National Excellence in Romance Fiction Award for best first book.

—

*"Have you ever found yourself reading a really exceptional book and you find that you're forcing yourself to slow down on your reading because you simply don't want the book to end? That's exactly how I felt with Eve's debut novel."* - **Shannon Kuhn, Writer and ARC Reviewer**

*"I loved, loved, loved it! Jo and Janus have captured my heart. Definitely in my top 5 romance novels! I can't wait to see what comes next in the series. Eve M. Riley may be a debut author but she's right up there with the great romance authors. This book is a definite must read!"* - **Clare Murphy, Romance Author**

*"Let's all take a moment of silence now that I've finished this book and it's truly over until book two is released."* - **Beauty and The Book, Book Blogger**

*"I loved this book. I finished it in one day because I couldn't put it down."* - **All the Romance, Book Blog.**

*"I have to say, first of all, DAMN! This book was sensational!"* - **Pride Prejudice and Pups, Goodreads Reviewer**

*"Reading this book is like watching a really great romance film, with substance. The author writes with such energy and heart, the story ends way too soon . . . If you read one romance novel this year, make it The Refusal by Eve M. Riley."*- **Readers Views, Book Awards**

*"Run, do not walk, to your nearest retailer/ computer and get this book. Yes, it's that good. I'm not sure what else to say other than "devoured," "book hang-over," "amazing," and "need more." Did you get it yet? What? Not into tech heroes? Don't usually do modern romance? Listen, great writing is great writing--trust me, you'll be swept away."* - **Nicole Wells, Romance Author**

*"I barely even know how to send an email (lol). BUT-I loved ALL of it: the slow burn, the characters, the way the relationships developed."* - **Bookish in Town, Book Blog**

# THE OUTCAST

## *EVE M. RILEY*

*THE* TECHBOYS *SERIES*

EVEMRILEY.COM

Published by Eve M. Riley.

ISBN: 978-1-9163982-3-8

Ordering and Enquiries Information:
Quantity sales. Special discounts are available on quantity purchases by corporations, associations, and others.
For details, contact the author at www.evemriley.com

Cover design and interior formatting:
Mark Thomas / Coverness.com

# *NOTE TO THE READER*

*Warning: This book is intended for adults and incorporates sexual scenes.*

*The book also contains references to drugs and drug use, and explores themes around generational trauma. Several scenes in the book are based in a hospital and show patient resuscitation as well as discussions about patient death.*

*To Grace, my very own Techgirl.*

*I couldn't ask for a better daughter, or be prouder of the person you are.*

# PROLOGUE

There's an unconscious man in front of me on the hospital stretcher, and a familiar sickness washing through my stomach. His long messy hair is tied up in a knot on his head, and sinewy muscles rope all over his body, long winding tattoos running down his arms and up his neck. Young. Rail-thin. *What's wrong with you?* The notes on my clipboard swim in front of my eyes: airway, breathing, circulation. No obvious signs of trauma. The form says: "found lying on a bench next to Prospect Park."

*Breathe, Kate, breathe. You're all he's got.* Above the oxygen mask strapped to his face, long dark lashes sweep down his cheeks. Will everything I've worked for go down the tubes if I don't lose this jitteriness that appears every time the doors to the emergency department swing open?

The new nurse, whose name I've forgotten, starts attaching him to monitoring. I pull out my stethoscope and listen to his lungs and the thump-thump of his heart. I check his pulse, lift his mask to check his airway and smell his breath for alcohol, and finally add to his notes. The nurse finishes placing the sensors on his chest, and the monitors spring to life. No arrhythmia. His blood pressure is low, but not unreasonably so. He's either incredibly fit or … I study the wiry muscles again. *Okay.*

"Sir, can you hear me? Sir?" I say, bending down and touching his hand. I'm sure the paramedic tried this. His tattoos are a blend of script, scenes, and birds that swirl into elaborate patterns.

The nurse glances at me as she moves around the bed.

"What blood tests do you want?" she asks, chin jutting as she checks the canula in his right arm.

*Think, Kate. Think.*

"Do a full set," I say, stalling for time, and she frowns.

"I guess he could be hypoglycemic?" She raises her eyebrows.

Of course. *Sugar. Diabetes.* I grab the glucose meter and test strips. "Yes. Did the EMT find anything in his pockets that might indicate anything about him? Diabetes or allergies? His name? We might be able to contact family."

"I think they searched him."

"No other belongings? Nothing at the scene?"

She shakes her head. "We should check him for drugs."

Jesus. Young guy … unconscious … of course! Where's my head? "Good idea," I say. "Let's take a urine sample."

I've never done this on an unconscious patient before, but she nods as if she understands, and I stare down at his translucent skin. *I'm sorry you got an intern.*

"How did he get here?" I say. What a stupid question. I wonder how long he's been unconscious.

She shrugs. "Someone called an ambulance. They couldn't find anything wrong with him, put an IV in his arm, put him on oxygen because they were concerned about his breathing, and monitored his vital signs. They wondered if he'd been hit by a car, but there's no bruising."

I look up as John Harvey sticks his head around the curtain.

"All right in here?" he says.

I purse my lips at him, and he comes through to stand beside me. As an attending physician, he's bailed me out on more than one occasion, so I give him a quick rundown of where we are and what I've done. He nods, bending over the patient.

"Pupils? Reflexes? Breathing pattern?" He leans forward and lifts the guy's eyelids. "Hmmm. Pinprick pupils," he says.

And my stomach drops. I didn't check those, and we've covered them time and again. I bite my lip. *That's so basic, Kate!* Every day I'm skipping over stuff like this. I nod at him slowly.

But John's gaze just flicks over the monitor and then scans his body. "Normal stats, no obvious trauma … hmmm."

He gives a long sigh, like this night has been too long already. "Well, you seem to have followed protocol." And he's being generous here, so I open my mouth to protest, but he carries on, "unless this is something unusual or he has an unknown preexisting condition, then I'd guess narcotics of some kind." He peers over my shoulder at the form. "Prospect Park? Drugs then. Sometimes people bring a bug or tropical disease back from abroad because New York is a travel hub, but given where he was found … He's stable, is he?"

His eyes flicker over the monitors again.

"So far," I say.

He nods. "Then follow the drugs angle, give him some naloxone, and let's see where that gets us."

I need to do a whole ton of research on drugs along with brushing up on basic protocols.

*

I open my eyes to a low beeping noise and blink up at round stains on square ceiling tiles. *Not my apartment.* The bedcovers are bathed in a dim green light. Unmistakably a hospital. *Fuck.* How did I get here? I was on the street next to the park. As I sit up, the room tips alarmingly, and I grab at the side rail, swallowing down the nausea. Something tugs on my chest, and I look down at pads and wires before ripping them off one by one as an angry beeping starts from the bank of machines by the bed. Examining the catheter going into my arm, I apply pressure and pull it out: I'm very comfortable with how to get things out of my veins.

Hurried footsteps echo down the corridor, and a nurse bursts through the door.

"Sir, what are you doing? You need to …"

A blonde woman in navy scrubs follows the nurse into the room, and my eyes land on rose-colored lips then drift across her porcelain skin up to a pair of sharp blue eyes: unfriendly eyes that are fixed on me. I stare back at her.

"Sir …" she starts.

I shake my head at her, and the room swims again. *Fuck.* I put my head in my hands, still trying to keep the pressure on my elbow where I've ripped the IV drip out.

"I need to get out of here." My voice is full of phlegm, and I cough in an attempt to clear my throat. "I can't stay here. No insurance."

She walks over to me, and small soft hands lock around my wrists as she moves them downward and looks into my eyes. A buzz runs right up my arm.

"Are you dizzy?"

She takes something out of her pocket before shining a light in my eyes, and I blink, turning my head away from the glare.

"Turn around."

Something about the way she says it, or perhaps because she's wearing blue scrubs, makes me shift around on the bed. The movement causes another wave of nausea, and I gag. A plastic tray is thrust into my hands as the doctor shifts my hospital gown and the cold of her stethoscope presses on my bare back.

"I can't stop you from leaving, but I wouldn't recommend it," she murmurs. "You're really in no state to go anywhere. What's your name?"

"Fabian," I say, "Fabian Adramovich." I understand they need to know, but then the beautiful doctor will look me up, discover my history, and become even more disapproving. I have to leave. "Where are my clothes?"

The nurse heads out of the room, but the lovely doctor ignores this. "Did you take something? Do you have a health condition?"

"Why do you want to know?" Medical professionals always ask these questions. It's my body, my lifestyle. But all my response garners is an impatient sigh behind me.

"You were brought in here unconscious."

I peer at her over my shoulder and narrow my eyes. I've never liked the idea that my records are on some hospital database: The less information people hold about me the better. She shifts my gown back together and moves back as I turn around to face her.

"Do you need a diagnosis for your files?" The last word comes out with a derisive snort.

"I'm curious," she says quietly.

I shrug, and she folds her arms.

"If you're going to be a dick and leave this place when you're in this state"—she waves her arm at me—"then at least give us the satisfaction of knowing what happened. We've spent time on you, and you've had us all worried."

I laugh. Well, she doesn't give a damn about her bedside manner, but fuck I like it, I like assertive women. Tests, though—how much money might that involve? My chest tightens. I've had to fight so many legal battles recently that my meager funds are all but wiped out, and I am not going to Janus for another bailout.

I sigh. "I took something," I mumble, not meeting her eyes.

"What did you take?"

I just shrug, and she tips her head back to look at the ceiling.

"Seriously?"

"It's none of your business," I say, starting to cough. As I lean forward, I retch into the plastic tray again.

"A recreational drug?"

"There are other kinds?" I say, trying to smile.

And her face softens as she laughs. "And you want to leave?" she murmurs, taking the tray and handing me another one as her eyes scan my face.

How am I going to survive a journey home? Fuck, I can't think like that. I nod.

She presses her lips together. "Let me find some medications to take with you and give you something for the nausea before you go. Do you think you could keep some tablets down?"

I look up at her and nod. I was expecting a lecture and form filling. Not this. She gives me one last glance before disappearing. Queasiness rolls down my throat, so I lie down again and close my eyes: I need to gather myself for heading out. In minutes she's back, clutching packets of drugs in her hands.

"Okay," she says. "This is for the nausea." She places everything on the locker by the bed and passes me a tablet and a glass of water. My hand shakes as I lift it to my mouth. This better get me home before I pass out again.

She purses her lips, before handing me a small packet. "Here's some more anti-sickness meds to take home. I'm not sure what the base of what you've taken might be. We gave you naloxone which would have helped if what you took was opioid based. Cocaine is more difficult, although, if it was a serious overdose, you'd probably be dead by now."

My eyes roam her creamy skin and blonde lashes, and a reluctant grin breaks free. "How come you know so much about illegal drugs?"

She straightens and squares her shoulders. "We have to learn about all the drugs that end up in the human body; they're pretty well known to the medical profession." She shrugs, then grins, looking a bit bashful and leans in like she's sharing state secrets. "We actually have a database called TOXBASE that tells you all about drug interactions and the effects on the body. There are chemists that make their own stuff, but that's very rare … and dangerous. You're not a chemist, are you?" I shake my head at her. "Many things are poisons in quantity. You'd have to be good to make your own."

Well, fuck me. I glance at her name badge: Dr. Thurman. A doctor who happily swears in front of a patient. And could I be any more of a cliché? I think I'm doing something alternative, but the truth is I'd know a lot more if I could have been bothered to study medicine or even chemistry. Turns out Janus was right: I *am* an idiot.

*

Something about this guy has loosened my mouth. And three things have become abundantly clear: He's a real worry, he's smart, and he's cute. Why do intelligent guys mess around like this? The analyst in me is watching every muscle twitch under his decorated skin, but all the doctor in me sees is red flashing lights. I've only been working in the ER for a couple of weeks, but I've had a few people walk out after treatment, and I understand the money thing.

The nurse, whose name I've now remembered—Melanie—comes back in with a set of scrubs and pieces of the patient's clothing. She raises her eyebrows at me.

"Ah, we had to cut off your clothes," I say.

He blinks at me, and then his lips turn up in a wolfish grin, gray eyes dancing between his thick lashes. My cheeks burn.

"Did *you* do that?"

I fold my arms and open my mouth, but he shakes his head and flaps a hand at me, taking the scrubs Melanie is offering.

"It's fine. It's fine."

I learned in my first week here that we can't stop people from leaving; they just need to sign the piece of paper that absolves us of all responsibility in case they expire on the way home. I don't think this guy is going to die but getting home might be a struggle.

"Where do you live?"

"Brooklyn."

A slight tremor is running through his hands, and his eyes go unfocused every now and again. He's also wincing from the nausea cramps in his stomach, but they seem to be growing farther apart as the meds kick in. He strips off his hospital gown, and although I've seen his body already, I look away. What am I doing? I'm a doctor! Amusement flickers through his eyes. And there's something about him—the sharp stare, long ropey muscles over a skinny frame: He's like a panther, all coiled strength and danger. But cold memories of another man, a disaster like this one, seep up in me. Melanie coughs, raises her eyebrows at me, and hands me a clipboard.

"I need your signature on this form to say you've checked yourself out against medical advice."

He nods, and the way he inclines his head and doesn't ask any questions makes me think he's done this before. He pulls on the pants, not in the least bit embarrassed, and his right bicep bunches as he takes the clipboard from me and scribbles on the form. He knew where to sign; there was no hesitation, no looking for the box. Have I missed something here? I scan his body. Maybe these tattoos are hiding other things, marks on his skin? Dammit, I need to check whether we've got any notes on him on the system.

"Be careful, okay?" I say. "You're likely to pass out if you try and move too quickly; go as slow as you can and rest often. Can you afford a cab home?" The thought of him going under the tracks on a subway line because he lost his balance doesn't bear thinking about.

He nods and waves his hand. "Yeah. And thanks. Thanks for everything. I probably seem ungrateful, but I'm not. I just hate hospitals."

"Why's that?"

He shakes his head. "I'm fine. You don't need to worry about me."

I narrow my eyes at him. "That's not how this works. You're my patient. Promise me you'll come back if your symptoms deteriorate." I give him my best doctor smile, but he just rolls his lips together. I glance down at his feet as he stands, the small, strange marks all over them. His chest is still bare. Close up, the tattoos are some combination of a script I don't recognize plus tiny words that look like they're in English. He coughs, and my eyes shoot up to find him smiling at me. I swallow.

He grabs the top from the bed and shrugs it on, swaying a little, and I grab his elbow to steady him. His skin is smooth and damp under my palm.

"What made you want to be a doctor?" he asks.

I laugh. "I'm not quite one yet. I'm still training."

He stares at me. "Seriously? Jesus, I'd have been more worried if I'd known." His face relaxes into that grin again, and he winks, leaning forward conspiratorially. "Are you sure you gave me the right stuff?"

I shake my head, laughing. This is not the usual way I engage with patients at all. Why am I finding it so hard to maintain my professional distance?

He presses a shaky hand to his chest. "Shit, I'm impressed—given you're still learning."

I'm not going to tell him how little I really understand about drugs or how proficient I've become at bullshit since I started in the ER.

# THREE MONTHS LATER

# CHAPTER 1

## *Kate*

My phone buzzes as I'm standing by the desk looking at the patient list. As I glance down at the screen, the word *David* flashes across it. I don't hear from him often now, but he still sometimes calls.

"Hello."

"Kate!"

His familiar warm voice fills my ear like he's pressed against me whispering right into it, my hands on his warm skin and in his tousled hair. My chest aches, and I close my eyes.

"How are you?" He says, his voice a soft rumble. "How's it feel being a proper doctor?"

I don't want to talk to David. *But you knew that before you picked up the phone, Kate.* That's me, always responsible and buttoned down, doing the right thing. And I'm not a real doctor yet, I'm part way through the first year of a four-year residency to get my medical license. I roll my lips together and stare at the computer screen.

"Oh, you know." I give a fake laugh. "Real patients, rotating around different specialties, that kind of thing."

"Sounds like fun, and it's what you've wanted your whole life. That must be great. And how are you doing otherwise?"

So polite after everything—it's like we're strangers. And medicine no longer feels like what I've wanted to do my whole life.

"Did you call for a reason?"

There's a long silence on the other end of the phone.

"Just to say hello, to stay in touch with you, Kate." I hear a long, controlled breath on the other end. "After everything, it would feel very weird not to even be in touch with you."

I fiddle with the stethoscope around my neck. It's been two years since David and I ended things, and I'm over him now.

"Ms. Thurman." A nurse appears at my side, face slightly flushed.

"I've got to go. I'm at work."

"Call me later, Kate, yeah? It'd be good to catch up."

*

There's a rosy-red tint of dawn in the sky as the bus rattles over potholes and through green lights, and every bone in my body screams at me to lie down. Coming home from the nightshift is the best part of my day: The streets are empty, and there's seats on the bus. But my normal quiet contemplation of Manhattan is impossible this morning. Last night was nonstop carnage. Someone came in with an axe wound on his head and his back. A dispute with another guy, he said. Who does that? But that wasn't the worst incident of the night by any means: six cardiac arrests, four of them we couldn't save. Time stands still during an arrest: It's just you, a body, and the equipment.

All the medical rotations I did during college were fine, but working in emergency medicine is shining a cold harsh light on every decision: *Get it right*. There's no time for thinking or planning; just surviving on my nerves and minimal skills. Confronted with symptoms I don't understand, ice freezes my insides and my thoughts disappear down a rabbit hole: Did I make a mistake? Maybe medicine is not for me. Maybe I'm not smart enough.

The graffiti-covered rolling shutters whip past in a colored blur. A call from David! What the hell? A shiver runs down my spine. It must be six months since he last called. So many charming, troubled men, like that guy I treated months ago. Fabian. Yes. Fabian Adramovich. I wonder what happened to him. Those tattoos! I'm not into long hair, but his was curly and thick and he had all this scruff on his chin … A long breath seeps out between my teeth. I've dated sensible hard-working guys, interns and residents, but there's always something *missing*; and then all it takes is one look from a brooding, unstable guy and that fluttering starts inside. I rest my head on the cold windowpane and stare out at the empty streets. You think I'd know better by now; I don't need any more drama. The ER is more than enough.

When I'm back in the apartment, I putz around making toast and taking a long hot shower. I've been avoiding my email for days, so I sit down at my computer—God forbid there's something from my mom or, worse, my dad. And there are a few emails sitting in my inbox, none with the surname Thurman attached, though, thank God, but there is one from my residency director, Mike Rodriguez, that's headed "Emergency Medicine Internship," and I click to open it.

> *Dear Kate,*
>
> *Apologies for sending this on email, but I've not managed to catch you in the emergency department. I've had some feedback that you've been struggling with your current rotation, and I'd like to talk to you in the next few days. Please fix an appointment to come and see me.*
>
> *Mike.*

My breath whips away in a sharp exhale, and I slump back in my seat and stare at the words blurring on the screen. He wants to see me? I knew I wasn't doing that well, but I never thought that it was bad enough that I'd be called in to see the residency director. And I've been better lately, I know I have. Neil said only two weeks ago that my decision-making was much improved.

A wet splotch lands on my keyboard, followed by another, and I try and suck in a breath as my throat closes up. *Kleenex.* I stand, and in two steps I grab a handful from the box by my bed and blow my nose. *Holy shit.* All my life, I've fought tooth and nail to get through everything. I sink back down into the chair again and look at the words on the screen.

Nope. Nope. I click the email shut. What am I going to do now? Ugh. I think this calls for ice cream, maybe alcohol. *At 8 a.m., Kate?*

It's just the perfect end to the shittiest night.

# CHAPTER 2

## *Fabian*

The hit I've taken kicks in as I walk away from the fire burning in the metal drum. None of the guys down by the river even raise their heads. A damp spring chill seeps through my coat, and I pull it tighter around my body. I want to be on my own for this one. Out of the corner of my eye, I see one of the grubby prostitutes who hang around giving out free sex in return for drugs struggle to her feet. She pulls down her short skirt with a wrench before she follows me, and just like that, I've got a hard-on. I groan. My subconscious has gone from seeing her to fucking her before I've even rejected what a bad idea it is.

But almost as if she knows what effect the drug is having on me, she puts her hand on my arm and trails her fingers down to wrap them in mine. And I can't move away, everything fades in and out, and fuck, I'm so turned on. She grins at me knowingly, leaning forward to press her breasts to my chest.

"It will blow your mind," she says, licking her lips as she runs her hand down my stomach, squeezing my cock. Fuck. Why has she followed me? I've got nothing to offer her: no cash, no drugs. I try desperately to pull up some restraint, to drag my head back into the game.

"I've got nothing to give you," I say. Maybe this will encourage her to go away.

She strokes me through my jeans, and my whole body goes wired.

"You've got this. Most of them can't get it up—I have to work for it. I want one I don't have to work for."

My cock is alive and electric, and my mind snags on STDs, followed by what effect this drug is having on my penis: like Viagra on steroids. One of the most painful experiences of my life at college, and not something I want to repeat: My erection lasted three days. But my head is full of cotton wool, and, clearly sensing weakness, she pulls me into an archway out of sight of the bridge rattling overhead and swiftly unbuttons my jeans, taking my cock out and stroking. I squint down, groaning. I am desperate not to do this, but I can't halt the runaway train. In seconds, she's rolling a condom down my length, and thank God—because I've got no thoughts in my brain, no ability to keep myself safe.

Her hand slides lower wrapping around my balls, and something must kick in because, all of a sudden, I'm lifting her and pushing forward roughly. Then I'm inside, and she's hot and tight. It feels like the best sex I've ever had. I push her back against the brick wall of the bridge support, hard and fast, but she just winds around me and doesn't seem to want me to stop. Within seconds, I'm coming. My head goes light, and I gasp, tipping my neck back as everything narrows to a pinpoint. The world swims before it all goes black.

*

When my eyes open, I'm lying on my back on the ground, water dripping down from above, and I blink up at the brown metal beams, weeds growing out of the rusty rivets, turning my head toward the dark shadow of the path. As soon as I sit, the whole world swoops and dives, and I take a quick glance at my crotch—no penis hanging out, thank God—before collapsing back down. What the fuck? She clearly tucked me back in but didn't help me otherwise. I grin up at the overpass. My cock still feels hard, but I can't detect latex, so I slide my hand down my pants and, sure enough, she's tidied me up. A laugh bubbles up. I should thank her for that. *Jesus.* The traffic is a steady thump bump above me. How long have I been out? What the hell was I thinking? Why do I keep doing this shit? But I've no answer for any of it, so I spread my arms out on the thin grass as the damp seeps upward, cold seeping into my bones. A sharp shiver shoots up my spine, and I gingerly push myself up into a sitting position, propping my head in my hand as I look across the pathway to the river and the buildings beyond. Dark clouds are gathering, and the druggies and the girls are nowhere to be seen.

If I've missed that high, I'll be mad, but I'd love to take it with someone I was into. Like that uptight doctor from months ago who looked like she'd never put a foot wrong in her entire life, and the desire to fuck again washes through me, as strong as before. This stuff I've taken … I shake my head. Shuffling my ass around, I lean against the cold wall, but the earth tips sideways, so I clamp my hand to the brick, breathing hard. I hope that girl was okay. Underneath the bravado and the tricks, these street girls can be pretty messed up, and what in God's name was she doing, following me and asking for that?

I don't think I can stand unsupported, so I just stare out over the gray water. Eventually, I peer at my watch. 3 p.m.: I came out at twelve. Jesus, I must have been lying on the grass for what … an hour? More?

The shivering is taking hold now, and I need to head home. Pushing my boots out, I shuffle my body up the wall until I'm upright. Something about experiences like this make me feel alive: My blood is thundering through my veins, and my mind is buzzing. I rub my cock through my zipper, the desperation to come still there—crazy goddamn side effects. Leaning on the stone of the bridge, I drag myself up the steps from the river to the street, eyes darting up the road for a cab, and giddiness rolls through me when a yellow light appears almost immediately. I wave my arm and weave toward the cab as it pulls in.

Once the cabdriver's got my address, I sprawl in the back as the warmth starts to penetrate, stamping my feet and rubbing my cold stiff hands, staring out at the traffic and the swarm of people. Where do they all come from? Sounds fade in and out: the radio the driver is listening to, the honk of horns, the rumble and woosh of truck brakes behind. I absently pat my pockets for my wallet and come up empty. *What?* I shove my hands in my jacket, my jeans pocket. Nothing: no cell phone, no cards. *Oh, fucking hell:* She's cleaned me out. I slam my hand into the window, and the guy glances at me in the rearview mirror. *Fuck. This.* I can't afford to lose my phone, and Jesus, all my cards. My foot connects to the seat in front of me.

"Fuck!"

"Hey, what's your problem, buddy?" the cabbie shouts, and I shake my head at him, subsiding back and burying my head in my hands. Thank God it was a cheap smartphone, not my adapted one.

Jesus Christ! I've no cash, nothing to pay this taxi with. I let out a loud groan, and the cabdriver scowls at me in the rearview mirror. I've no family to speak of and, the type of life I lead, few friends. What the hell am I going to do? I eye up the taxi driver. Push comes to shove, I could outrun him—he must be forty pounds overweight. That fucking … *calm. Think.* I've two friends, two options here: Adam is the one who always bails me out, but he's in debt up to his eyeballs with his company, and I'm not burdening him anymore. It's going to have to be Janus.

"Take me to Maiden Lane and Front Street," I say, and the driver eyes me in the mirror again.

Taking a deep breath, I take him through the situation, and he shouts a lot—bitter complaints about wasters in New York and derogatory comments about guys with long hair and tattoos—before grunting unhappily at me. After some negotiation, he agrees to take me to Janus's offices with the promise of three times his normal fare. Then he threatens to come in after me and beat the shit out of me if I don't return. I'm sure he'd make good on his threat.

The receptionist eyes me as I approach the desk through the soaring marble-and-steel office entrance, smiling one of those false smiles that all receptionists seem to specialize in. I'm not quite steady on my feet, and she's fading in and out. I also realize, too late, that I'm filthy and disheveled like I've been sleeping on the street—which I guess I kind of have.

"Call Janus Phillips and tell him Fabian is downstairs and urgently needs his help. You need to get that message to him as soon as possible. I'm a personal friend."

Did that sound sensible? Resting my head on the marble of the desk, my legs start to shake, and I slide to the floor, leaning my back against the reception desk as my eyes close.

Then someone is urgently saying my name.

"Fabian. Fabian!"

My eyes pop open to find Janus crouched down beside me, all smart suit and tousled hair, eyebrows pulled tight. *I love this guy.* No one has ever cared about me like my two friends from college, and I'm warm with whatever karma brought them into my life. Janus is so all-round good, loyal as they come. I'm the hopeless friend, the guy he tolerates with an amazing amount of good grace. Something about the smart attire jars on me, though, and I grimace at him: I've probably seen him in a suit twice in my life.

"I've pulled you out of a meeting," I groan. "Shit, I'm sorry." I close my eyes, the world swinging around in an alarming fashion.

He laughs, and I crack open an eye to see his face has cleared and he's smiling. "It was bankers," he says. "Fucking spectacular timing."

He sits down next to me and rests his back against the reception desk, and out of the corner of my eye I notice people gawping at us. I'm sure they're not used to seeing the CEO sitting on the floor in the lobby with a down-and-out, and my lips curl up. Something is niggling at my brain though, and the more alert part of me remembers that Janus hates bankers.

"Wankers, did you say?"

He laughs loudly and I grin at him. We're a couple of fucking teenagers. I straighten.

"Shit, I came in a cab …"

But Janus puts his hand on my arm. "I sorted him out. He told me you had no cash and promised him ten times the fare to bring you here."

My eyes widen. "The fucker! I said three times!"

Janus grins and nods. “I’m just messing with you. He did say three—I gave him $100.”

“I’ll pay you back. Fuck, that’s more like five times the fare.”

The receptionist appears before us with two cappuccinos in fancy cups—saucers and everything. I can’t hold back the laugh now. This insane day just got officially hilarious. I’m sitting here in my filthy gear looking like God knows what, and someone is giving me bone china?

“I’ve got a story to tell you,” I say, inhaling as I knock back a huge gulp, wincing as it scalds the back of my throat. I need caffeine like I need to breathe. “You’ve got to go back to your meeting, though, right?”

Janus shakes his head. “Don’t worry about it, my afternoon is free.”

I narrow my eyes at him. “You fucking cancelled them, didn’t you?”

He turns to look at me, gaze roaming over my face, warm and grinning. “You’re my best friend, you idiot. You passed out in my reception—of course I ditched my goddamn meetings.”

Ugh. This shouldn’t be such a one-sided friendship.

“Would you like another coffee, sir?”

The sharp-suited receptionist in her pencil skirt is standing looking down at me, so I nod at her and she scampers away. We’re sitting in his fancy glass atrium, being served cappuccinos by professional, no doubt highly paid, people. Talk about going from one end of New York life to another.

“How much does all this shit cost?”

“What?” he says.

“This?” I swing my hand around at all the marble and chrome.

He laughs again. “I’ve no fucking idea. I’ve got a department that sorts all that stuff out.”

Janus was the relaxed, lively one at college, and my partner in crime. I reach out and tap his arm.

“Are you okay? Doesn’t it all drive you a bit bonkers?”

He looks down at his hands, blowing out a long breath and then shrugs, crossing one leg over the other on the floor. “Sometimes. But I’ve got a team of amazing people, which is the best feeling in the world. You know me, Fab, I love working with people."

I never did. I've always been a loner, skating around the edge of everything all the time: life, other people, eating, looking after myself. And now fucking look at the state of me.

"Have you heard any more from those hackers?" he says.

Two weeks ago, Jo and I chased a bunch of hackers out of Janus's company systems: Some people I'd annoyed started taking his company's systems down and wanted me delivered to them in return for stopping. Like Janus, I'm not holding out hope that we've heard the last of them.

"I can still get into their system, so I'm keeping an eye on it. I'll keep Jo in the loop."

He looks away, nodding.

"I took this drug that gave me an insane hard-on," I mumble into the steam rising from the rim of my cup as I take another gulp of coffee.

Janus doubles over laughing, just as another cappuccino appears in my peripheral vision. Heat rises up my cheeks; I hope to fuck she didn't hear that. I don't want to offend his employees. I'm already sitting like a hobo in his reception, so surely that's offensive enough. He seems to have the same thought as me.

"Can you stand?" he says.

"Why?" I ask as he pops to his feet, grinning down at me.

"I think a large burger is needed for this story."

My stomach emits a loud grumbling noise as I look up at him. I haven't eaten since yesterday morning. No wonder I'm feeling odd. I hate him paying for me, though—it makes me even more conscious of my self-destructing life—but today I know I'm going to let him feed me.

"How come I don't give a damn about money?" I mumble into my new cup of coffee.

I can't be with Janus and not compare his life to mine, and he hates this conversation. Oh, I could make some cash if I put my mind to it. The Russians would pay millions for some of the places I've hacked into and the documents I've seen. I'd be charged with treason, mind you, but even a little bit of industrial espionage could be extremely profitable. Maybe this South Africa thing I'm working on at the moment will turn up trumps.

Janus squats down again, laughing at my question. "Because you like your freedom?"

"I'm fed up working for the love of doing something."

"If you want to be a wage slave, come and work for me. I'd employ you like a shot, you know that." He narrows his eyes at me. "Are you short of money? You're okay?"

"Yeah, I'm fine." I wave my hand. I don't want Janus to find out how close to the edge of collapse I live all the time. The trouble is I want to do my own interesting projects, not the stuff that pays me well. And he's right: I do love the freedom of what I do.

# CHAPTER 3

## *Fabian*

A week later, I'm outside Janus's apartment building. Why was he so insistent that I come around for dinner tonight? I hope he hasn't invited anyone I'm going to have to talk to: I'm a hermit. I read about tech stuff that no one in their right mind would be interested in. I have no small talk, no views on politics. I don't even keep up with the news unless hacking reaches the front pages. Janus and Jo's conversation about companies, however—now that is a joy to listen to, along with their good-natured bickering. The everyday chitchat that's a million miles from my upbringing.

Maybe the incident at Janus's office has led to this invite: He has a tendency to step into my life when he's concerned. I push through the main door of the building, and the doorman lets me up in the elevator and then I'm down the dark-papered hallway, banging my fist on their metal door.

"Fucking trendies with your distressed industrial doors," I shout. "At least the vandalism on my apartment door is real."

Silence. Then feet shuffling on the other side. The door opens suddenly, and I take in the wide china-blue eyes and pink mouth of the woman standing there, as her hand flutters up to press against her chest. I shake my head, look at the number on the door, and then back at her, blinking. Her face relaxes as she holds out a hand.

"Hello, Mr. Adramovich," she says. "You're still alive."

She looks amazing out of her doctor's scrubs. The short blonde bob shines under the hall lights, and her eyes glint with mischief. A soft green dress is wrapped around an incredible body—she looks like a Greek goddess. Why oh why did I grab scruffy Levi's and a barely clean tee from the pile on my floor? Oh yeah, I was coming to a friend's house, and it didn't matter. Fucking Janus—he might have warned me.

Like I summoned him, Janus appears behind her with a small frown, gaze flicking back and forth between us. He holds out a hand for the bottle of wine I'm carrying.

"You two have met?"

I shrug, and she raises an eyebrow at me as if to say, 'Well?' So, I turn to him and say, "The lovely doctor here treated me in the ER a few months ago."

Janus makes a face at me, grabbing my arm as he pulls me into the warm apartment. The smell of spices and roasting meat curls around me, and my mouth waters. Today was another day of hours of coding and forgetting about food.

"Now why doesn't that surprise me? Is there an ER staff member in New York you haven't met?"

"Fuck off," I say.

Janus wraps a friendly arm around my doctor, and I eye his hand on her shoulder. "Tell us how many times you've been admitted over the last six months?"

I raise my eyebrows. "Classified information, man."

This is a terrible joke from college that has worn smooth over time like a pebble; if I'd taken enough illegal substances to be arrested, that was always my response.

She raises an eyebrow as she surveys me as if she's asking for permission, and when I nod, she folds her arms and says, "The notes on the system said twelve times."

And something about the slightly sanctimonious tone of her voice and the folded arms gets my back up. Is this woman with a stick up her ass really the same person I met in the ER?

I widen my eyes at her. "Dear God, is that all? That's less than once every couple of weeks. I'm slipping. Becoming a square. I need to go on a proper bender; I wasn't sick enough on the last one."

Her eyes soften, crinkling into laughter, and the way they dance around my face makes all the tension seep away. It's a glimpse of what lies beneath the blue scrubs; all her secrets shimmering below the surface like light catching a fish in water. I'm guessing she's a sweetheart under that upright pillar-of-society exterior.

"Doesn't passing out classify it as a real bender?"

And something about the way she says the words "real bender" with relish makes me think of sex and what she might look like out of her dress.

I shake my head and grin. "No, I think a real one would be waking up having lost two days with three women in your bed."

Janus raises his eyebrows. Okay, I get it. I don't talk to women this much. I can't stand the chat about friends (I don't have any) or celebrity gossip (who's even interested?), or TV shows (I don't watch any). Jo is the one notable exception to this; I could chat to her for hours. But I certainly don't flirt. Janus alternates between telling me I'm a hermit and a sexist pig, and he's closer to the truth on both counts than I'd care to admit.

"So," Janus says, "let me make proper introductions since the last time you were introduced you were clearly horizontal." He winks at me, and I groan.

"Tell me you're not going to make jokes like that all night."

"If he does, I'll kneecap him," my doctor says, and here's some more of the dry, cool person I met in the ER.

"And if you do, you'll be qualified to fix it," I say, and the throaty laugh she makes in response is like a depth charge going off inside me. *Fabian, you don't get to be thrilled, you dick; she's way above your league.* My level is more like that prostitute down by the riverside, and I'm still trying to sort that mess with my cards.

"I'm Kate Thurman. Jo and I were at college together," she says, holding out her hand.

As I wrap my fingers around hers, a zing runs up my arm. Her palm is warm and soft, and she blinks down at our hands with a small smile on her face.

"Well, Dr. Thurman, you know who I am"—I pull her hand forward and lean into her—"intimately." This gets me an eye roll. "Nice to meet you out of uniform, Kate."

Her small pink lips stretch wider, and I smile back, still holding her hand.

"I was at college with Janus," I add.

"Oh!" she says. "Did you study tech, too?"

"Well …" I say, my mind flashing back to the unattended lectures and the litany of abuse I received from my professors. "I'm a programmer."

Janus snorts. "Study! I'm not sure you went to a single lecture or even read a book." He leans in to whisper to Kate. "And he's still the best programmer I've ever met. He does all this stuff for other people too, but I bet he won't let me talk about that either."

"Moving on," I say and Janus laughs.

I look down, frowning. I haven't let go of Kate's hand yet. I can't seem to bring myself to do it.

"And you have a death wish?" she asks, smiling and squeezing my fingers, and I'm aware that she means my propensity to experiment with drugs, but I can't resist teasing her a little.

"Why? Are you a black belt who's going to take me down for holding your hand a bit too long?"

I've not flirted for a decade, and what's coming out of my mouth feels old and rusty and makes me want to disappear into the floor. But Janus's astonishment is burning a path down my left-hand side and it makes me want to press a bit further, to show him I can do this shit.

Kate wraps her fingers more intimately around mine, her skin warm against my hand. "I thought I was the one holding on to your hand?" she says softly, and my laugh catches me somewhere deep and empty.

"Beer?" Janus asks, and my eyes flick down to Kate's as I purse my lips.

"You've nothing stronger?" I say.

Janus gestures to Kate to lead the way, and I reluctantly let go of her hand.

Jo appears at the end of the kitchen island, her face breaking into a big grin. I'm still envious that Janus got her; she's a tech security expert with long trailing red hair and a petite frame—and as sharp as they come. He had to pull out all the stops to win her, and he's head over heels, so I don't begrudge him her really. I grab hold of her and spin her around as she shrieks, small nails digging into my shoulders.

"Tell me some amazing tech fact," I say, putting her back on the floor.

"Oh no," Kate says from behind me. "Jo's already told me all about this game you play, and I'm here with three techies. Have mercy on me. We're only playing if we can include medical facts as well."

"Okay," I say, turning toward her. "Let's try a different game. Sex facts."

A pink blush starts on Kate's neck, but Janus lets out a loud groan as he opens a wall cupboard and pulls out some wine glasses. I prop myself back against the pale wood cupboards that face out over the island toward the lounge.

"Didn't we play this game one night in college?" Janus says.

I ignore him and bowl right on in. "Did you know a quarter of all penises are bent when erect?"

"I've seen more men's penises than I care to think of," mutters Kate, and my mind screeches to a halt as we all turn toward her.

"What?" she says as the pink continues to climb up her neck, and she glances around all our faces. "Hello? I *do* work in the ER."

"But how many erect ones?" I say, raising an eyebrow, and her unrestrained smile bursts through again.

"Not a lot of them are erect when I examine them. Most guys are so terrified of what a medical professional might do to their penis that they—their penises, I mean—shrivel up. Either that or most men have tiny penises."

Janus and I catch each other's eyes. I'm sure we're thinking the exact same thing: We've exaggerated our size, and we've been very nervous around doctors. Something warm creeps through me. Home was a terrifying place for me, and in this safe apartment with easy company, the kernel that always sits tight inside starts to unwind.

Janus peers into the oven while Jo opens the wine and pours. Alcohol isn't my drug of choice, so there's the risk I'll get drunk embarrassingly fast like I usually do.

"This reminds me of that old joke: Why are women so bad at parking?" Jo says.

"Why?" says Janus, looking up from where he's examining a pot on the stovetop.

"Because they've been lied to about what eight inches looks like their entire lives."

I snigger at this as Kate says, "Actually, the average length of the erect penis is 5.16 inches."

Like slow motion in a movie, all three of us turn toward her. I'm thinking: *No, that can't be right*. Janus's nose is scrunched up like the same thing has occurred to him. She grins proudly despite the blush staining her cheeks. She's so fucking cute.

"What? I had to learn this stuff! I'm glad my medical training is coming in useful—for this game at least," she says, slugging back her wine.

Janus leans in to kiss Jo. "Aren't you lucky you're getting something so much better than average, honey?"

She snaps at him with a dish towel.

"I'm saying nothing," I say, holding up my hands.

"Yeah, that's because you've got less than me, man."

I grin at him. "How about we take them out and measure them?"

We did this one drunken night in college, and my memory was that I won by an eighth of an inch. The girl we were with was adjudicating, and for some reason she wanted to go to bed with me rather than Janus; the first and only time that's happened.

"I wouldn't mind judging that. Sounds like the perfect Friday night, measuring two hot guys' penises," Kate says, and even though this conversation is embarrassing her, she's going down this road farther than any of us. The risks she's taking here … I shake my head.

*Wait a moment, she thinks I'm hot?*

"Isn't it penii?" Jo chips in.

"What is the collective noun for penises?" Kate adds.

Janus whips out his phone and sips his wine and scrolls then snorts. "A clutch?"

"No way," I say, peering over his shoulder.

Janus opens more windows and types something in. "Okay, here's another fact: There are seven calories in a teaspoon of semen."

Jo shrieks in disgust. "Urgh, gross! Who started this game?"

"Glad to hear I'm not risking my diet on a regular basis," Kate says, her flush subsiding somewhat. But now I'm riveted by the idea of her giving oral sex to someone, that someone being me. Of grabbing on to that silky hair while she … *Woah, woah! Knock it off!* I surreptitiously adjust my jeans. Does this mean she's with someone or having a lot of booty calls? My stomach plummets.

"Kate!" Jo growls.

"Okay, okay. I'll stop being bad," she says, rolling her eyes.

I blink at her, grinning. "Oh, please don't," I say, and she grins back at me, eyes locking with mine. *Fuck.* She clears her throat and turns to where Jo is standing by the stovetop, breaking the spell.

"What can I do, Jo?" she says, eyes flickering over the pans.

Janus is still scrolling on his phone, and I ease forward to stand beside her, placing my glass of wine on the countertop. Jo hands us serving dishes full of vegetables, gesturing at the pale wooden table and dangling lights beyond the island. Side lamps illuminate the comfy couches and thick rugs, and outside the windows that run along the far wall, Manhattan twinkles at me invitingly. By the time everything is laid out and we sink into our seats, Janus has managed to dig up another fact.

"Okay, here it is," he says. "In a magazine survey, given the choice, 75 percent of readers said they would prefer to sleep with one man in their lifetime rather than have sex with a hundred men."

"No surprise," says Jo. "Who'd want to put up with a hundred guys' egos? Jesus."

"I'm definitely a one-woman guy," I say, holding up a hand, and Kate's eyes snap to me. She's surprised? Surely most people want to find that significant person. I can't resist teasing a little, though. "Imagine all the shit you'd have to take from that many women, all that jabbering."

Janus glances at me. "Yeah, even talking to one woman … you know, having to act like you're listening when you're really not."

I link my hands behind my head and lean back into my chair. "The tuning out while still nodding your head is a real skill," I say, taking the ball and running with it.

"All the talk about shopping," he says, looking at the ceiling.

"All the advice about tech," Jo murmurs, handing a well-stacked plate over to me. I inhale the most delicious beef stew I've ever smelt, and my stomach growls.

I catch Kate's grin as she dips her head. "Oh yes! The having to act like the size of their penis is okay to protect their egos, the pretending they're good in bed."

"Just a minute," I say, "the pretending …?"

"Oh yeah," says Jo, interrupting me. "Faking orgasm."

This is too much for Janus. He puts his cutlery down and turns to frown at her. "You have never faked it with me." He states this categorically, and my mouth curls up.

She laughs, wrinkling her nose at him. "That would be telling," she says with a wink, and he pins her with a stare, jaw tight. There are going to be words behind closed doors later. Honestly, I love these two, they're so cute, and, as I shift my eyes away from them, I catch Kate studying me. Her eyes drop down to the plate in front of her, and I try and tamp down the answering vibration in my body.

"Guys," I say, holding up my hands, "too much talk about sex."

"Is there even such a thing?" Jo says, lifting a forkful to her mouth.

Kate shakes her head and smiles. “I think the men are feeling threatened,” and she reaches out and pats my arm over the table.

And in this moment, I know I’m royally fucked. I really like this woman, and there’s no way on earth I’m good enough for her.

# CHAPTER 4

## *Kate*

Heads lift up around me as I pull out the chair and it scrapes across the gleaming floor of the McNally Jackson Café, and Jo looks up from her phone. Jo and I became friends as freshmen at NYU, along with Liss, who I shared a dorm with. We adopted Jo because she lived next door and had a terrible roommate, and I think she ended up hanging out in our room more than we did. Jo now lives in Brooklyn, and I'm still in the same apartment Liss and I shared in sophomore year. Liss intermittently shares it with me, but she's been away in Africa since January. Jo's built a company out of helping people out at college, and I'm slightly envious, but it's a good envy. And I know things always look easier from the outside: She gripes about how hard it is doing her own thing, and I tell her how stressful it is in medicine.

She puts down her phone and taps my hand. "Before we talk about other things," she says as I sink into a seat opposite her. "I want to find out what's happened about that email?"

After I'd eaten a ton of ice cream, I sent Mike's email on to her and later cried on her shoulder.

"Okay, okay, Mom," I say. "I talked to Mike. He was very supportive, but a few people have passed on to him that I'm below proficiency, he didn't say who. One of the attendings then took me through case by case where I'd not done what was expected. That was really hard to hear … He said I lacked confidence and didn't ask enough questions or ask for help when I needed it." I blow out a long breath.

"Oh God, Kate, that sounds shit."

"I've always done okay at school and on my previous rotations. What he said was just so negative. It's the first time in my life I've failed so badly."

"I'm sure you're not doing badly," she says, stoutly. "What do they do in situations like this?"

"I might have to redo the rotation or the year, or they could fire me. None of it's good."

"Or you might get better? You can ask questions or ask for help, can't you?"

"How do I get my confidence up, though? I don't know why I struggle so much in the ER. Maybe I've reached my limit."

But Jo just shakes her head. "Don't think like that. You just don't know. You've not failed yet."

I know there are people who don't anticipate the worst, but how do they do it?

"I'm sorry, Kate. Can I do anything to help?"

I shake my head. "Listening is good."

She eyes me for two beats then nods, leans forward, and folds her arms with a smile. "On a more positive note, our Mr. Adramovich is the guy you told me about who you treated in the ER months ago. How exciting is that!"

I loop my bag over the back of my chair, not meeting her eyes. I'm going to let her have that subject change. With my hand in Fabian's the other night, my body vibrated like I was plugged into a socket. I've never felt this kind of zinging heat before. Dammit, Jo can always read me better than anyone.

"I don't think that I—"

"Oh, come on!" she says, laughing. "All those loaded looks? All that chitchat? You guys cut Janus and me completely out of the discussion over dinner."

I curl away. The questions he asked: What did it feel like cutting someone open? What was it like when someone died? How do you deal with the emotion? What about all that *blood*. No one ever asks about things like that!

And was I *that* obvious? But Jo's grinning. "He seemed just as into you by the way. Janus says he's never seen him like that with a woman, hasn't witnessed him flirting like that … *ever*." "Ever" rolls around on her tongue like she's relishing it.

My chest is hot and tight as I smile at my lovely, helpful, curious friend. She's not my family, or someone out to judge me, and she helped me through the aftermath of David. She's not going to turn this into something I can't handle.

"How come I haven't met him before?" I try and deflect. "I mean you and Janus are still pretty new but …"

"From what I can gather from Janus, Fabian's a recluse. I only got to meet him because he worked with me on that hack into Janus's company. I don't think he socializes much. Fabian turned up at his office in a bit of a state over a week ago, and Janus was worried about him, so he leaned on him to come to dinner."

"What kind of state?"

"I think he'd taken something."

"Okay," I say, staring out the window behind her. He was cagey when I saw him in the ER. What does he take? But I guess the more interesting question, though, is why? The sunlight of a warm May day bounces off the sidewalk, warmth burning into every crevice, chasing away any sign of the ice and cold we've sat through for months.

Jo taps her spoon against her cup. "Tell me what you like about him."

I survey her red hair and freckles: *confession time.*

"Perhaps I should start with the tattoos that snake around that lean body of his, which I've seen all of by the way." I waggle my eyebrows, and Jo laughs. "He's intense, laser-focused when you're talking to him with those gray eyes that figure everything out, plus of course the scruff and the long curly hair …"

"Yes, I'm getting it," Jo says, nodding and smiling.

"But really"—I pause for effect—"it's his hands."

Her mouth forms a perfect O.

"The long tapering fingers, the way he moves them when he's talking, drums them against his thigh. The short square nails. That script tattoo all the way down the outside of his left hand that runs up his arm and disappears." I laugh, shivering.

Jo bites her lip. "There's something about Janus's hands, too."

Is this a thing? A great thing for women everywhere, like reaching the Promised Land? I lean forward conspiratorially. "Programmer hands," I whisper.

She snorts just as she lifts her coffee to her mouth, and brown liquid sprays all over the tabletop.

"Oh my God!" She giggles, grabbing a napkin and plopping it onto the biggest puddle. I bend down and pull a tissue from my purse, dabbing up the remaining spots.

"Sorry about that." She reaches out and squeezes my arm. "We just came up with that! Programmer hands are a *thing*."

Her eyes drift off to the doorway, and I can tell she's reliving something about Janus right now, and I shake my head at her. I don't want to picture what he might do to her with his hands, and I really don't want to think about what Fabian could do to me with his. I don't need to start imagining …

"What other profession might have hands that …?" Jo starts, and oh, this is why she's one of my best friends. I want to bounce over the table and hug her.

"Rock climbing?"

"Oh, you're so bad!" She tips forward, hugging her arms around her tiny body, before rocking back. "Climbers need all this strength in their fingers. I think I've read somewhere that they do specific exercises so they can pull themselves up. And they're roughened, too, from all the rock abrasion …"

"Imagine what sex would be like with a guy like that."

"I think it would blow my head off," she says, and we're both quiet for a minute. How many rock climbers have I met? What talents might they have that I have never appreciated? Aside from insane muscles and the ability to scale impossible cliffs.

"Not a lot of climbers based in Manhattan," I mutter just as she says:

"You need some profession where they have to use their tongue." She's grinning like an idiot now, and I snort into my drink, narrowly avoiding a repeat of the earlier mishap. She has no filter.

"You're filthy." But I'm nodding, too. "I can't think of any sport that requires a man to use his tongue that much."

"There should be," she says. "How amazing would that be?"

"The people who run these sporting events are sadly lacking in imagination. What about those people that do eating challenges, like burgers on strings or something?"

Jo laughs. "Holy shit, yes. Strong lips, tongue and jaw, I guess, for a challenge like that." She shakes her head at me. "Burgers on strings? Where did that come from?"

"No idea."

"Do you think we could devise some exercises for guys to do … I'm going to suggest it to Janus."

I freeze. "Oh God! No way, Jo. Don't you dare tell him what I said about Fabian. I'll never hear the end of it."

She shakes her head, standing up to head over to the counter. "I know: He's like a dog with a bone when he gets hold of something. I won't say anything to him. I promise."

I eye up the people at the next table. How much have they heard?

"Seriously, though, what are you going to do about Fabian?" she says when she returns, placing a flapjack in the middle of the table. She slides into her seat and cuts it up, and I absently pick up a piece, pop it in my mouth and chew.

"Oh God, Jo, nothing. Absolutely nothing."

"But why? He'd be perfect for you."

I stare at her again. "You're kidding me, right? You *do* remember David?"

I met David at college, and he was my biggest champion, and maybe that's why he was so addictive. He was one of those people who paid attention from the first moment you talked to him. I thought it was because of me: It took me a while to realize he was that way with everyone.

"Fabian is so not David. David was a slimeball."

"Well, thanks for telling me now," I grumble, though I know I'm not being fair. Jo *was* dubious about David. She saw how he was trying to be good for me, and worried that the effort would fall apart. But why wouldn't the same thing happen with Fabian? "They are so alike, that whole car-crash, bad-boy thing. I can't do that again, Jo. I've just got myself back together."

At the end, when I found out what David had done, I realized how often he would say he had told me something and that I must have forgotten. *Lies by omission.* Even now I wonder whether I got certain things wrong, the self-doubt pressing in around my heart. I was too honest, too open, and he exploited that. It felt so real, so right what we shared. The pain hits me sharp beneath my ribs.

Jo shakes her head. "I don't think that Fabian's like David. Janus has known him a long time. I think he's a gray wolf."

"A *what*?"

"A gray wolf—they mate for life."

"Where do you come up with all this stuff?"

"I watch too many wildlife programs when I'm at home and need to zone out and forget about networks and security."

The light reflects off the red and purple storefronts opposite. Two women are laughing as they exit, one peering into a shopping bag. Manhattan suddenly feels full of the possibilities of spring. Is she right? An awful wild hope claws up my chest that in the last few years I've buried under my career and my medical degree. But I don't want to reawaken the desire for *that* connection, for an *amazing guy*. My expectations are stupidly high, and it sits raw in my gut that David put that expectation there, and then wasn't that person. Guys like the one I want don't exist.

Jo must read something in my face because she reaches out and touches my hand. "I understand, Kate, and I have the utmost sympathy for you. But don't be held back by David or your goddamn parents, okay? They demand so much of you, don't give them your relationships with other people as well. Maybe

David wasn't the right guy, but perhaps you'll find someone like him who *will* be right for you."

I've sworn to myself that I'm not going down that road again. Men like this, who derail their own lives and carry everyone else along for the ride, the ones who never think about other people, are a liability. I'm touched that she sees me and the pressure from my parents so clearly, that she's stuck her neck out to be blunt with me, but the last thing I need is a gray wolf.

"I won't," I say. "I promise I won't."

# CHAPTER 5

## *Kate*

I glance down at the number making my phone vibrate. *Mom*. Over half of my family work in medicine, and although that's good because we can discuss problems and cases, their combined expertise is impossible to live up to. There was never any question about what I'd do for my career, and I'm fine with it; most of the time, I love it. But I never want to take their calls. Oh, I'm sure they care in their own peculiar way, but it all comes with a raft of expectations. Conversations are loaded: They appear to demonstrate a concern for me, but they also burrow down into my life until I'm pinned against a wall with nowhere to go. And I'm struggling in the ER, so talking to them could just make it all worse. I'm not having panic attacks, I remind myself firmly as I pick up the phone.

"Mom."

"Sweetheart," she says. "How are you? How's emergency medicine?"

I examine the pale blue paint on the kitchen wall. My mom rarely phones for a social chat. As a family physician, she's often preoccupied with patients, and I understand this. Someone who's sick always takes precedence. There are people who would tell you that your family should come first, but the person I'm saving has loved ones too, right? Why should I put mine before theirs?

I give her an update on what I'm doing, omitting any references to problems in the ER or Janus and Jo, or a certain guy who seems to be occupying a lot of my thoughts.

"How's that lovely friend of yours … Jo? The one who works in technology?"

My mom says "technology" with a weird emphasis; like tech is some new-fangled thing that young people do that needs to be endured, as if she doesn't use it to treat her patients and work with it every day of her life.

"She's doing well. I was round there the other night for a meal."

"Oh! How lovely of her to feed you."

"Her business is going well," I say, and I stare at the pile of mail sitting on the kitchen counter, the textbooks waiting for me on the table. Jo has finished college and has a successful company and has hooked one of the best men I've ever met. No one would describe Fabian as a good man. A lunatic perhaps, even dangerous … but good? No. But unfortunately, that just makes him all the more attractive. Ugh. I need to stop with the Fabian daydreaming.

"That's nice. Not quite medicine though, is it, darling?"

I grin at the blue wall now. I could debate that with her, and sometimes winding her up by reminding her of very successful people who left education at sixteen is fun. Today, however, I don't get a chance.

"Anyway, I'm calling about Javier's wedding, darling. It's a month away now and well … your aunt called me."

I inwardly groan as I move toward the lounge looking for the embossed cream invite—the kind of thing you'd put behind a clock or above a fireplace if you had one, which I don't! Javier is my cousin, and we've always had this insanely competitive relationship with my uncle's family: The stories are legendary about my dad and his brother when they were young. I'm sure I've stuffed the invite in a drawer to forget about it, and I move through to my bedroom, opening and closing drawers, my hands damp and slipping on the handles. A month! Where is the damn thing? Where is this wedding even going to be?

My father will want to demonstrate how well we're all doing. This is the first reason I hadn't responded; the second is that Javier works on Wall Street and is a pretentious asshole. I'm failing at Emergency Room 101. How can I sit with them all and pretend everything's fine? I grip my phone tighter. My mother is so proud of how many of us have chosen to be doctors, and there'll be so much questioning and posturing. *Yuck.*

"Are you thinking of bringing anyone?"

My mom's voice is hesitant, and my search falters. Oh God! Why didn't this occur to me? Ever since an ex answered my phone early one morning (so clearly sleeping with her daughter) and she gave him the third degree about his major (art, for which he scored, like, minus three million points) and his prospects (which he didn't take too kindly to), I have not mentioned another man in my life. The artist, Euan, and I split up not long after. He was chilled and fun, but he started to question why he was with me after my mom gave him a grilling.

My mother and I dance around things in an effort to keep the peace, but not Euan: I blamed her when we broke up. Maybe it wasn't fair of me. I don't think the relationship would have lasted, but the way he was treated made my blood boil. He was lovely and kind, and they made him feel inadequate. I didn't tell them about the David debacle, and I thank my lucky stars for whatever made me keep that romance out of the parental spotlight when I was so besotted with him.

"Of course, Tod is coming with his family. Seb is bringing his girlfriend, and I think Georgie has invited her latest man."

Bless my siblings. And Georgie is seeing someone? Why didn't I know this? I rub my eyes, and it's on the tip of my tongue to say something, but I don't want to give my mother an in with Georgie: She wouldn't thank me. I need to call her. Tod is my eldest brother, an amazing surgeon and married to the good-natured Lily, with a pair of recently born twins—my first, gorgeous, nephews. Seb has been with the girl he's with since he graduated and is refusing to marry her, much to my parents' chagrin.

But Georgie is our rebel. As the youngest, she rejected all the Thurman academic pressure by first becoming a hippy, then spurning college and turning into an environmental activist. I envy her. But as all this news sinks in, I suddenly realize why my mother has called. Fucking hell. Why is everything a competition in this family? She wants me to bring someone, so I don't stand out among my siblings, so it looks like every part of my life is successful.

I squeeze my eyes shut. "There is someone I was thinking of bringing," I say, my throat dry, and as soon as the words are out of my mouth, I want to kick myself.

"Wonderful, darling," she says, voice light. "I'll let your uncle know. Lovely to talk to you and catch up."

Mission accomplished, she hangs up. I sit and turn the phone over in my hand. Does anyone else have calls like this from their mother? Do they hang up without an "I love you"? Did we catch up? I told my mom I was taking someone to Javier's wedding: who is that going to be? The blue wall looms over me, the abundant herbs running along the kitchen windowsill that I've been keeping alive for Liss while she's been in Africa. Complete blank. I don't have any male friends. I push up from my chair, fill the kettle with water, and place it on the stovetop.

I press the button to call Georgie, but it goes straight to voicemail. My parents would think they'd died and gone to heaven if there was the prospect of me marrying someone from college or from the hospital. *Another doctor, darling—how wonderful!* I skim over the guys I know better than just a nod in the hallway: nope. They'd all think this was the oddest thing in the world to ask them to do.

And despite the flirting at dinner the other night, I suspect Fabian will have figured out by now how uptight I am. I was never the cool, hippy chick who I can see would be much more his speed; I can really see him with someone wild and fun. And I absolutely don't want to go there, I remind myself, but that still doesn't solve the problem of the hole I've just dug myself into.

# CHAPTER 6

## *Kate*

A week later, I shoot out of the ER to escape a night where I lost count of the patients who didn't make it, and I jump onto a bus to go and meet Jo and Liss. My God! *Liss.* Liss is back. I text Jo that I'll be there in thirty minutes, and collapse into a seat beside a large man who's breathing heavily, eyes closed. I watch the in-out in-out of his chest, before giving myself a shake and staring out of the window.

Liss arrived back in New York yesterday from her water project in Africa, and the apartment has been dead without her live-wire presence. She did a degree in civil engineering, but decided to use it in the developing world, so now she disappears off to Africa as often as she can, and I have a rotation of temporary roommates. Her family is a lot like mine. I'm the conformist; she's the rebel like Georgie. But where my sister is a campaigner, Liss is a builder, never happier than when she's knee-deep in dirt and sweating on a construction site. I don't think her father has ever forgiven her for using her degree to do good in the world.

I scroll through my phone, grinning as I find the place I'm meeting them.

Liss has chosen a typical hipster hangout close to the apartment, all nonsense detox juices and chai tea, and the medic in me is already rolling my eyes. They charge a fortune for flavored water.

"Oh my God! Look at you!" she bursts out when I arrive, almost leaping over the table to hug me as my arms come around her, and my eyes prick, inhaling her warm scent of earth and patchouli. Student nights dance before my eyes, both of us in our tiny apartment with whatever drink she'd forced on me in an effort to loosen me up. Jo grins at the pair of us as Liss steps back and tracks me up and down. "God, how straight up you are! You look like a real doctor, K."

I laugh as the stress of attempting to keep everyone alive, of trying not to worry too much that I've made some awful mistake, washes out like the tide. Have I changed that much in four months?

As is Liss's way, I've no time to breathe before she launches right into it.

"Oh my God, K, you have to save me." She squeezes my hand. "I was just telling Jo. I've got to move out of the parents' house. I've been back twenty-four hours, and they are already on my back. "When are you going to do something decent with your degree?' Yada. Yada. Yesterday my father said, 'I don't think you're going to make very much money in Africa, Alicia.'"

I laugh. "What did he say when you told him that wasn't the objective?"

"You see this is what I love about you guys." She circles a long finger between Jo and me. "You understand! When I told my dad the aim was to make a difference, he said, 'Well, you can't live off making a difference, Alicia,' and we got into a big argument about what 'making a contribution to society' meant." She rolls her eyes.

"You can come and camp on my couch," Jo says.

"Or come back to the apartment," I say. "You can camp on my floor. In fact, your old room might even be up for grabs. I've not seen Lucy, who took your room, for ages. How long are you back for?"

"Actually," she says, eyes meeting mine, "moving back into the apartment would be amazing. I'd love to be close to campus. I ran out of money, and I need to save up again before I can go back. That's why I'm at home. That's why my parents are giving me such earache; they think I'm here to start planning and building a career." She makes a face. "I've got a temporary job with my old professor helping in the department. They want someone to fill in while one of the staff members is on maternity leave."

"God, that sounds perfect," Jo breathes.

"I know, right? And the pay is good, too. It was a total fluke. I was heading to the library to look at some research on irrigation design, and I ran into him."

I study Liss's glowing face and deep tan. She's pursuing her life's dream while here I am treading water, floundering in my first job.

"You look so brown and healthy," I say, and she doubles up laughing.

"Oh no way! I'm tanned because, duh it's Africa! And I'm thin because I've had the most god-awful illnesses. There are drugs for all the ones the West is familiar with, but Africa has other bugs and they're dreadful. I have been through the mill physically."

My brain kicks into full gear. "Are you okay? Do you want me to check you over? What meds have you been given?"

She grins at me and waves her hand. "Stop being a doctor, I'm fine."

"Can't stop doing that," I mutter, and although I'm itching to examine her and get all the details and sort her out, I tamp it down. What would it be like to be a medic out there?

Liss points a finger at me. "Don't even think about working in Africa. A lot of the Western doctors out there"—she shakes her head—"they burn out so fast. The day-to-day decisions you make about people who are starving and dehydrated … they're tough. Don't get me wrong, the work is important, and it sounds awful to say it, but you have to be realistic about the toll it takes." I grimace at this: I already feel burned-out working in the ER. I've learned really fast that you can't save everyone.

I glance over at the line at the counter and catch a guy looking over at us. He's kind of cute but posh looking in his smart suit and my mind immediately leaps to Javier.

"Oh God, I've got my own awful parent story."

"Spill," says Liss, grinning. We've swapped stories about our manipulative families for years.

"My cousin Javier is getting married at the end of May—"

"Is this the competitive cousins?" Jo interrupts (and bless her for remembering the nuances and the politics in my dreadfully pushy family).

"The posh asshole?" Liss asks, and I nod at them.

"My mom rang to chase me about going to 'The Wedding.'" I make air quotes. "And all my lovely brothers and sisters are bringing their partners …"

"Hang on, Javier's getting *married*?" Liss says.

"No one would marry him," Jo adds. "Wait, what do you mean, *all* your siblings are inviting their partners? *Georgie* is seeing someone?"

I wink at Liss, and she frowns at me. "Come on, I'm not as rebellious as your baby sister," she says, and I'll give her that. Georgie takes rebellion to an art form.

"Oh, I'd love to see who she brings," Jo sighs. "I bet he's going to make your parents' hair stand on end."

Liss nods. "Dreadlocks, do you think? Was your mom ranting about Georgie's man?"

I pause, frowning. "No actually." Hmmm. Interesting. "Anyway, I felt so much pressure to live up to their expectations that I said I was bringing someone."

"What?" Jo says, groaning, but Liss beams at me. "Oh! Great! Who's the lucky man?"

Jo frowns, and I shake my head. "That's the point, Liss, I don't have anyone to take."

"Oh well, that'll be easy. You're stunning and smart and any guy would be happy to go with you." Her eyes sweep around the café as if she's sussing out who we might ask, right here, right now.

"I'm flattered you think that, Liss, but trust me, I'm stumped."

But she claps her hands. "I'm thrilled! I love the fact I've just got back, and this is the problem I've got to solve."

"Is there anyone at the hospital?" Jo asks, humming.

I shake my head. "I'm not friendly enough with any of them. They'd just think it was weird of me to ask."

Liss tuts. "I'm sure they'd be delighted to be asked by you, Kate. What about exes?"

I roll my eyes, but I know what's coming next out of her mouth.

"What about David?"

I sigh. Liss liked him better than Jo, and, like me, she's a bit of a sucker for that kind of guy. Jo is much more logical and demanding; she always wanted someone who would support her career and was incredibly picky at college.

"He called me a couple of weeks ago."

Jo's eyes go wide as Liss says, "Well, then, that's perfect."

"Liss. He asked me to marry him and then cheated on me," I say as scathingly as I can.

"And it was *two years* ago, Liss," Jo says, rounding on her indignantly, "and we really don't want to be opening up that can of worms again." She turns back to me. "What did he say?"

"Not a lot, just asked me how I was. I was at work and couldn't really talk to him. He told me to call him back, and I didn't."

"Good," Jo says.

The sharp ache takes me by surprise. After we split up, he tried so desperately; I would come back to the apartment and find roses laced through the handle of the door, notes pushed under it. And the poems … God, his poems. What disturbs me most was that I liked it: After the devastation of finding that card in his pocket, I wanted anything to prove that I hadn't got it so wrong. He would accost me outside lectures, and so I stopped going and watched the recordings instead. God, I scraped through that year. Some of the things he gave me are still buried in a box in my cupboard. Should I be keeping them?

I come back to the conversation with a jolt to find both of my closest friends observing me with matching expressions. They were wonderful through the whole David thing. I wave my arm at them.

"I'm fine, you guys. Stop looking at me like that. I'm over it. I'd just like to have that again with someone someday." And God, I miss it. I miss the chat, the giggling in bed. It's the most depressing thought in the world that I might not find that again.

"Oh yeah definitely," Liss sighs, looking down at her hands. There's something about the way she says this …

"Meet anyone in Africa?" I say, raising my eyebrows and catching Jo's eye.

"Kind of," she says, cheeks pinking and ducking her head. My eyes go round.

"Oh my God! Why are we only hearing about this now?" I look at my watch. "We've been here for twenty minutes! It should have been the first item on the agenda. Spill."

Jo holds up a hand. "Before we launch into that, I have a suggestion for the wedding."

"Who?"

She raises her eyebrows. "Fabian?"

"Who's Fabian?" says Liss, while I start to laugh.

"He's Janus's best friend," Jo whispers, and I shake my head.

"That's an insane idea," I say like it hadn't already crossed my mind.

She leans forward with a wicked grin. "Yes, but think how much upset he'd cause."

"Why would he do that?" Liss asks.

"He's a bad-boy hacker, covered in tattoos, and he experiments on his body with unusual drugs," I say, folding my arms on my chest and staring at Jo.

Jo puts her hand behind her ear. "I didn't hear you say he's also incredibly hot and you get on with him like a house on fire."

"Oh, he sounds perfect," Liss breathes, eyes wide and thrilled.

"You guys were setting sparks off each other when you came round for supper—just imagine what might happen over a weekend," Jo says, grinning.

"I don't need another car-crash relationship. One was enough."

"Seriously?" asks Liss, like I haven't spoken. "I'm gutted I missed this."

"You can come and see the show next time," says Jo. "They were flirting like crazy with each other, and Janus says Fab never even talks to women."

Hope. It kills you every time. *For God's sake.*

Jo turns to me. "And why would it be a car crash? Don't you think you need a man like that? Someone to help you loosen up?"

I'm vaguely insulted by this, but Jo does just say what she thinks 90 percent of the time. I can imagine traveling with him to the wedding, right beside me in the front seat of my car, that lean body with those tantalizing tattoos. A whole weekend. I wouldn't survive. What would he do to my parents' blood pressure?

I shake my head. "Not going to happen."

"Oh, go on," says Liss. "Live a little. Have a hot fling, don't take life so seriously … it doesn't have to be serious."

Could I ask him? I hardly know him! And I can't believe he doesn't have women falling all over him. I need to call my mom and just tell her that the guy I am seeing doesn't want to come, or some nonsense that she'd buy into, or perhaps even be honest for once and say that I'm way too busy panicking at the hospital to be dating anyone.

"Stop, you guys, all right? I'm not asking Fabian." I rap the table with my knuckles. "Moving on. We need the scoop on this guy of Liss's."

*

Later that afternoon, when Liss and I are back at the apartment, a text drops into my messages:

Looking forward to all the dorky doctor speak in three weeks!

Tod, my eldest brother. And where has this week gone? This wedding is only three weeks away now, and I have so little time to sort anything out.

You enjoying emergency medicine?

*Goddammit.* My hand hovers over the typing button.

All good.

*Liar.*

Have you killed my nephews yet? Fed them too many of the wrong drugs? Poisoned them with your cooking?

A picture drops into the text stream of two small toddlers asleep in a double buggy.

> Just out walking the little shits. They were awake all last night.

Then:

> You think medicine is hard now. Wait until you've got children.

I laugh. I haven't even got a boyfriend.

Then the phone rings in my hand. Oh God, I hope Tod's not ringing to chat about the ER.

"Hey, Pudding, I hear from ice cube number one that we're going to meet your new man." His deep voice curls into my ear.

I close my eyes. Of course. This is not just Javier's wedding. It's an introduction to the whole Thurman family. Why did I think I could invite some hapless guy into that? And I wish he wouldn't call me Pudding.

"Don't call Mom *ice cube number one*."

He laughs. "She's a robot. And I know you play your cards close to your chest, sis, but you need to fill me in. You don't want me meeting this guy for the first time and challenging him to pistols at dawn at a wedding."

Oh shit. Now he's in Seattle and I don't get to see him that often, I keep forgetting what a big brother he is, how he stepped into the role of being an understanding and invested parent for the rest of us.

"Are you bringing a gun on the flight with you?" I say sweetly.

"I want to know if I'm going to have to give him a warning to treat my sister right."

"It's a surprise." It's the best I can come up with.

Silence. "Seriously? You're telling me *nothing* about this guy?"

"Tod. For once, cut the bossy big brother act. Just chill. You'll meet him when you meet him."

"Okay, but …"

"No buts. Just ..." A sharp wail of a distressed child cuts through the background.

"The call of the Valkyrie!" Tod shouts in my ear.

"You've killed them, haven't you? Pushed them into the street without looking."

"They're good, sis. Better go." Another wail joins the first. "Okay, I'll let you off the hook, but he better be an amazing guy, that's all I'm saying. No one deserves better than my Pudding." And he rings off.

Holy shit. Did I dodge a bullet?

I dodged a bullet.

Later in bed that night, my eyes stray to the illuminated numbers on the clock beside my bed: 2 a.m. In the dim light, I can make out the shape of the blinds covering the window. Three hours until the start of my shift. The apartment is quiet apart from the faint sound of the steady drip from the showerhead, and the cars on the road making a distinctive *thud thud* as they go over the manhole cover outside the building.

I punch my pillow again and turn over to find the cold bit for my hot head. I can't stand up to my mother, and I can't pluck up the courage to ask Fabian. But whatever, I'm done giving myself a hard time. I have to bite the bullet and do one or the other, and I'm going to talk to Fabian because Liss is right: It doesn't have to be this big thing, and out of all the people I know, he gives me the impression he'd understand how I've fucked all this up and would play along. I just need to engineer an opportunity to talk to him.

# CHAPTER 7

## *Fabian*

Solas is a three-in-one bar: a typical neighborhood joint with a long, polished counter down one wall, a food place with awesome tacos, and a dance joint with a space upstairs where a DJ spins tunes. I drag a shaking hand across my forehead, peering down at my sweaty clothes before hitching myself onto a stool. My mind slices through the parkour route that got me here after Janus texted me to meet him for a drink. So many leaps and slips, a collection of bruises coming up on my shins and my elbow.

A warm Friday night in May, and no surprises, it's busy in here. I pat my pockets and come up empty. *Dammit.* No cash or cards. But before I can say anything, Salvatore the barman nods at me and slides a bottle of beer onto the glossy wood. I sip it gratefully: twelve fucking hours of trying to hack into a system today with nothing concrete to show for it.

"Stop sweating on my clean bar," he says, snapping a dishcloth as he heads off to serve a guy sitting farther down, and I laugh.

Then a hand lands on my shoulder, and I grin. *Janus.* But I turn to find

Darren, a gym pal and parkour friend, smiling down at me. He's wearing a sling around his left arm.

"I thought it was you," he says, just as I say, "What the hell?"

He makes a face. "Slipped on a wall," he mutters as he crumples into the stool next to me and studies the shelves at the back of the bar. Injury is seen as an admission of failure among the committed parkour crowd.

"You never were that brilliant at walls," I say deadpan. Darren can scale up almost anything, and he relaxes and meets my eyes with a grin.

"What have you been up to?" he says.

*Dreaming about a woman I can't have.*

"Work okay?" he adds.

To most people, I'm a programmer. A freelancer. Boring. Same old, same old. I haven't told Darren that I'm a hacker. Don't get me wrong, I'm happy to talk, but trusting people is different. Not that I think that anyone would pose a threat or deliberately incriminate me, but there are people I've rubbed up the wrong way and keeping information tight is second nature now.

"Yeah, great. Wrestling with a tricky bit of code." I pinch the bridge of my nose. Being evasive is like wearing my coat inside out.

Darren jerks his chin up at me. "By the way, someone was asking after you."

*What*?

"The night I did this"—he lifts his elbow—"some guy was watching us, as people do, y'know? I thought he was security, but then he came up and asked about 'a long-haired tattooed guy who was sometimes with us.' He said he was a friend from college, which seemed fucking odd to me because, if that was the case, how come he'd watched us and not said anything? But Mark just said, 'Fabian,' right out before I could stop him."

I sip my beer, cold dripping down my throat. "What did he want?"

"Just if we knew where to find you." His eyes scan over me. "I just said no, but it felt off, y'know? An odd thing to ask."

I shake my head. I can't tell him about the threats and the hack into Janus's company. That's not the kinds of friends we are. "What did he look like?"

"Dark. Short. Built like a boxer."

Yeah, I don't know anyone who looks like that. There's a shout behind us, and I jump, but when I turn Janus is heading toward us, grinning. Fuck. I can't tell him about this, he'll go into damage limitation mode, and I'm not sure I've forgiven myself for how they tried to close down his company.

"Why so serious?" he says, lifting his sweaty running top from his body and flapping it. Then he cuffs me across the head and smiles at Darren.

I frown at him in mock annoyance and try to cuff him back, but he dodges out of the way.

"Janus, this is Darren, a parkour friend of mine. Darren, Janus and I studied together at college."

"Dangerous sport that," Janus says, grinning at Darren's arm. "I keep telling Fab he should stick to running."

Darren makes a face. "Running's too boring, man. Why run when you can climb and run at the same time?"

He flexes an impressive bicep, so I drag up my sleeve and flex mine against his.

Janus tuts and has just started to pull up the arm of his jacket when a soft voice behind him says, "What are you guys even *doing*?"

I grin over Janus's shoulder at Jo, and my whole stomach drops when I see who's standing behind her. *Kate.* Why is Kate here? My eyes snap to Janus, and I glower at him, but he just raises his eyebrows, a smug expression on his face.

Kate's dressed top to toe in black. A tight T-shirt hugs her breasts, and some kind of metalware is holding her jeans together, and fuck, her skin is visible underneath. Her normal sleek bob is tousled into disarray and her dark makeup gives her a sultry air that's so unlike the prim doctor that I've seen before. All I want to do is stare and stare. I have to stop myself from examining her chest and I want to slap my head. Could I be any more sexist? I give her a half smile hoping it comes across as an apology, but I think she's oblivious to my ogling because she grins back at me with a smile that makes me want to push past everyone and kiss away all that pearly nonsense on her lips.

"Table?" Jo says, waving her arm, and Darren and I grab our drinks from the bar and follow her while Janus leans over the counter and chats to the barman about beers.

"How are you doing?" Kate says softly from behind me, and I turn and smile at her, trying to look anywhere but down her torso.

"I'm good. You?"

She purses her mouth before she nods, and with that hesitation, I suddenly want to hear all about her day.

"Kill anyone today?" I say with a wink, and she laughs shaking her head.

"Not that I'm aware of," she says, "but I can't rule it out just yet."

Her eyes dance at me as she licks her lips, and I track the progress of her small pink tongue from one corner to the other, tripping over my feet. I swing my gaze back toward Jo. Jesus Christ.

Jo snags a table on the long wall by the dance floor. If I sit with Kate, I'll rub up against her like a cat in heat, so I gesture to a seat and move around, sitting on the opposite side of the table, and lean over to chat. But Darren levers himself down, right next to her, and introduces himself, and within minutes she's asking him about his arm and they're too far away for me to comfortably join in their conversation. I shift back and stare at the few couples who are dancing.

Darren's hair flops over his forehead, and he keeps tossing it back as he gives Kate open white smiles, leaning in like he's telling her state secrets. She taps his sling and cocks her head, and he starts twisting his body as if he's describing the exact moment he damaged himself. He's taking full advantage, the bastard. I want to jump over the tabletop and damage his other arm … tell her that I do parkour, too … tell her that he's not interesting just because he's injured. Why didn't I sit beside her? Why didn't I think that Darren would chat her up? I blink away from her smiles and his answering grin, the way his eyes roam her face, cheeks, mouth. Dammit, I'm crap at all this, and so out of practice. I grind my teeth. So what? I'm not her keeper—if she wants to be chatted up by a decent guy, who am I to intervene?

As if he realizes that I'm torturing myself incessantly in my head, Janus leans into me and gives me a nudge. "You going to let that carry on?" he whispers, nodding at the pair of them.

"What?" I say, scowling.

"He's chatting up your woman."

"She's not my woman." This is not fucking helping.

"Come on, Fab, she likes you. Don't let her slip through your fingers," he says, and I growl at him in return, eyes skimming over where Darren's head is bent toward Kate's.

"I'm not going to behave like a caveman," I say.

"Ask her to dance."

"You're kidding, right?" I nod at the few couples on the floor. "Have you ever seen a techie that could do that?"

We're all terrible dancers. Not that it hindered our ability to pick up women at college, but in a wild moment one day we decided to go to a class—our dancing was appalling, but the women were a revelation.

"Well, you've got to drag her away from him somehow. Why didn't you sit next to her?"

"Because I'm a fucking idiot," I mutter, tipping back my beer. "I'm not making a play for Kate."

"Just get up off your butt and go talk to her," he says, and before I can think any more about it, or listen to any more of the crap in my head, I push up and walk around the table. And her eyes stray to me and dart up my body like she hopes no one is watching. Her eyes meet mine, and her cheeks go pink. Fuck, yes.

I stand behind her and lean over her shoulder. Darren glances up and frowns, but I stop looking at him and concentrate on her, leaning right in, my lips on a small mole right under her ear. She does a whole-body shiver, and suddenly I'm high as a kite.

"Want to dance?" I murmur.

Darren sits back, mouth a flat line as he folds his arms across his chest, but she nods and presses her hand into mine as I pull her to her feet.

Her fingers feel small and rough wrapped in my palm as I pull her forward toward the music, beat thumping through my blood as we make our way to the back of the floor, close but not touching, and I splay my hand across her back, the tip of every finger on her spine. *Salsa music.* That's a fail on exhibiting any kind of dancing skills.

"I can't dance to salsa," she mumbles, grimacing, and my lips curl up.

"Me neither." I shake my head. "Don't worry about it, just swivel your hips." And she raises her eyebrows at me, making me laugh. And somehow between the pair of us we manage to settle into some kind of rhythm.

"I think Darren's plotting my murder," I say.

"He seems like a nice guy," she says.

Did I completely misread this situation? She likes him? *Fuck.* I study her flushed cheeks.

"Have you been friends long?" she adds.

"We do parkour together. I did that on the way here, hence the workout clothes and the sweat." Damn, I probably smell terrible. I step away from her. "Sorry."

But she just smiles up at me, and the urge to place my lips on hers is almost overwhelming. "I don't mind," she murmurs.

My breath leaches in and out of my body like I can't expand my lungs. The beat of a song I half recognize encourages me to move my hips more, and we drift together again. And Kate's cutely awkward as I urge her closer, my hand hot on her back, and I move it in slight circles, pressing my fingers into her skin. Sweat trickles down my spine.

"Do you like him?" I say in a low voice. "Is it okay that I asked you to dance?"

She grins up at me. "I'm delighted that you asked me. Darren is nice, but probably not my type."

And something warm explodes inside me, and having her so close, her undivided attention, Janus's insistence echoing in my head, makes me feel reckless. "What *is* your type?"

I focus on her with laser intensity: Whatever comes next out of her mouth is the most important thing in the world.

"You," she says.

# CHAPTER 8

## *Fabian*

"There's no way, Janus."

When I swing round in my seat, Janus is staring at me from where he's hunched over in front of my bank of computer screens, eyebrows raised. We're supposed to be having a quiet Sunday evening programming at my place, but after watching Kate and me talk at dinner and in the bar on Friday night, he's been making comments about the two of us ever since he walked in the door.

"No way what?"

I've just launched into this after an hour of coding silence, but it's bursting out of me like a wriggly fish I can't hold firm in my hands. He's my best friend, but he's also Jo's other half. Will talking to him make it better or should I keep my big mouth shut?

"No way it could work," I mutter, turning back to my screen. The comment she made on the dance floor has been running through my mind like hot metal for days.

"Who? Kate? Why the hell not?"

"Because … man. I'm a wreck. She's beautiful and sorted, and works hard and is organized … and did I say hardworking? Fuck!" I undo my bun and shake out my hair: My head is sweating. "I'd ruin her life."

He pivots on his chair and fixes me with a stare. Shit. I hate it when he gets that expression on his face: A speech is coming. Janus has this uncanny ability to beat the drum and make people pull together; this is why he's running a business and I'm not. I pick up a pencil from the desk and start tapping out a rhythm on the arm of my chair. Janus sighs.

"You're a fucking genius, that's what you are. Look at the way you helped Jo sort out the attack on my company—"

"A problem *I* created," I talk over him.

" … And she'd be damn lucky to have you." His eyes drop to my drumming pencil, and he gives me a smile before he pivots back around to his screen, fingers flying over the keyboard. "Anyway, I don't think you've got a choice. You two strike sparks off each other every time you're together." He grins over his shoulder at me, face full of mischief.

"Fuck off," I say, turning back to my own computer. The liquid heat of her voice whispering "You," lips and breath painting patterns against my ear. A flash runs right through my body like a detonated grenade. She's everywhere, in my dreams with her golden skin and hair, slipping forward over her cheek as my fingers track across every part of her.

"She's not interested." Now I'm lying to him. I know she is. Why am I pushing this conversation?

"Yeah, right. Funny she spent so long talking to you the other night."

"Perhaps she's just curious about why I experiment with drugs." I turn to face him, dropping any pretense of working. To his credit, he swings around again to talk to me properly.

"Yeah, I'll bet she does that with the hundreds of other patients in the ER who've taken an overdose." He smiles at me sarcastically.

"I didn't OD; it was just a bit of a weird trip."

"Anyway," Janus says, leaning back, "I've seen you two together. Why don't you just ask her out? The worst thing that could happen is that she says no, and then you just get more persistent. Look what happened to Jo and me."

I sigh, because Janus was incredibly patient with Jo, becoming her mentor and her friend before they ever got together. I'm kind of pissed he thinks this can work for everyone. He has an ability to play the long game that I just don't have.

"I don't think Kate and I would be anything like you and Jo. We don't have anything in common for a start. We're complete opposites in every way." Janus opens his mouth, and I hold my hand up to stop whatever is coming next, shaking my head. My gut is already churning. This is an *impossible* idea. She's the type of girl who would only settle for a kind, steady, *sensible* guy. And she'd be right to do that.

"I'm way too impulsive, you know this."

He stretches back with a thoughtful expression, and the chair creaks in protest. Code is scrolling up his screen behind his head. The sky beyond the window is reaching that inky evening darkness. My stomach rumbles.

His eyes narrow. "This isn't about Nadine, is it?"

My only attempt at a long-term relationship. A girl like me, and a wild, soul-destroying two years.

"No. Fuck, no."

"Because you deserve someone so much better than her."

"She was just messed up, like me."

"You are not like Nadine. Man, the manipulation—"

I hold up my hand.

"Why don't you just take a chance and see where it goes?"

Falling for someone like Kate and losing her … I am not the kind of person that could walk away. When you lose someone good, it's all on you.

"I experiment with drugs, Janus. She's a doctor."

"Then why don't you let her help you kick the drug habit?"

He's always been ambivalent about my propensity to experiment on my body.

"I don't have a habit. I try out different drug combinations like a chemist, but that's all it is, man. I'm not an addict. I don't take anything regularly. I don't use drugs as a prop: too much lying, stealing, bodily decline. I've had periods when I've ditched the experimentation and been totally okay with it."

He grunts at me unhappily. "And yet you keep ending up in hospital? You have to admit it's a bit of a worry."

"Why is it any different from alcohol? You wouldn't turn down a cocktail you hadn't tried before, would you?"

He sighs. We've had this conversation many times before. "It's a lot more dangerous than a bit of booze."

But I like the danger, I don't say. Some people scale cliff faces; I like testing my body in other ways. Oh, I know the trips to the hospital are not the actions of a sensible man, but I like understanding how my body responds. Pushing myself, emotionally and physically, takes me out of my head and into the moment; all the voices and the noise and the running video of my father's looming face and evil grin disappear. It's like diving off a cliff into deep water. I pull myself up at the thought—are all these things replacing some emotional space in me that they shouldn't? I need to return to that idea when Janus is not messing with my thoughts.

Janus coughs. "Anyway, I think you're protesting a little too much about Kate," he says.

*

Later on, after he's left, I take a cold shower and curse myself as I pad around the apartment. *Dammit, what am I doing?* The hot burst inside when she told me she liked me. And asking her to dance? Fucking Janus. I think about the courage it must have taken for ice queen Kate to tell me she liked me, and I ran away, knowing in my heart that, while she might *say* she likes guys like me, the day-to-day reality … well … she wouldn't stick around. She would come to see me as I saw Nadine—a loose cannon, a liability. And I couldn't bear the hope. This is like when I was trying to get into college, every time I got closer, did a test, the terror would take me over that someone would whip it away or I would say the wrong thing, *do* the wrong thing. *Fucking hell.*

I clean my bedroom, play several games of *Valorant* and eventually start watching *Kill Bill* on HBO. But even the body count doesn't distract me from the pounding in my head. Forty-five minutes in, I pause the film and fling the remote onto the couch, walk across the warm wooden boards into the kitchen, pull a cup from the cupboard, and grind coffee beans, inhaling their bitterness.

Never mind whether this could go somewhere—I like Kate. She's good people, and I've probably hurt her feelings by backing right off after she said she was interested. And you don't treat decent people like that. I need to apologize and explain.

# CHAPTER 9

## *Fabian*

My phone lights up on the desk, and I stare down at it, hands stilling on the keyboard. The number for this phone is known by very few people, and I'm looking at a number I don't recognize. *Fuck, it's compromised!* How did they find the number for *this* phone? I pick it up, and the desire to throw it across the room is almost irresistible.

"Hello," I growl.

"Umm, Fabian?" The uncertain tilt to her words makes my whole body swoop.

"Kate?" I pull my phone away from my ear and inspect it. "How did you get this number?"

"Janus gave it to me. Is that okay?" she says, breath whispering down the line. The hairs on the back of my neck prickle. Janus wouldn't realize this was any kind of special phone—how mundane is giving out a number for everyone else? Most people don't live in my paranoid little world.

"Yes, of course! It's great to hear from you."

She's called *me*. I sit back in my chair, chest expanding. This hack I've been doing is going backward rather than forward, and despite the fact that I need to explain and apologize to her, I love chatting to Kate. A miracle in its own right.

"How's the ER?" I want an update on everything. "What's happened with the asshole physician?"

She laughs. "I've not been on with him since I saw you." Her voice dips a bit, and I'm straight back to the bar dancing in front of her, hand on her back, her hip. "Thank God. But the ER is fine. I'm fine. Just … fine."

Her voice tails off, and I have a feeling that she's not fine at all, but I don't know her well enough to push. Now I'm even more determined not to add to her problems. I suck in a deep breath.

"I'm glad you called," I say. "I'm sorry I rushed off the other night."

"Oh! That's okay. I had too much to drink, and my mouth ran away with me."

Sweat trickles down my spine. "It was all good, Kate. I'm highly flattered, but I'm not what you need."

Silence ticks down the line. I have no radar for poor decisions, no inner compass that says this is a bad decision and this one is better, but something about this feels off, like a cymbal clashing in the wrong part of the music. I stand up and pace away from my desk.

"That's okay," she says quietly.

And I groan internally. I don't know what I expected but it wasn't this. This is worse: She's taking it as a rejection. I don't want to reject Kate. I don't want her to feel that she's not worthy or interesting or … I'm the one at fault here.

But before I can say anything else, she says, "Friends?"

I come to a halt where I'm wearing a familiar path across the rug. *Friends*? God, no.

"Okay," I say because my head is empty of any other sensible response, and how can I explain all that is my life, my past, over the phone like this?

"Actually, I rang because I've got a favor to ask, *friend*," she says.

"Oh yeah?" Ah! A tech question. I should have known. People always call when they need help with their computer. Although … why didn't she ask Jo?

"I've got a bit of a difficulty with my family," she says, and I stare blindly at the window that overlooks the street.

*What?*

She's so together I can't imagine her parents as anything less than organized and kind. And I am *not* the person to consult about any sort of family problem. All my life I've kicked sand over my fucked-up history and buried the trails. Dad was a violent offender with terrifying anger problems, regularly careening into the house completely plastered to take whatever was eating him out on us with his fists. He was in and out of jail, and we were *always* fucking delighted when he was behind bars. He went there permanently when he went crazy one night and killed my mom in a jealous rage when I was sixteen. He's been in there a long time. Zach—my brother—and I testified against him.

A shiver runs down my spine, and I swing around, taking in the empty room. I stretch out my throat. The ghost of his hand always sits on the back of my neck, his whisper in my ear saying, "What you doing, boy?" in that way he had. He used to tighten his hand around our throats if he didn't like the way we answered his questions, my mom's hysterical voice promising him anything, anything if he'd stop.

Killing my mom, I suspect, was an accident. Oh! I'm not trying to excuse him. He was way too drunk most of the time to ever think about anything he did. But holding on to the rage I felt afterward ate away at me. I have no idea whether he's still alive or not, or even still in jail, although he should be—he got life. Zach and I ran wild after she died: burglaries, drugs, booze, out of reach of the authorities. Unhinged and free, we could have killed ourselves and not cared. We both felt we could have saved our mom if we had known, if we had acted sooner: If, if, if.

Kate clears her throat. And oh shit! My silence has gone on way too long.

"Okay," I say.

And a whole story comes tumbling out about her cousin's wedding, about her family's expectations, the pressure they place on her, and how she told them she was bringing someone along. I put her on speaker and sit down to listen. Is this what normal families do? My dad used his disapproval of us to fuel his anger and excuse his violent behavior: Somehow it was always our fault. Is this just a different, more civilized, condemnation?

"God, Kate, they sound …" well, at best they sound "… manipulative?"

"That's about right."

Footsteps scuff in the background, a cupboard door opens and closes, a spoon clinks against a cup, and I stare at the dark outside. She's probably in a soft T-shirt and sweatpants. I would stand behind her, lift that blonde silk, and kiss her neck. As I examine my weary reflection in the window, the warm glow of the lamp by the couch, the penny drops, and my heart takes off.

"Just a minute, let me get this straight. You want *me* to go along?" She wants the unstable, tattooed hacker guy to go with her to … "*Why?*"

I stand again and pad across the worn floorboards and kilims to the kitchen. If she's drinking coffee, then so am I.

"I don't think—" she starts, as I say: "I'll do it if you want me to but"—her breath drifting down the line brings goosebumps up on my neck—"why me? I'd go down like a lead balloon." I tuck my phone under my chin, turn on the tap, and pick up the brush to clean out my coffeemaker. "I mean I'm hardly the most appropriate …"

She laughs. "I like your company, and I think you'd really annoy them," she says.

Swallowing hard, I fill up the water chamber. She enjoys my company? Positive comments don't come my way in the normal run of things, which is why I like hanging out with Janus. I see myself in a different way when I'm with him; he pulls me out of my tendency for negative introspection. I screw the top back on the pot and place it on the stovetop, gripping the edge of the counter and closing my eyes as warmth swarms through my chest. I'm not insulted by the idea I'd rub them up the wrong way: No family on earth would approve of me.

"Why do you want to annoy them?"

She sighs into the phone, and the sound of her breath tickles my ear before running all the way across my shoulders and down my arms. I flick the switch, and the blue flame roars to life under the coffeepot.

"I just think they have a narrow view on how people should live their lives, and I like to shake them up every now and again." I can imagine her shrug over the line. "That makes me sound like a terrible daughter."

This is a mad idea, but I've not met her family and they could all be assholes. The thought of spending time with Kate … I'm so tempted … but I'm also not supposed to be going *there*. But this would also be the perfect distraction from the systems I'm trying to get into, and from wondering who the fuck was asking around about me.

"I've never been to a wedding."

"You've never been to a …"

Way too revealing, that little comment. I barrel on. "How many days?"

"Probably two or three, a weekend?" Her voice lifts, like she's hoping I'll say yes.

"When is it?"

There's a long pause. "The weekend after next actually."

Only two weeks away? Woah. "You want me to do this? I might not behave very well. I'm not known for my subtlety or my impulse control. I experiment with drugs … you know that."

She laughs again. "It'd be fun though, right?"

"Anything with you would be fun," I say, as the pot starts spitting and the coffee bubbles up inside.

Her laugh is infused with joy this time. "You're an unusual guy for thinking that," she says, and I raise my eyebrows at the orange cupboards above my head. Surely, guys have been falling over themselves to tell her she's great since the dawn of time.

"Normally, I'm told I'm uptight. I don't think anyone has seen me as a fun person before."

She does come across as serious, but I can see the twinkle in her eye; she's lively and knowledgeable and …

"Jo calls me 'Dr. Dull.' We joke about it but—"

"Well, I'd say you're anything but dull. I'd love to spend a weekend with you, Kate." Because goddammit, I would.

"That sounded like a yes," she says, and I can hear the grin in her voice.

"It's a fuck, yes," I say, and oh! "… Wait. Do we get to share a bedroom?"

There's silence on the other end of the line. Like she's wondering why the hell I'm suggesting this when I've told her this is going nowhere. And did I foolishly agree to be friends? This is already an accident waiting to happen. The whole weekend will be torture.

But all I get is a dry chuckle. "Guys," she says, "why does it always come back to that one thing?"

# CHAPTER 10

## *Fabian*

Three days later and a day spent pacing the apartment, doing a thirteen-mile run and not concentrating on any code, I ring Kate and ask her to meet me for dinner to discuss logistics. So now I'm in Rocco's, a little Italian place that sits midway between her place and mine. I'm taking in the red-checkered tablecloths, candles, wooden chairs, and the bar, and wondering if the vibe's a little too romantic for this … whatever *this* is. *Friends*, Fabian. I groan. I'm crap at keeping to any kind of rules. If there's a line, I will always step over it.

I glance out of the window at the street, trying to work out whether anyone is watching the restaurant. All the way here I was wondering whether I was being followed. I diverted a couple of times, but nobody looked in the least bit interested. *Stop being so paranoid.*

My phone buzzes on the table, and I pick it up to see a dark head bent over a sidewalk: a picture of Janus throwing up the one time I took him out to do parkour.

"Janus."

I'm too stressed to hand him any shit, so I'm not surprised when all I hear is a sharp intake of breath on the other end of the phone.

"I've called you to give you crap but you're being far too polite and so now I'm freaked," he says.

"You're the mother I never had."

"That's more like it," he says. "So, I understand there's a date happening tonight?"

Fuck the grapevine, how did he know? Probably Jo. And now he's baiting me.

"Lucky you," I say. "Who's the lucky lady?"

His chuckle warms my ear. "Were you hoping to keep it quiet from me?"

He's ignoring my comment, as he should.

"Yes, because you're an asshole and you'd give me shit about it."

"I'm proud of you, Fabian. Proud that you plucked up the courage to ask her out."

Hmmm. Do I want to come clean about the "friends" agreement? No. No, I don't.

"Yes, Mom," I say. "Actually, she asked me first."

He lets out a low whistle. The grapevine clearly hasn't passed on everything. I raise my eyes to the ceiling. The polystyrene is covered in splatters and weird stains—how did those get there? It looks like someone in this place has been twirling their spaghetti too vigorously.

"As your dating coach I'm pretty pleased with that," he says.

"Wait." I straighten and pick up my fork, spinning it through my hands. "When did you become my dating coach?" And ugh, we don't hide things from each other. "Anyway, calm down, this is just a briefing session; she's asked me to go to her cousin's wedding with her."

"Fucking hell! Are you going?"

I laugh. "Society wedding? There was no way I was saying no to that."

"It's tuxes and shit? This I have to see. I want pictures of you in a tux."

Oh shit. A tux? I take the phone away from my ear and pull up the notes app and add it to my list of things I have to ask Kate when she gets here. I glance at the door. No sign of her. But it's only 7.30 p.m. I was so worried I'd get engrossed in code and forget that I made sure I was really early. I've got ages to chat with Janus. I relax back into my chair and put my phone back to my head.

"I think she only asked me because she wants to create trouble at this wedding with her family."

"Yeah, that'd be right. You're not interesting at all." His breath whooshes out. "No woman would want a guy with your tattoos or six-pack, plus, of course, you lead a seriously dull life."

"Fuck off," I say, looking up and opening my mouth to put him straight on this whole thing. But I'm stopped in my tracks when I see a head of golden hair in the restaurant doorway. My stomach tightens. She's early, too.

"I need to go," I say.

And I hear that start of what sounds like "Good luck" before I hang up.

Kate glances around before her eyes land on me, and the way her face lights up has my gut clenching. She turns with a smile for the waiter as he takes her coat. She's in tight jeans and some kind of lacey top that molds to her breasts. Her blonde hair is styled like someone's already had their hands in it. The waiter's white teeth flash as he gives her smile after smile, and I want to head over and do damage to his face, then the douche stares at her ass as she heads toward me. I stand up and glare at him over her head, and his gaze flicks to mine as his face reddens and he ducks into the back of the restaurant.

"Asshole," I mutter, sitting down.

"Fabian?" Kate says.

"He was staring at your butt."

A rose tinge appears on her cheeks as she laughs, then she does a little shimmy of her hips and turns around. Her bottom is pear-shaped and fits her dark jeans perfectly.

I run my hand down my face, clearing my throat.

"Fuck."

"What?" She peers at me over her shoulder and shrugs. "Well?"

"Well, what?"

She spins back and sits down grinning. "Is it worth staring at? I don't see my butt much."

*She's flirting with me?*

I lean in so my lips are inches from hers. "Your ass is sensational, Kate. I want to see it naked."

And with that one comment, I throw the whole friends thing right out of the window. Heat sweeps right up her cheeks. Even when I talked to her half-naked in the hospital, she didn't blush like that. I've also let my leery thoughts spill out over our nice polite evening. *Shut the fuck up, Fabian.*

I sink back and shake my head. "Sorry, I'm not very good at …"

But she leans in and presses a finger to my lips, causing a shiver to run all the way to my toes.

"Don't censor yourself. I like who you are. I like the compliments."

There's nothing quite like the buzz of hearing a girl you like say something like that to you. We are careening down a new path now at a hundred miles an hour. What am I *doing*? I kiss her finger, and she raises an eyebrow at me, so I give her my best cocky grin, trying to ease the syrupy tension. *Come on, Fabian, you can do normal chitchat.*

"I forget to eat most of the time so I'm starving. I hope you don't mind if I order half the menu."

She nods. "Likewise. We see too many patients and too much trauma in the hospital to spend time eating."

Perhaps, in some odd way, her days are just like mine.

"How was it today?"

She puts her head on one side and purses her lips. "I often go home with a mountain of diagnoses buzzing through my head and the worry that they could all be wrong. I keep thinking: Will I always think like this, or will I be more confident and care less when I've got more experience?" She waves a hand, her silver bracelet catching the light. "Today I'm not too worried, so that makes it a decent day. How about you?"

"Well, I didn't try any interesting drugs today."

"Is that a good thing or a bad thing?"

And I raise my eyebrows. She's not passing judgment here. *Interesting.* She was the same in the ER. "It's good *and* bad."

I don't want to explain why I experiment with my body, why I want to get out of my head, so I'm going to stick to what loosely passes as work for me.

"I'm working on a complicated hacking project that has a few problems at the moment."

"Can you tell me anything about it?" she says, and the intense expression on her face makes a smile creep around the corners of my mouth.

"Without having to kill you, you mean?" I say, and her lips twist to the side as she wrinkles her nose. She's earnest, Kate, but in the best way. Perhaps you don't realize when you first meet her, but the fun is bubbling away under the surface like a geyser looking for an escape valve. I take in the tousled hair and the pink cheeks and straighten my cutlery. How much should I divulge about what I do, the state of my finances?

"I hack because I love it, and I like projects that are challenging or interesting, rather than things that pay well. Unfortunately, that doesn't cover the bills, so I also need to do paid contracts. This is one of those."

"Illegal?" she asks, and I shake my head.

"I don't do stuff like that for other people. Well …" I correct " … I have sometimes. For organizations where I believe in what they're doing: exposing corruption, criminals, bad environmental issues people are lying about. That sort of thing."

I'm often hiding behind the scenes. The difficult jobs come to me eventually, as other people try and fail. But I'm not special: I've just got a good head for it and a lot of experience and, surprisingly, patience for this type of work. People like me are hard to find: Everyone is motivated by money.

"Some of it I've done outside the States, but occasionally I'm asked to do stuff on criminal cases here. This one is all about corruption in South Africa. Knowing which side is in the right is harder than you'd think. Sometimes people aren't guilty even if the FBI or CIA would like to think they are. Having said that, I can usually prove it either way. People leave a trail of evidence a mile wide. Even the best people struggle to close down the kind of digital footprint we have nowadays, and tech companies make it difficult. I've worked for a couple of celebrities who were being hounded … That was pretty interesting."

This is the longest explanation of my work I've ever given, and, when I focus back on Kate, her eyes are round.

"You realize how thrilling all that sounds?" she whispers, and I get the feeling she'd take more risks if she ever allowed herself to.

"Yeah?" What else can I say? Then I laugh. "It doesn't feel exciting when you've spent three weeks trying to locate the backdoor into a secure system and failed. What I do is all about failing, over and over."

She nods. "Me too. And they carry on living with you, the failures. The beaten women who go back to their husbands, the homeless drifter you fixed up who was so lovely and grateful, who then turns up in the morgue …"

"Oh God, did that happen?"

A watery look creeps into her eyes. "Yeah. This old guy used to come into the ER every couple of weeks roughed up. The routine was to fix him up and give him a hot meal. He's been doing this for years apparently. He died last week. Everyone was gutted."

"Oh shit."

"Someone on the unit told me. It was his heart. He'd been living rough for a long time."

"The street is a fucking terrible place to be. I've slept there myself; I don't know how anyone can do it long-term." I realize what I've said when her eyes widen on me again.

"You've lived on the street? Why?"

A chill hits me. I wasn't planning on telling her all this history. Even though she shared some of her family background with me on the phone, it's nothing like what I experienced growing up.

"It was an experiment of sorts."

She's still staring.

"An experiment? Why? How long were you on the street for?"

"A couple of months, but it was years ago. I was determined to keep going that long. It taught me a lot, I have to say: about drugs and dealers, about how to find food when you don't have any, about how to keep warm. I know all the sweet spots of Manhattan now." I half-grin at Kate. She isn't taking this the wrong way, is she? She leans forward, face soft.

Okay then.

I take a deep breath. "I also learned about crime, and about how people treat you when you're at the bottom of the heap. But I know how lucky I am to have the choice of whether to be there or not. My brother Zach never did: He was a drug addict who lived and died on the street. I wanted to understand what his life was like.

"Zach and I used to do a lot of daft shit together when we were younger, and one night we were at a friend's party, high as kites, when the cops bust in. I sprinted off over the backyard fences, only escaping because I was fast and I was good at parkour even then. When I got back to the room Zach and I shared, I expected a knock on the door any second, but it took them a while, and ultimately they had no proof I was at the party.

"It's kind of why I got involved in computers. I realized I could go down the same road all those people were on, partying their lives away, or try to come up with something else. I looked at things where I could escape my upbringing and make money and started messing around with software, taught myself how to code, and eventually wangled a scholarship to college. After the party, Zach was caught and arrested. They were lenient as it was his first offence, but it left him with a record and he struggled to find work. He drifted, got more involved in that world despite everything I fucking did to keep him out of it, and when I moved to Manhattan he followed me, which was disastrous as he was already into cocaine and that's so easy to buy here. He stayed with me for a while and I tried to help him, but he stole my kit and sold it to feed his habit. We had an argument, and he stormed out."

I scrub my hands over my face. "It was my fault, what did the kit matter, really? And keeping tabs on him was hard after that. He didn't want to speak to me. I knew where he was on and off for a couple of years. I got to know this guy, Steve, who runs one of the hostels and knows everyone and anyone on the streets here, but even he struggled to help me find Zach toward the end."

The warm glow in the restaurant reflects off the wood and the glasses on the table. In the end, Zach was in a terrible place: addicted, ill, always tricking to get money from me, from anybody. God knows I tried to take care of him. There isn't a day that goes by when I don't remember his grinning mischievous face, the way he would grab my shoulder, shake me, and laugh. I told Janus this same whole sorry history one night after Zach turned up at our dorm looking for cash and we had a fight. I got stoned and threatened to fly off one of the school buildings: Janus talked me down.

A sudden loud crash in the kitchen, followed by excitable voices, jerks me out of my thoughts to Kate's furrowed brow across the table.

"After Zach died, I wanted to see what he'd been through. If I'd slept out sooner, maybe I would have known how to find him, who to talk to." I can't meet Kate's eyes, so I watch the waiter as he moves from table to table. "You've no idea how much I regret that. He OD'd, and no one was there. When they found him, they said he'd been lying dead for a couple of days."

An ache tightens the back of my throat, and I stare at the serving hatch, trying to swallow down the elephant-load of feelings. I've been way too honest.

"I can't even … I'm so sorry, Fabian. Sounds like you were really close to him."

She's not flinching away. I pick at some skin on my hand.

"We were as thick as thieves. At least until we argued and the last nine months when I couldn't fucking find him. It ripped us apart, but I understand why he did it." I shake my head. "Why am I telling you about such a depressing subject?"

Why am I dragging Kate through the misery that was my family?

In all the pressure her parents put her under, are *they* honest with her? What's their deal? I hate the idea that there's this rivalry that her parents actively encourage. Why compete with people you're supposed to be close to? I'm willing to bet it destroys a family, in a different way to mine for sure, but destruction nonetheless.

She stretches over and touches my hand. Her skin is cool, and something burns through me that I don't quite understand. I curl my fingers around hers. I'm anchored here. Safe.

"I think I started it by talking about the homeless guy. And I like that you can talk to me honestly." She stares at our hands as if she doesn't know quite how that happened. "Some guys aren't that open, and believe me, it's"—her pale throat moves as she swallows—"great when they are."

The light catches on the golden strands of her hair, and I shift in my chair. Am I honest? I play my cards close to my chest most of the time, but something about tonight has loosened my tongue.

I squeeze her fingers. "Tell me more about this wedding."

# CHAPTER 11

## *Kate*

When I imagined driving to the wedding, I don't think I really thought it through. Being in a confined space with Fabian is like being on a long run along the East River, a strong wind whipping the breath out of your body and dumping adrenaline into your veins. In the dim light from the dashboard, his long body is curled into the car seat next to me, a worn white T-shirt with a faded logo wrapping around his body like bindweed every time he shifts—and boy, is he a shifter. His torn jeans cling to muscly thighs and a tattered pair of Doc Martens adorn his feet, currently tapping away in the footwell. I focus back on the inky gloom, headlights dancing across the tarmac.

We're in an odd place now. When he sat on the opposite side of the table at Solas, I thought I'd misread the long chat we had at Janus's apartment and I had bored the pants off him talking about work. But then he asked me to dance, and having all that skin and his tattoos right there, his long fingers pressing into my back, and Jo and Liss's encouragement echoing in my head … it made me reckless. I wanted to lean in and lick all the way up his neck. Then he rebuffed me but ended up holding my hand and was suggestive and flirty all through dinner at Rocco's. I have no idea what he's thinking. He turns his head and smiles, and my breath disappears.

"I should have worn something different. Smartened up a bit," he says, looking down at himself, misinterpreting my ogling. He pats his chest. "This T-shirt has seen better days, but it's clean." And it makes my mouth curve up, shaking my head. He doesn't need to smarten up.

"I had my hair cut," he adds, with a grin, and I risk a glance at the man bun that is holding it back from his face. "Only a trim, though, to remove the split ends."

A big smile splits his face as he pulls the band out and runs his fingers through the thickness. I chance another look away from the road to his wayward curls, and I can't resist.

"I like your hair."

"You do?" A sweet thrill slides through his words.

And this is the trouble with Fabian: He's delighted every time I pay him a compliment. "It fits the bad-boy image."

His warm gaze roams my face. "Tell me all about your week in the ER," he says, and I laugh.

"You really don't want to know?"

"Oh! believe me, I do. I love hearing about heart attacks and old homeless guys and grumpy doctors and anything else you want to tell me."

I shift in my seat, and his gaze drifts down, and when I blink down to find what he's looking at, I realize that my shirt has pulled tight on one side. Because I'm not wearing a bra, everything is visible through the thin cotton.

"Whoops!" I say, laughing and sitting forward to loosen the material.

Fabian tips his head back and closes his eyes. "This weekend is going to go south very fast if I see things like that." He takes a deep breath before propping his feet on the dash and resting his arms on his knees, hands dangling. "And we can't do this."

*But he wants this?* A hot thrill shoots through me. Is he talking to me or himself? "Can't do what?"

He stares down between his legs. "You're such a golden girl, Kate. I'm this no-hoper with a chaotic life and very little impulse control."

He's said things a bit like this before, but I wouldn't describe him as a no-hoper. He's always so confident, with a great handle on himself, even when he's taking huge risks. This is like my parents' view on life. Black, white. Good, bad. You can easily twist things one way or another, say this person or that person is a loser or a success, but it's rarely so straightforward. On one level I've achieved a lot: I've climbed the academic mountain that got me into college to study medicine. On the other hand, I have panic attacks in the ER and flirt with failure every day. And when I fail, people die.

"I like you," I say simply, and he groans.

"Kate. You're beautiful, smart, funny, interesting. You could have any guy you want. You don't need a man like me."

*Funny?* Is he high? And how can he view himself so negatively? "Firstly, I've had relationships with those guys you might say would be 'right' for a girl like me. And I've not met one yet who wasn't an asshole. Secondly, you're *not* a downbeat, messed-up wreck. You're a brilliant programmer and hacker, a kind, honorable man who I'd give my right arm to spend more time with."

He starts laughing. "You're crazy, Kate, do you know that? I'm none of those things."

He reaches out and runs a long finger down from my shoulder to my wrist where I'm gripping the steering wheel, and tingles run in the other direction back up to my throat. I risk a glance at his thick dark lashes and thin, firm lips. His scruff looks soft and edible.

He squeezes my hand. "Goddammit, I don't need to think about this. I'm going to be uncomfortable this whole journey. We've got three hours in this car. I warn you I've never been able to ignore an erection. I might have to rub one out while you're driving." And oh my God! I love this outspoken honesty. Something warm and wicked rises up.

I wave my hand at him. "Be my guest. We may have to stop, though, because I'd like to watch."

I don't dare meet his eyes, and he leans over and presses his nose into my jaw, growling into my skin.

"You have a filthy mouth. How am I going to keep my hands to myself all weekend?" he says, sitting back in his seat and staring out at the darkness.

A filthy mouth? I have *never* been described that way. "Who said you had to keep your hands to yourself?"

He groans. "Stop it, all right? We're going to be with your family, your parents. Let's do a crossword." He twists and leans into the back, pulling *The Washington Post* out of his battered rucksack.

He does *crosswords*? "A crossword?"

"Yeah. Don't you like them? Perfect for relaxing and taking your mind off things. Tricky bastards, though."

"You might have more in common with my family than I thought," I mutter, switching on the wipers as a light rain starts to patter across the windscreen.

"Why's that?"

"They are big crossword doers, too."

"Finally, some good news," he mutters, rifling through his bag again and pulling out a pen.

"Why?"

"Well, I can't really talk about drugs or hacking, so it will give me a topic of conversation."

He pauses for a minute as he searches through the paper on his lap, folding it open when he finds the right place.

"By the way, Kate, we've talked about your family and what the form is for this wedding, but don't tell them I'm a hacker. Tell them I'm a software engineer, programmer, electronics … whatever. I don't normally tell people what I do for a living."

"Why's that?"

He shrugs. "Too many questions, too many assumptions about it all being illegal. The fewer people who know, the less exposed I am."

"It's that dangerous?"

He stares over at me. "I try not to do the data people would kill for or kill to protect, but you don't do this and not come to the attention of people you'd rather not be on the radar for. I can handle myself; I just don't want anyone I know to be sucked into something they shouldn't be. I'm just being cautious."

He's such an incredible combination of risk-taking and common sense.

"Anyway," he adds, taking a deep breath and looking down at *The Post* again. "We'd better get a move on: We've got a crossword to do, and I'm sure you've got more stuff to brief me on before we arrive."

*

Two hours later, we pass by ornate entrance pillars into the middle of a large turning circle graced by a fountain. Gravel crunches under our tires. Fabian lets out a low whistle at the cream Italianate building with a beautiful wrought-iron porch. Yeah, the Wheatleigh is just the type of place I imagined Javier having his wedding. We leave the car with the valet and head up the steps to the entrance, the roar and clink of the pre-wedding party drifting out through the front doors.

Fabian's face is a mask, and through the lobby and plush velvet seating, I can see people milling around under a pavilion out back. A lady sweeps across the floor and trots upstairs in a long turquoise gown. A hotel employee steps forward with a small bow, and a taut expression creeps over Fabian's face, so I reach out and squeeze his arm.

He glances at me and winks. "Good job I brought a clean T-shirt," he leans in to murmur in my ear as I give the woman our details. I've no idea what my parents have arranged for us, but when she hands over the keys, I stare down at the single set of room keys and a shiver runs down my spine.

"I bought a tux for tomorrow, Kate, but I didn't bring much else," Fabian says, peering at the throng outside the double doors. "This looks pretty smart to me."

"I'm not sure where this desire to conform is suddenly coming from," I say.

His eyes are shuttered as he looks at me. "I just don't want to embarrass anyone."

Oh God! "When you said yes to this, I was relieved. I didn't think about how it might make you feel. I'm sorry." *Stupid, Kate.*

Fabian undoes his man bun and ties it up again with a frown. Out through the open French windows, a man in a pinstriped shirt with his back to us wraps his arm around the shoulders of the suited guy next to him, laughing loudly.

"I'm always the troublemaker, Kate, even when I'm not trying to be. You don't have to apologize for it."

I squeeze his elbow. "Every woman will be envious of me this evening. You'll be the only person here who doesn't look like a banker clone."

He laughs at this.

I catch the profile of the man in the shirt through the French windows. *Javier*. He looks just as obnoxious as I remember. As we watch, his other hand lands on the back of the dark-haired woman next to him and slides down over her ass, squeezing.

*Is that Cassandra?* I clear my throat. "I need to go and shower and change. I smell of hospital antiseptic," I say. Fabian nods, and I lean forward and kiss him on the cheek. "Don't worry, you always look great."

His eyes warm, but he shakes his head at me. "I'm going to get changed, Kate."

He takes my hand and uncurls it, looking at the single key lying there, and his slow-growing grin is a work of magic, lighting up his whole face.

*

Kate's singing in the shower by the time I'm ready, and how out of key it is makes me grin. I tap on the door.

"I'm going to explore, Maria Callas. I'll see you in reception."

She laughs. "Sorry about the singing!"

"It's all good. I'll see you down there."

I slip out the bedroom door. Going straight down and throwing myself into something so foreign doesn't appeal when I can see beautifully manicured grounds out of the windows that look out over the rear of the building. I wander along the corridor away from the main stairs, eventually finding a fire door with a sign that says, "STAFF ONLY." When I push through it, a set of service stairs winds down toward a rear extension. *Perfect.* But as I start down, a giggle drifts up to me.

Then unmistakably a man's voice, muffled. I pause on the step and peer over the railings. I can just make out two heads of dark hair, tucked away in the bottom of the stairwell.

"Come on, you know you want to." The man's voice becomes clearer as he lifts his head.

"You're wicked—we can't do this here! What if someone finds us? You're getting married tomorrow."

*Getting married?* Shit. This is *Javier*? The man smooths the woman's hair back from her forehead, and as I lean a bit farther, I get a better look at his face. His other hand is cupped around her jaw.

"So? You think that's going to change anything?"

I can hear the pout in the woman's voice when she answers. "You decided to marry *her*."

*What?*

"Babe. You don't think I'm going to get lots of breathing space? I'm buying a place out of town. It won't be long before she's living there." His voice drops. "I'll have endless excuses to stay in town, and she won't be breathing down my neck. We can spend all night. Just imagine." He nuzzles into her neck again. "I've got something for you."

She arches against him. "Yeah?"

He puts his hand into his back pocket and draws out a slim box. The woman takes it greedily and opens it up. Something catches the light, and she gives a little squeal.

"Shhhhh!" he says.

"Oh, it's beautiful."

"You see? That's my commitment to you. Cassandra's getting nothing like that from me."

*Sonofabitch.* I watch as he takes something out of the box and then clips it around her wrist.

"Promise me." she says, still pouting.

"Of course. You know you've always been my best girl."

I bet she fucking is. Out of how many?

"I want to see that on your wrist as you go down on me."

As I watch, he leans back and her hands come to his belt. I stare in horrified fascination as she unzips him and sinks to her knees, and shit, I feel like a slimy voyeur, but getting evidence of this is just too tempting. I fumble in my pocket for my phone. Then checking around, I sink down on the stairs, stick my hand through the railing and start videoing.

*

Fabian has left the bedroom by the time I'm out of the shower, so I throw on a lick of makeup and head out of the door. The red dress that I flung into my suitcase at the last minute curls around my legs, clinging to my damp skin and revealing far too much at the front. Some of Fabian's attitude must have rubbed off on me tonight because it matches my mood.

As I descend past stained-glass windows to the lobby, still trying to walk properly in my high heels, I lose my breath when I catch sight of Fabian leaning against the reception desk, idly chatting to the lady who checked us in. He's in smart black jeans and a tight black T-shirt that clings to his ropey chest, long tattoos trailing out from beneath the short sleeves, an assortment of leather around one wrist. His hair is up, his scruff suspiciously tidy on his chin. As I head across the parquet floor, he props his elbow on the desk, and I can't tear my eyes away from the way his muscles tighten. The woman on the desk flutters her eyelashes at him, so I sneak up to him, my hand coming to his hip and sliding into his back pocket as I press against his side. I'm not sure whether I'm staking my claim on him, pulling his attention from the flirty receptionist, or something else. Liquid-silver eyes tip down to my face, then his eyes widen and he pulls back to examine what I'm wearing.

"You can't wear that," he says.

I laugh. Am I offended? "Why not?"

"It's way too sexy. I'll have my hands up your skirt in two seconds flat."

My eyes flick to the receptionist as she looks away, mouth pursed, and red heat drifts up my cheeks.

I grin at him and raise my eyebrows, and he closes his eyes and groans, leaning in to sniff my neck, lips brushing my skin.

"I'm not taking advantage of you this weekend, Kate," he mumbles. "I swore I'd be on my best behavior."

I pout at him, and he steps farther into me and slides a hand around my waist. "I'll just imagine what's underneath." He whispers right by my ear. "I'm only just managing to keep my hands off your ass." He peers down the front of my dress, and I grin, shivering a bit when his fingers make contact with the edge.

"Kate?"

The voice of my younger sister echoes behind me, and I spin round in Fabian's arm, taking in Georgia's bouncing brown curls and broad smile as she heads across the lobby. A strapless cream lace evening gown clings to every curve, red shoes flashing beneath its long straight skirt. I step forward to pull her into a warm hug. *My family ally*. Thank God.

"Are you trying to upstage the bride?"

"As if. Have you seen Cassandra's dress?"

I catch a glimpse of her expression as I draw back: Her eyes are big and fixed on Fabian over my shoulder. I immediately step to the side.

"Fabian, this is Georgie, my younger sister, and …"

I've been so caught up in seeing Georgie that only now do I notice the man behind her, and now I'm gaping. He's the most straitlaced person I think I've ever seen. Good-looking in that way a lot of preppy guys at college are: soft wavy blond hair, clean-shaven, polo shirt, taupe chinos. The kind of guy I would never have pegged for her. No wonder my parents were quiet about this relationship; I'll bet they're secretly smug their wayward daughter is with someone so wholesome.

Georgie clocks me staring at him and steps back quickly too. "This is Brad," she says, beaming, and I almost laugh. Even his name is straitlaced.

Perfect white teeth flash at me, and two very clean-shaven dimples pop out, and now I see why my sister is interested: He's devastating when he smiles. But he's a puppy next to Fabian, who is looking more and more like the wolf Jo said he was.

"Great to meet you, Brad," I say, holding out a hand, which he clasps in a jock-like shake.

"You and I have some catching up to do," I lean in to whisper to Georgie, my eyes widening meaningfully, and she laughs.

"Definitely," she says, raising her eyebrows at Fabian.

"Where is everyone?" I peer behind her, as Fabian shakes hands with Brad. But she's still focused on Fabian and smiling widely, and I have seen that smile throughout our whole childhood; it appeared on her face every time my mother, fists clenched like she wanted to hit her, confronted Georgie in our family kitchen. She can see how much trouble Fabian is going to cause: It's coming off him in waves. She gestures vaguely toward the back of the hotel, eyes dancing.

"Somewhere near the bar outside, I think," she says.

"Let's go find everyone then," I say, looking up at Fabian as he gives me a reluctant half smile, rubbing a hand around the back of his neck, and I'm warm with the idea that perhaps he cares about this.

*

To start off with, my family is unfailingly polite to Fabian. Apart from a flicker of an eyebrow from my mother, and my father spinning his drink in his hand and quizzing Fabian about what he does, both their faces are like masks. My brothers, however, stare at him in undisguised glee. He cottons on to my father's prejudices about success and money pretty fast, and he starts talking to him about his love of alcohol and how recreational drugs aid relaxation. Seb winks at me with a broad grin as he keeps refilling everyone's glasses.

My dad's face turns redder and redder, and he gets more and more strident while Fabian dodges questions about his job and his lifestyle.

"So, tell me more about this company you work for—Xeracorp?" Fabian says, knocking back another whiskey Seb has placed in his hand.

I blink at him, but his gaze is trained on my dad. I'm sure that my father hasn't mentioned Xeracorp at any point in the conversation, and although I briefed Fabian on my parents on the way up here, I didn't talk about my dad's job. He's a successful corporate man through and through, and his chest puffs out as Fabian tilts his head toward him. When he begins to ask my dad about overseas contracts, I tune out.

Out of the corner of my eye, I see Javier, in a sharp dark suit and shirt, working the room with his fiancée, Cassandra. She's gorgeous in that plastic way: contoured makeup; fake blonde hair, perfectly styled; immaculately manicured; thick penciled-in eyebrows. I look down at my torn, unpainted nails and slide my hands behind my back. As they approach us, her long black lace dress swishing around her ankles, she's all simpering charm, saying how delighted she is to meet Javier's family, her red claws curling into his arm. But she's also clearly not the owner of the ass he was squeezing earlier on.

My father turns away from Fabian, face clearing as he asks Javier about his work on Wall Street with drunken bonhomie. I groan inside. Tod coughs into his drink. Javier is a patronizing pain in the ass about his role as a corporate raider, and he straightens and launches into how much he's earning in a loud voice. My eyes skim around the room, clocking all the rich bankers. Fabian must be hating all this.

"You see, Tod? Seb? All the money you could be making?" My father booms, slapping Javier on the back. He can be snide at times about my mother's propensity to encourage us into medicine, but we're not exactly in a poorly paid profession.

Fabian's tension radiates through my dress at my side, and I steal a glance at him. His eyes are fixed on Javier, color high on his cheeks like he's seen a snake. Something is working behind his neutral expression.

As if realizing he's the subject of scrutiny, Javier's eyes stray toward Fabian, scanning over the tattoos escaping from the edges of his sleeve before asking, "And what do you do?" in the kind of hard, flat tone that suggests he really couldn't care less.

"Amphetamines mostly," Fabian says in a drawl, and Javier blinks for a second as heat begins to build under his already flushed cheeks.

In the pause that follows, Fabian smiles tightly at Cassandra. "I'm sorry to say this, but he watches far too much illegal porn to be healthy."

Silence hangs in the air like smoke filling a room, and then we all try to talk at once. Javier's face turns slowly puce: He's not going to let the comment go. *Be careful what you wish for, Kate.* Fabian might well annoy my family, but he's also perfectly capable of annoying everyone else as well.

"Don't insult my fiancée like that or I'll have you thrown out," Javier's clipped tone rings over the raised voices. Several heads turn from a group standing near to us.

"For telling the truth?" Fabian eyes him distastefully. "You're insulting her way more than I ever would." He turns to Cassandra again. "Check his computer, and if he tries to wipe it, he won't be able to—it always leaves a trace."

I'm watching Javier as Fabian says this, and I catch the twitch that runs across his forehead and his eyes before he attempts to hide it. Fucking hell, he's worried. A bolt burns right to my toes. Fabian *knows* this?

*But of course.*

I'm so slow. Fabian is capable of hacking into anything; an individual computer would be child's play to a person like him. I place a steady hand on my chest, studying everyone standing around as cold realization drips into me. How many people's computers has he hacked into and how much does he know? *Holy shit.* What must it be like to be him? To have the skill to find out everyone's secrets so easily? Is that awesome or terrifying?

Javier's beady eyes land on me, and he leans forward hissing, "How could you bring someone like this to our wedding party, Kate? You're a disgrace." His eyes dart over us all. "Your whole family is an embarrassment, actually. My father always said as much." He snatches Cassandra's hand to sweep away, but Fabian's hand lands on his arm.

"Leave Kate the fuck alone. The only one here who's disgracing this family is you."

Fabian's eyes narrow as Javier shakes him off and stalks away, like he can't escape fast enough, dragging Cassandra behind him. But no one is watching them: They are all staring at Fabian as if he's a tiger that's suddenly appeared in the middle of a shopping mall. Fabian stares after Javier's retreating back with cold, dead eyes.

"I hope she checks," he says. "That man is sick."

I catch the unrestrained delight on Tod's face just before he steps forward and claps Fabian on the back.

"I've endured that guy looking down on me my entire life. That was the best ten minutes I think I've ever had with him."

My father pulls himself up to his full height, jacket rising up around his ears as he forcibly tucks his shirt into his pants.

"Tod," he says in admonishment before turning to Fabian. "This is Javier's wedding. That was incredibly rude," he says. "I don't know who you are, young man, apart from the fact that you're a friend of my daughter's, but I don't think that gives you the liberty to come in and throw accusations at people when you know nothing about them. This is a family wedding, a special occasion. You have no right to …"

Fabian is watching him, face relaxed. "I know everything about him," he interrupts quietly. "I don't say things that aren't true." He shakes his head. "Especially not things like that."

"Well, I don't see how you can …"

Then he leans toward my father, voice quiet but the anger simmering under his skin like the hum of an electricity cable stretched tight.

"This is a friendly warning. I don't know how familiar you are with the illegal deals your company is doing in South Africa, but you're clearly in a senior position and you either need to be very careful or find out what's going on."

In the total silence that follows, the alcoholic redness in my father's face drains away, replaced by a mottled flush that works its way up his throat. His eyes swing to mine, and two spots of color appear high on his cheeks as his lip curls. I realize with astonishment that his scorn is aimed at me. *He's disgusted with me?*

"I never want to see this man again, Kate, and if he shows up at the wedding tomorrow, I'll make sure he's thrown out."

His gaze swings to my brothers and sisters. They are all looking completely stunned like they can't quite believe the car crash that has unfolded in front of us.

"I expect you to support me in this," he says, eyes scanning their faces and not looking at Fabian. He turns sharply and stalks away. My mother's hand is pressed against her throat, and with a darting look around us all she shoots off after him, heels clicking on the parquet floor as she follows my father out through the French windows. We all track the back of her dark blue evening dress as she disappears. Tod swings back to Fabian.

"Holy shit," he says, looking down and swilling his whiskey in his glass before knocking it back. A group of people have gathered under the awning on the patio, and are eyeing us curiously. Fabian presses two fingers of one hand against either side of his nose.

"How did you find *that* out? Is it all true?" Tod says.

Fabian squints up at the ornate ceiling, and then his eyes drop to meet mine. "Shit. I'm sorry, Kate."

Tod starts to laugh. "I don't know who this guy is, Kate, but I really fucking like him."

Georgie grins as if she can hardly contain herself. Brad is staring at the floor.

Fabian shakes his head sheepishly, the tight flush of anger dropping away as quickly as it arrived, and he runs his hands over his face.

"I can't bear men like them. I can never resist bringing them down a peg or two. I should never have come here with you, Kate." He shoots me an apologetic glance. "I'm a liability with alcohol. I can't keep my mouth shut when I'm drunk." He leans into me and inhales my neck. His lips are warm and insistent on my skin.

Tod laughs. "Stop molesting my sister and talk to me about how you know this stuff."

Fabian straightens waving his hands. "I'm a programmer."

Tod's eyes narrow. "A rather unusual one, I'm guessing," he says. "Is it all true?"

Fabian studies the floor like he's trying to work out what to say.

"Yeah," Fabian says, looking at me. "Fuck, I'm sorry, Kate. I thought I'd do some research before I met everyone. It was superficial stuff to start off with, but then a couple of things came up, and when I pulled on those threads it was like opening Pandora's box."

I grin at him. He certainly has an interesting definition of "research."

"Don't apologize," I say. "That was kind of amazing."

"I thoroughly enjoyed that," says Tod. "Dad's an asshole."

I frown at him, but he waves a hand at me.

"Why are you so disapproving? You know what he's like. He patronizes everyone he meets. Do you think he's involved in that South Africa stuff?"

Fabian opens his mouth and then shuts it again, and I catch his eye. I'm guessing that he's found out more than he's letting on and the answer is yes, my dad's part of it. Fabian was holding back in not exposing him.

"I hope she doesn't marry him," Fabian mumbles, clearly wanting to distract us back to Javier. "He's pretty sick."

"Really?" Tod says, voice thrilled again. "Fuck, no longer do I need to hear from him, my aunt and uncle, or our parents about how much money that asshole has made. Hallelujah! Fabian, I can tell you don't want to talk too much about what you do, but I'm getting you another whiskey." He grins evilly, turning around to beckon to a waitress. "I think this amount of excitement in one evening requires us all to get totally wasted."

# CHAPTER 12

## *Kate*

A skinful of bluebird is right under my eye, and I blink at the ink and the delicate lines and shading before rolling onto my back. I'm in bed, with *Fabian*? A dim light cuts through the gap in the curtains, and my eyes drift across his back to the script on his arm and the white sheet lying over his hips. He's naked. The curve of his ass is just visible and my mouth waters: The urge to run my hand over it and squeeze makes me dizzy. He's sex on a stick. I blink down over my bra and panties. Did we …? The previous evening shimmers just out of reach. This weekend has gone downhill so fast. I'm contemplating the ceiling rose when there's a sharp rap on the door. When I sit up, the whole room swims alarmingly so I collapse straight back down again.

"I'm coming," I shout, rolling over and shifting out of bed gingerly. Fabian doesn't stir.

My phone says 7 a.m. I think I've had about three hours of sleep.

Staggering upright, my foot lands on something soft and slippery: my red dress. A vision of tossing it over my shoulder and collapsing face down shimmers through my mind. There's no sign of a bathrobe so I pull the dress over my head, tipping over, and my hand shoots out to land on a chair as my head swoops. I remember Tod buying round of shots after rounds of shots, Fabian and I supporting each other up the stairs, bouncing off the stairwell to the banister and back again.

I prop myself against the wall, groping my way along to the door, and when I open it, my stomach drops. Cassandra is standing there in a black polo neck, black pants, and full makeup. Her mouth is a set slash of scarlet.

Before I can say anything, she grabs my arm. "Is he here?" she hisses.

"Who?"

"That man you were with."

I nod at her, and she hustles in, eyes widening on Fabian in bed. She strides straight up to him and shakes his shoulder, bold as brass.

He grunts and rolls over, eyes opening then blinking fast when they latch on to her. He clutches at the sheet, pulling it up to his chest, and I grin at his bashfulness. His eyes sweep around the room and land on mine, and I grimace at him in apology, but really I want to bust out laughing.

"What did you find on his computer?" she snaps at him, and his eyes swing back in near panic to her, then he shakes his head, groaning and rolling over again and burying his face in the pillow, saying something that sounds suspiciously like "still drunk."

So, we're both feeling like crap. I sink down on the other side of the bed.

"You have to help me," she says, planting two fists on the edge of the mattress as she leans over him.

"Your fiancé is an asshole. Don't marry him," he grunts into the pillow.

She tips her head down and breathes out heavily through her nose. When she lifts her head, her voice turns pleading. "You can't let this wedding go ahead without me knowing what you found."

"Only if you pay me," Fabian mumbles.

Her eyes narrow. "Fine," she snaps. "How much do you want?"

Seriously?

"I was joking," he grunts.

"Well, I'm not," she says.

"Fuck. Why don't I just keep my big mouth shut."

I shouldn't be enjoying the drama of this weekend as much as I am. Life with Fabian is anything but boring: He's impulsive and mad. How crazy is all this? I'm beginning to understand that he can uncover anything. Jo was right, he really *is* nothing like David. David would never have done anything like this. He would have been polite, aiming to curry favor, not hauling my family over the coals. Fabian isn't trying to impress anyone; I don't think he works that way. I've never been with someone with so little need to conform, who *really* doesn't give a shit.

He rolls over onto his back sighing. "I'm only helping if you promise me that you won't say anything to anybody about where the information came from."

She eyes him shrewdly but nods.

"I'm serious. I'm doing this so you can see what kind of guy he is, but if I ever found out you told anyone I'd done this, I'd come after you too. I can find out everything about you. Do you understand?"

Something passes over her face when he says this—a shadow, a beat of hesitation—but eventually she nods.

"Pass me my bag." He waves at the beaten-up old bag on the floor. When she fetches it, he pulls out two laptops and places them on the covers, opening the lids and powering them up. He closes his eyes and gestures to a carafe with two glasses sitting on a mahogany table by the window.

"Get me some water."

Cassandra dutifully trots over and brings him a glass of water, which he downs in one.

"Are you sure you want to see this?" he says, resting his head back against the headboard like the mere act of being upright is costing him dearly.

She frowns at him, and he sighs again, fingers flying over the keyboard before he points at the screen. "This is Javier's sign-in screen, yes?"

She shifts to stand near the head of the bed, eyes skipping over his laptop. "Yes, God, yes," she says, pressing her hand to her chest and looking at Fabian. I don't know what she was expecting, but I don't think it was this. "I couldn't get into it this morning; he'd changed his password."

Fabian's laugh vibrates through the bed. He studies the other laptop, the code running down the screen.

"This might take a while," he mutters, tapping keys, then he laughs again. "He's such an idiot; he changed one number in it. Clearly not the smartest tool in the box."

Windows pop up as he searches through the files. Fabian grunts. "He's been busy, though; he tried to delete it all last night."

"Seriously?" Cassandra's eyes are huge, with fear or excitement I have no clue, like she's relishing the idea of discovering her future husband's innermost secrets.

"Yeah, but you can't do that properly unless you know what you're doing. The disk always has temporary files. I kept copies of it all anyway."

Clicking through some folders, he looks up at Cassandra. "Are you ready?" he says.

Suddenly porn fills the screen, some with very young girls. I turn away.

"There's worse stuff," Fabian grunts.

"Show me it," she says, mouth a grim thin line like a crack in granite. I can't imagine what it must be like for her seeing what he's been doing. I wouldn't want those images in my brain.

"That's enough," she says suddenly, straightening. "Thank you," she says to Fabian. "I'm going to need some proof," she says. "Can you provide that?" He nods wearily. Perhaps this is the first question everyone asks him.

"But my role in this is confidential; there will be no trace back to me," he says. "I'll tell you what you need to do to collect the evidence, retrieve and store the files, gather a digital footprint of his use. Do you understand?"

She narrows her eyes at him. "Yes. I'm going to pay you very well for this, and I'm not taking no for an answer."

Fabian sighs and nods at her like he's had this kind of conversation before.

"What are you going to do?" I say. "Call it off?"

She laughs. "Oh no, just think how I can manipulate him for the rest of his life with this. He'll do everything I tell him from now on, or he'll end up in jail.

How ideal will that be? Like the perfect relationship. Total control."

Holy shit, is she serious?

"Thanks," she says and turns on her high heels and taps out of the room as fast as she entered it, the door closing with a soft click. I stare where she disappeared. Did that just happen? Cassandra was in our room for twenty minutes, tops.

Fabian drops his laptops onto the floor and rolls onto his front, groaning. "Looks like the wedding is still on then," he grunts into the bedding, and I lie down next to him, the room swinging around dangerously. My stomach cramps and sweat starts to prickle on my forehead.

"I think I'm going to be sick."

I throw myself out of bed and through the en-suite bathroom door, hands sliding on the toilet bowl as liquid splatters out of me. Sinking down, my hands tremble on the edge, tiles cold under my knees. If I've felt worse, I can't remember it. Another spasm has me leaning forward with a groan.

A soft hand lands on my back, and I twist my head. Fabian slumps down by my side on the floor against the vanity cabinet beneath the sink, eyes closed, face pale, hand now moving up and down my back. He's pulled his jeans on, but the tattoos around his shoulders and arms are on full display. Somehow, he doesn't look like a technology wizard under the harsh lights.

"Are you waiting your turn to throw up or comforting me?" I crack.

He smiles. "I think I abuse my system so much that my body has given up trying to reject anything it doesn't like."

"Cassandra is mad," I say. My stomach pitches, and I lean over the toilet again.

He makes small circles on my back. "Jesus, yes. Imagine knowing that about a person and marrying them anyway. Insane."

Despite the crazy behavior, day to day, Fabian both understands people and rejects the kind of nonsense that other people indulge in. But perhaps he is like David, saying one thing and living by another.

"He's a trader, right? Lots of traders view hardcore porn, don't they?" I say.

"Yeah, I'd say it's pretty endemic in the finance industry. I got a contract once to clear it all off a company's server. One of the most difficult jobs I've ever done—that stuff is impossible. It leaves a trace everywhere."

We lapse into silence. I'm cuddling the bowl like it's my favorite comfort blanket.

"How are you doing?" he asks eventually. "Still sick?"

I nod.

Fabian closes his eyes and waves at a black toilet bag on the countertop. "I've got an emergency pack in there, enough for the two of us."

Dragging myself upright, I run the tap and wash my hands and mouth before grabbing the bag and collapsing back down next to him. I open it to find four plastic pouches of white powder.

"What is it?"

He turns his head from where he's propped against the cabinet, and opens one eye to peer at me. "My magic formula," he says, mouth quirking, long eyelashes sweeping his cheeks as his eyes flutter closed.

His fingers are pale against the blue denim of his jeans, gnarly like they've spent years grabbing on to the loose concrete of windowsills. Three star tattoos decorate his right hand, one by the base of his thumb and two others on the outside edge by his little finger. I'm curious about the abrasions and scabs on his knuckles, a cut along one side of a nail that has been half ripped off. I peer into the bag again and take the pouches out.

"I'm not sure I …"

My eyes dart back to discover he's grinning widely, and God, I want to kiss him. Would his lips be hard or soft? He cracks open an eye again.

"Do you trust me, Kate? Would you take it if I didn't tell you what it was?"

I look at the bags in my hand. "Are you testing me?"

He shakes his head.

"Not really. Sorry, I'm just messing …"

He's asking a question here, though. Something important. He's seeing if I'll hand control over to him, if he's earned that right. I'm on a roller coaster at the top of the ride, staring down the drop. As an intern, I could lose everything if I got caught taking something illegal, but I want to believe in him. He appears honest and straight, but I'm not sure if he's really like that and I am concerned about drugs.

"Okay, I'm going to give you some ground rules here," I say, and he laughs, shaking his head.

"No way. I'm not trying to test you, Kate. I was just kidding. I do that shit sometimes, just ignore me."

I examine the white packet again. "No seriously. I want to trust you. I'm just not much of a risk-taker, and I could face disciplinary action for taking something illegal."

"Okay," he says slowly, as he chews the side of the battered nail I was examining earlier. "I'll make a deal with you. You trust me and I'll not do anything that could get you into trouble."

I swallow. Am I going to do this?

"How do you take it?" I ask.

"Empty it into your mouth and wash it down with water," he grunts.

I stand again, and before I can think twice I'm filling up the cup from the back of the sink and crouching down on the floor again, handing him a packet, watching as he tips it back and downs half the water before making a face.

I lock eyes with him, open the plastic bag and tip it into my mouth, then without thinking too much I gulp down the rest of the water. It tastes foul … like acetaminophen and …

"What was in that?" I say, and he shakes his head, shifting to stand and dragging me back into the bedroom. He shucks his jeans as I collapse down, and he follows me, curling around my back and pulling me into him, a strong hand pressed over my stomach.

"Sleep," he says. "I'll tell you later," and something about his warmth and my churning stomach keeps me silent. I close my eyes, shutting out the way the world is tipping and dipping, sliding back into the darkness.

My eyes blink open to the same view of a mahogany chest of drawers and a damask-covered chair. Fabian's heat is like a furnace at my back. A gentle tap, tap, tapping noise is coming from the door.

"Kate! Kate! Are you up?"

Georgie. I swing around to sit on the side of the bed, and then I'm upright and goddamn I feel almost okay. I look down at the red dress as I head to the door: Nothing too bad on display.

Georgie grins in delight at me when I open the door and peeps around my shoulder to where a half-naked Fabian is lying on his side, fast asleep. Her eyes dance.

"Wow!" she says, unabashedly ogling my … my … What are Fabian and I to each other now? "That is the best thing I've seen in a very long time." She giggles and gives me a wicked smile. "Those tattoos," she whispers. "You are a badass sister. I'm envious."

I laugh, looking at the script that runs all over the muscles on his right-hand side and the smooth bulge of his bicep. I want to crawl back into bed, straddle him, and bite him. I never check out guys and think thoughts like this. Maybe he gave me a mind-bending drug cocktail in that powder?

"We should stop ogling—he's sleeping," I whisper.

"I can hear every word," Fabian grunts from the bed, eyes closed, and Georgie giggles again. He rolls over, and his sleepy eyes lock on her. She covers her eyes, and I see he's got morning wood.

"Put that away," I hiss at him, grinning, and he chuckles, rolling over again.

"Still in last night's clothes, I see," Georgie says.

"Why are you here?"

"You were both pretty out of it last night. So was Brad by the way, so I thought I'd do the rounds and wake everyone up. The wedding is in an hour."

"Oh my God, seriously?" I shoot across the room and grab my phone from the nightstand.

"Thank Christ I don't have to go," Fabian mumbles.

"Oh no, you do. Apparently, Cassandra has insisted you're there. Well, that's what she said at breakfast this morning."

"Fuck," Fabian says into the pillow. "It always backfires when I help people."

"You've been helping Cassandra?" Georgie asks.

I hustle her out the door. "Let me get ready. It's a long story. I'll tell you later, at the reception. We'll need some entertainment to get us through today."

Once she's gone, Fabian rolls onto his side and studies me with sleepy eyes, then pats the bed.

"Come here," he says, and in two steps I collapse back down next to him.

"I feel surprisingly okay," I say, and he laughs. I turn my head on the pillow. "Turns out, you *are* a magician."

He winces and closes his eyes. "We should compare notes on drugs some time." Rolling into me, he presses his nose into my throat, inhaling as he did in the car. His erection is a solid presence at my hip.

"How about we do that thing you suggested on the drive here where you watch me getting myself off."

I grin at the ceiling. "I'm down for that."

A groan rumbles up from deep in his body as he nuzzles at the red fabric at the side of my neck.

"This is the hottest dress I've ever seen. Every time I see you, I get hard."

I'm dissolving into the mattress. He props himself up on one hand and studies my hair, then down over my eyes and nose, and I lick my lips as he leans in so close that we're sharing breath, his gray eyes swimming like oil on a pool. Encircling my wrist with his fingers, he brushes my skin, his thumb rhythmically pressing into my palm.

"Anticipation," he murmurs, his mouth curling up. "Taking it slow is my favorite thing."

And with that statement, my body freezes. *What?* This impulsive, thrill-seeking guy? He likes to take it *slow*? Will he hold off and hold off? Hold *me* off? I can almost taste it. I shift my hips, and he catches my top lip gently with his teeth, oil-eyes never leaving mine, and I want to know how he tastes, how soft his lips are. But I realize now that Fabian won't push.

"What do you like, Kate?" he says, releasing my lip and running his tongue over it, and I open my mouth chasing his kiss, but he shifts back ever so slightly. His eyelashes are long and spaced out, a small black dot sits in the colored part of his right eye, faint laughter lines fanning out from the far corner. The heat between my legs tightens into an ache.

“I think with you, I’d like everything,” I say, reaching up to stroke his eyebrow, as slowly as I can, and it moves under my finger as he frowns. My nail snags on a piercing hole and I press on it.

“I have a number of piercings I’ve got bored with. You can discover them all,” he says, leaning in to run his nose along the side of mine, lips brushing my face, the warmth of his breath drifting over the soft down of my cheek as strands of thread starts to wrap around us, pulling us ever closer. I nip his lower lip, body full of lightness and air. Who knew I could be this forward?

And then his mouth is on mine. I expect it to be brutal and aroused, but despite the hardness of his erection pressing into my thigh, his kiss is achingly soft. His lips are smooth and tart, the sharp tang of whiskey and the chemicals of whatever we took earlier. He brushes over in a broad sweep, pushing my bottom lip down, nibbling across the tender length of it, playing with the corner, growling. I realize that rumbling sounds have been coming from his body ever since he curled into me, and I want to growl right along with him. My mouth is open now, seeking more contact, and he licks my upper lip, then my lower one. He does this over and over again, never pushing forward or pulling back, our bodies pressing together as the ache inside gets worse and worse.

“Beautiful, Kate,” he groans. “Oh fuck!”

And he rubs himself against my hip, but the slow contained kisses don’t change. He’s such a mass of contradictions, and I smile against his mouth.

Propping himself up on his arms, he blows out a long breath, biceps popping as he smiles down at me, and I reach up to loosen the band in his hair. It flops around his face as I run my hands into the silk of it. Then he pushes up to sit, pulling me up too.

“We need to get ready for this wedding.” It comes out as a hot growl. “No time to do this now.”

I clear my throat, staring at the bedcover in a haze. “We don’t have to go.”

“I’m trying to be good here, Kate.”

“I’m not sure I want you to be good,” I mutter.

# CHAPTER 13

## *Fabian*

I drum my fingers on the door handle of the car, staring out the window at the Taconic State Parkway, full of finance drones returning to the city from their second homes upstate.

"Bored?" Kate says, her lips curling up.

Busted. We're only fifteen minutes into the journey.

I wave my hand around the interior. "I'm not used to sitting still unless I'm at a computer."

Despite all the nonsense of the last two days, nothing further has happened between Kate and me. We've curled around each other for two nights, drunk and ill, and shit, I didn't want to take advantage of her when she was wasted, notwithstanding the hot make-out session right before the wedding. The second night was not much better than the night we arrived, except I avoided Javier and her parents—surprisingly easy at a large function. And I've watched her body move under a nightgown, under shimmery slinky dresses, and now jeans and a sweatshirt. I roll my shoulders.

"Why are you staring at me?" she says, smiling.

"Why did you invite me to the wedding again?"

Kate grins at this. "No better options."

I wince, pressing my hand to my chest. "Oh, I'm wounded." I study my hands. "You said you wanted to annoy your parents. Did I live up to expectations?"

She laughs. "What do you think?"

What was I thinking checking up on her family before coming up here? It started off innocently enough, looking people up on LinkedIn, but before I knew it, I was hacking into Javier's computer to find out what he was really like. I shift uncomfortably in my seat. Kate's eyes are flickering between the rear-view mirror and the parkway as she drives, and I need to take my mind off this weekend, what I might have set in motion and the damage I might have done.

"I'm sorry."

"What? Don't be! I enjoyed it. It was anything but boring." She shakes her head laughing, indicating to pull out as she checks the road. "I can't quite believe all that happened."

"That's what I do when I'm bored and drunk: I cause trouble." I pick at some hard skin on my thumb.

"I think you caused trouble because you were confronted by a couple of assholes."

"Yeah, but one of them was your dad."

"He's been an asshole all my life. My parents are …" She hesitates. "If he's really involved in what you think he is, then warning him was the right thing to do."

"Maybe." I'm still not sure whether I should have exposed her father in front of his family like that. "Probably could have done it in a better way."

She shakes her head at me. "He's not the kind of guy who'll listen to some more reasoned approach."

And I get it, he didn't give me that vibe either.

The easy understanding we have is like an unstoppable force. What was I thinking pushing her away? My eyes wander over her. She's looking a little less than her usual perfect self and fuck, I like it. Her face is bare and she's wearing a pair of ripped jeans that are loose and slouchy and an oversized sweater that keeps falling off her shoulder. What is it with this girl and tops that slide off? The reaction it sets off in me is like tinder in dry brush. I'm guessing I've got weekend Kate now, and I don't want to let her go home: I want another night.

"I'm wondering where you're sleeping tonight," I say, the words bubbling up and out before I can stop them.

Her eyebrows raise, and she risks a quick glance at me before her eyes skitter back to the road.

"Are you working tomorrow?" I say.

"I'm at the hospital, a late shift. I start at midday. Are you inviting me for a sleepover?" A small smile dances over her face.

I grin at her profile. "I might be."

She nods. "Then I'm spending the night with you."

I blink at her. *She said yes.* Now the drive morphs into something else entirely; I'm no longer worried and bored, I'm torturing myself. I examine her bare shoulder, the creamy skin, and I shift in my seat, propping a dirty boot against the dash. What will she let me do? What might she do to me? I'm hardening in my jeans, unable to tamp it down.

By the time we've found a parking spot near my place, tension is thrumming through me. As I head to the back of the car, I scan the street but nothing trips my radar. I grab my backpack and her bag before reaching for her hand as she appears around the trunk. She squeezes my hand and grins at me, and I can't resist pulling her forward and leaning in, locking our entwined hands on her butt and hauling her right into my body, stopping just short of her lips as she tilts her head, eyes fluttering closed, expecting my kiss. Holding us there, I smile when her eyes pop open again, breath soft against my skin. Her eyes are a hundred different shades of blue, like a screen of pixels.

"What are you doing?" she says, crinkles appearing around the edges of her eyes.

"Anticipating," I say.

# CHAPTER 14

## *Kate*

If Fabian's apartment is anything like the inside of his mind, then I can see why he's an amazing hacker. Computers are everywhere, boxes and boxes of kit, stacked to the rafters. A label written in a neat script adorns every box: memory boards, ethernet cables, power adaptors. Everything is tidy and clean. When I question him about it, he just shrugs and says, "You have to be organized to be a decent hacker."

A set of shelves stretches from the door to the windows along the long wall in his bedroom, and there are piles of books and the kind of electronic boards you'd see in a computer with wires attached. Under the windows, a wooden desk is fitted tight against the brickwork with two office chairs and a bank of screens. A huge bed and two comfy red armchairs sit in the center of the large room.

In two steps, Fabian twists me right into the middle of his dark blue duvet and gray sheets, and hovers over me like a dog contemplating a meal, inspecting every part of me. Why isn't it embarrassing? I would say I'm pretty uptight in bed, but this feels different. I don't feel uncomfortable, not even a little bit.

Kneeling between my legs, he reaches behind his head with one hand and pulls his T-shirt up and off, pulling me up to do the same. The muscles in his arms pop out with the movement, and the tattoos on his torso shift as he trails a slim finger down my arm, creating goosebumps in its wake. His body is a map, intricate patterns of swirling ink, the bluebirds on his shoulder leading into winding decorative lines of script over his chest and arms. I trace them with my hand. I've never been able to live in the moment, always strategizing, always looking for problems to solve, but his skin quietens all the voices.

"Stop thinking," he says.

I laugh, closing my eyes and whispering, "But I have so much to think about."

His breath huffs out over me, and I know he's smiling.

When I open my eyes again, he's looking at my hand resting on his forearm and he shifts down to my side, picking my hand up and trailing his index finger over my knuckles, back and forward, back and forward like waves on a shore. A smile plays over his lips, and my whole attention becomes focused on my hand until my head is buzzing with it. How does he know that this will stop my head trawling through every little worry?

He bends down and murmurs into the skin on my neck. "If it's any consolation, I can't shut my head off either."

I turn my head toward him, shifting back so I can see his face. "Is that why you do parkour and try out different drugs? Does it take you out of your head?"

How bizarre that we both have too much head noise and our strategies for dealing with it are so different. He inclines his head as his tongue sweeps out to wet his lips.

"I suspect that taking myself out of my head is very different for you than it is for me. I do it partly for that, but mostly I do these things because they make me feel alive."

"Alive?"

"Sort of thrilled, high on adrenaline, I guess." He shrugs. "I don't understand it myself. I get bored easily."

"I hope this isn't boring."

Maybe Fabian has done crazy stuff in bed with women who were up for it and as into experimenting as him, not uptight like me: Ms. Missionary Position. Cold drifts through my veins like smoke.

But he blows that all away when he laughs. "You couldn't be boring if you tried, Kate. I'll never get to the bottom of what your mind is jumping through in a million years."

*This man.* That was kind of perfect. To say my value is not what we're about to do, but in me, in who I am and what I think. He strokes my hand lighting my nerves on fire.

"I'm not sure I even want to have sex with you," he mumbles, and my stomach drops out. He glances at me, away from where he's threaded his fingers through mine, and a broad smile creeps over his face.

"No, no, no. I didn't mean it like that." He leans forward again, his voice slightly muffled as he kisses my skin. "You're so fucking sexy, Kate." He presses into me, erection hard against my hip, and an answering ache starts in my pelvis. Propping himself on one arm, he strokes the hair off my face.

"What I was trying to say is that I'm so turned on with just talking to you that I want to keep doing that. I don't want the physical act of sex to spoil how turned on I get when you flirt with me, when I can see your body moving through your clothes but I'm not allowed to touch."

His eyes shift downward, lighting sparks everywhere.

"I'll have you know I don't flirt, Mr. Adramovich."

He shakes his head at me. "You're the biggest flirt there is for a guy who's looking for an interesting woman."

God, that's so untrue. And I've no answer, so I lift our entwined hands and kiss his knuckles. His face tightens around the jaw, and I trail my tongue down his index finger, playing with the tip, testing my teeth on the pad as his expression darkens.

"So sexy, Kate. This is going to be very, very, slow."

"All night?" I grin.

He doesn't smile back. "And as much as I have of tomorrow." He says this with a half growl, like a veiled threat. "I like to take my time." His hand comes up to cradle my jaw. "I've been thinking about this ever since I met you. I want to get lost in this."

*Ever since he met me?* He had a hand up and something about my invite, this weekend, has made him drop it.

But what he's said is a statement and an enquiry at the same time: He's asking whether I'm down for slow. I close my eyes and bring my hands to his waist, skin tight under my fingers, pent-up sexual drive seething under the surface, and my breath stalls. I nod and he groans, nuzzling into me.

"I want to put it off over and over again."

It comes out like a confession, like he's ashamed, and I've no idea why, so I curl into him pressing my chest against his: This gets me a sharp inhale and a frown as he pulls back.

"We agreed slow," he says, and the grin that has crept over my face wobbles.

"What if I get carried away because you're just too mouthwatering?"

He laughs and shakes his head.

"Then I'll have to tie you up," he says.

I laugh. I can't imagine what that would be like.

He starts tracing a pattern on my shoulder. "I want to draw on you," he mumbles, pulling back and moving off the bed. "Stay here." And he walks out of the room. I roll onto my back, listening to kitchen cupboards opening and closing and a few curses, and I grin to myself.

A couple of minutes later, Fabian appears in the doorway with something containing golden liquid. It looks like … God … honey? And he grins as he straddles me on the mattress, walks up on his knees, stops at my hips and holds the plastic bottle over my torso. I raise my hand, and he lifts an eyebrow. He's so cute right now I want to lean up and kiss him, so I start to sit up, but he puts a hand on my chest and pushes me back down.

"We're not at the kissing stage of the night yet," he says.

With a roll of my eyes, I say, "You're only doing this to me if I can do it back to you."

"You don't get to make the rules."

I raise an eyebrow at him, then not agreeing or disagreeing I say, "Just think how hot it would be for me to trace every tattoo you have with my tongue."

He shakes his head with a laugh. "You're an impressive saleslady."

He squeezes the bottle over my tummy, and a large warm blob lands right on top of a mole. *He warmed it up in the microwave?* I am not going to think about how he knew the right temperature. I stare down at the honey on my skin, but he draws a line through it and up … reaches my bra and stops.

"Take it off," he growls.

Sitting, I unhook the strap, and he swallows when the pale green lace falls to one side, eyes skipping over my nipples, his hand unsteady when I lie back down. He pours the honey up the center of my body and out across my shoulder blades; down one arm then the other, putting the cap back on the bottle and placing it on the nightstand before coming back to me.

He spreads and smears, licks his fingers and pushes them into my mouth, nodding. So I suck. I feel liquid and loose as he inspects me, judging his handiwork, eyelashes a dark fan against the slight pink tinge sitting high on his cheekbones. By the time he comes down on the first mole and sucks, I'm damp between my legs, but by God, it tickles. As I squirm away, he locks his hands onto my hips and twists me back down, not stopping. I gasp and blink at the ceiling, trying to relax into the wet and the warmth of his tongue and his teeth.

Tension drains away like water down a plughole. Does he feel like this when he parkours, all sensation focused on his body? I want to be in his bed forever with his intense dark eyes and his mouth on me.

He works his way up from my stomach to my chest, and I arch my back, but he follows the golden line straight up the middle, shaking his head.

"Quiet," he says, looking up at me. "We're taking our time, remember? What's the rush?"

His hand shifts up my ribs to under my breasts, and I lift my fingers to rest them on his torso. He's warm and damp under the pads, and my bones turn liquid as I trace one of his tattoos. "The rush is you're turning me on," I say, and he laughs, his erection a hard line behind the faded denim of his jeans where he's straddling me.

"This will get much more torturous before I've finished," he mutters, and I groan.

Leaning down, he works me over with teeth and wet licks, sucking the sweetness off my skin, nuzzling and inhaling.

"You smell like summer," he says. "I want to lick every last bit of this off you."

He sucks as he says this, tongue circling, eyes closed, and I close mine, sinking into the quiet, the pressure, the cool wetness on my collarbone. *How does this feel for him?*

"I want to put honey all over your cock," I say, and he groans, pressing his nose in deep with a sharp inhale.

His voice is a warning growl. "Kate."

"What?" I say, keeping my face straight and reaching up to remove the tie from his man bun. Curls cascade around his face. "I'm thinking about how slowly I'd be sucking it off, especially around the tip," I whisper, a smile on my lips as he slides his mouth over my left arm. He lifts up and grabs my wrists, pinning them on either side of my head, shifting forward to trap my hips under his.

"You don't get to dictate this," he growls, erection suddenly right where I want it, and I wiggle my pelvis beneath his, giggling as his eyes widen in mock outrage.

"Do you like being a bad girl, Kate? Do you want me to punish you?"

"Yes, please," I say, grinning.

What am I saying? I have no idea what form punishment from him would take but I would trust him with whatever he wanted to do to me. Fabian's emotions are right there—explosive, calm—he doesn't hide any of it. But I'm used to being the one who makes the decisions, not putting everything into someone else's hands.

I lift my head and kiss him, and he lets go of my hands, cradling my face as his mouth continues to explore, his tongue tangling with mine. I wrap my legs and arms around him like an octopus, taking his weight as his body pins me to the bed.

He rubs his cock against me. "You're so wet and slippery, Kate," he growls, nipping my ear, and a noise I've never made before slips out of my throat. He pushes up abruptly, unfastening my jeans and sliding them down and off. Then he flips me face down and, oh God, how did he do that so easily?

He trails a long finger all the way down my spine, the groove of my backside and around the leg of my underwear. Then he leans in and nips my shoulder, nuzzling into my neck.

"You have the best ass I have ever seen."

I snort into the pillow at this.

"That's an excellent pickup line. You should use it in …"

His hand comes down on me with a sharp smack. "Quiet, woman," he says in a way that is halfway between a command and a plea, and I close my mouth. *He's dominant in bed.* I think he'd back down if I wanted him to, but *Lord no*. This roughness … where … what do I know about his past, dealing with threats: Does he suppress it? A shiver runs through me. The men I've been with before have been sweet with me in bed, but Fabian is not treating me with kid gloves at all. And I don't want him to: I don't need it. Blood is thundering in my veins now like horses let loose in a field. Fabian's assuming I can take it, and maybe I *can* throw off the mantle of seriousness and responsibility that has dogged me all my life, be a little free and wild.

"Let me savor this," he murmurs, rubbing his nose into my back as he kisses down my spine to my lace briefs, pushing them up, then he stretches out to the table and the warm stickiness of more honey lands on the crease at the top of my thighs.

"Oh my God," I mumble into blue cotton.

His tongue curls along the fold, teeth sinking in, fingers soft on the inside of my thigh as he sucks. *Higher, come on, higher*. I stretch my arms right out at ninety degrees to my body, reaching for the edges of his big bed, curling my hands into the covers.

"Mmmmmmm."

"Kate? Talk to me."

The words are stuck in my head. I clear my throat. "Your teeth … right on the edge of my nerves … Oh!"

He leans over me, propping his body on one arm anchored close by my head, nibbling my shoulder as his hand slides in from behind and under the lace of my panties, fingers finding the wetness. He brushes down one side then the other, so I widen my legs and he reaches farther forward with his finger and presses on my clit. Just once.

"Here?"

I groan into the covers, and he removes his hand, resting his weight half on me as he nuzzles into my neck and whispers in my ear.

"Glad to know I'm having the right effect." His hand slides over my ass, long fingers cupping me as he moves his thumb gently over the crease at the top of my thighs, and God, I want him inside me.

"You're so *wet*, Kate." He's still all of a sudden, voice wobbly, and I groan, shifting my hips toward him, pressing into his erection, and he nips my skin, a low rumble vibrating in my eardrum. He's torturing himself as much as he's tormenting me.

Then his hand disappears, and he sits back on his heels and leans across the bed. I turn my head to peer at his arm muscles as he rustles through the wooden drawer in the nightstand, and a slow smile spreads over my face. *Finally*. But when he straightens there's a bottle of oil in his hand, not condoms. He drips it all over me and his strong fingers sweep down my back, digging in. Oh God. Vertebrae crunch; the strains of the day—fuck, probably years of overwork and late nights hunched over my desk—disappear as he kneads and pokes. He works his thumbs down the center of my spine, pressing on either side, just enough to make me wiggle as the tips of his fingers tickle my ribs. Goddammit, I want those warm hands somewhere else. But he focuses on the dips near my coccyx, pushing me right into the mattress.

*

Fabian holds himself above me suspended on his arms, muscles bunching in my peripheral vision, his ropey body sporting the imprints of where I've mapped his tattoos, traces of honey on his chest. His eyes are fixed on my face, sweat and honey sticking us together, and his hair is a halo of riotous curls as I've wound the strands around my fingers over and over again. I'm buzzing with distracted desperation. The sheets are oily. We've been here for hours, and he's taken me close to the edge time and time again. I run my hands down some scratches on his sides and follow the ridges of his abdomen, the dark curling hair between his legs. His distended cock distracts me, and I start to wrap my hand around it, but he shakes his head, batting my hand away.

"I'll come if you touch me, Kate," he mumbles, his voice gritty and coarse like he's holding on by the slightest thread.

I slide my hand over his thigh and in, and his eyes widen, thinking I'm disobeying him, but I cup his balls, stroking behind them, and he fixes his gaze on the wall above my head as he grinds his teeth. My other hand locks around his hip as I pull him forward widening my legs. I've tried several times to coax him inside me tonight: Is he going to allow it now?

He groans, bending to kiss me. "Don't. Just … this is … I can't …" He sucks in a long breath. "Christ, I don't know what I want."

I tug at him until his length is pressing against my wet folds, and he closes his eyes, swallowing. Then he rests his forehead against mine, opening his eyes, and I stare at their soft gray, the black in the center, his pupils blown wide.

"You're drenched."

I want to say something that might tempt him to push forward, but my mind is blank, floating with the tide, drowning in sweat and skin. We both watch as he grips his cock, and it strikes me that he's handling himself almost gingerly, so I grin up at him and his eyes crinkle at the edges in return: a smile and a grimace.

"I think I'm a bit wound up."

The cute vulnerability of that: My heart takes off at a gallop. He's such a surprise in bed. He's tender and slow, but dictatorial too. My God, I want to give him every relief I can.

He pushes forward pressing on my mound and I reach down to move him so he can press right where I want him. My fingers brush the tip of his shaft, and he grinds his teeth.

"Fucking hell, Kate."

When I tip my hips, his cock slips over my clit. He stretches out, leaning over and pulling a condom out of the nightstand, going up on his knees. *Thank God.* He rolls it on, wincing. Then he's back down and moving lower, finding my entrance with his cock but sliding back up again; pushing forward to press against me. After all the torture, to have direct pressure there gives me tremors down my legs. He smirks and repeats the movement, once, twice, and I'm shuddering, scrabbling at the damp skin of his hips. He slides back down again, this time holding himself unmoving in my opening. So, I relax my knees and rest my feet on his calves.

"Holy shit," he says and starts a rocking motion backward and forward just inside, just out, and I arch with the pressure and the stretch, pushing my breasts into his chest, gasping as I lift my head and my lips slide clumsily across his jaw. He instantly dips his head and nips my lower lip, tongue soothing along after his teeth.

*Just in, just out.*

"Oh, Kate. Fuck," he mumbles into my mouth.

He's going in a bit farther each time, teasing me open, and I can't believe after the hours of foreplay that we're actually doing this now. I shift my legs up over his waist, opening up more, wrapping around him like bindweed until I can't tell who's moving, him or me. Our hips lock together, and his mouth is all over my face, smearing and urgent, taking my face in his hands as he moves all the way inside and then he stills, forehead against mine, fingers wrapped around my jaw, my temple. He kisses down my nose; I know it's costing him to stay still. Is he doing it to relax me or …?

"This is incredible," his voice breaks, and I can hardly answer him. Are we stopping now? Is he going to pull out? I grab his backside to keep him where he is, and he smiles against my cheek.

"Fabian, please," I groan.

"Good," he says, and the smug ring of his tone lights a fire in me, so I slap his ass. His eyes widen, and he props himself up on his arms as he starts to move in earnest, pulling right out and thrusting back in again, watching my face intently. But I lose him as my eyes flutter and close.

"Open your eyes!" he says. "Goddamn it, Kate. After all this I want to see you fall."

His hand sneaks between us, and he's gently rubbing my clit and my eyes open on a gasp. And he's nodding at me. The intensity of staring at each other like this, with the half smile on his lips as I tighten up all the way along his cock, getting closer as his hips jerk and stutter as he pushes into me.

"Yes, Kate. Sweetheart, yes."

The endearment sends a sharp stab through my chest.

# CHAPTER 15

## *Fabian*

A thundercloud is building inside, waiting to dump all its rain; like no high I've ever had. Control is unravelling like a ball of wool. Kate is pink and disheveled under me, and I'm buried deep after hours of torture, of sitting back and tamping down the need to come, come, come. The contrast of my dark hand on her pale skin, the way she wraps herself around me like she wants to disappear into my body. She's close like she has been so many times tonight, tightening along every inch of my cock, so swollen and tender after endless friction and pain. My balls are tucked up, stiff, and I'm trying to think of other things, to last, to last, but my mind is fused, refusing to cooperate.

She flings her hands out to the side, arching up, and I can't take my eyes off her mussed hair and shiny face; *this* is the version of Kate I want to see every time I shut my eyes. The flush on her chest as she gets close. Holy shit. I can't take my eyes off the curve of her breasts, her hard pink nipples.

Her hand lands on my side and moves down and in between our bodies, sneaking over my hip and rubbing a finger all over the sensitive skin between my legs. No one has ever done this to me when I've been so close to coming.

Tight threads run from my feet to the apex of my thighs, cramping my calves, and I grunt, powerless to stop the orgasm climbing up my shaft. Her other hand grabs my ass, and she grinds up into me, crushing our hands between us, and my head spins as I laugh-groan into her neck.

"I want to lick every inch of you. You think this is torture now, Fabian, but wait until you've had my tongue on the underside of your cock," she whispers, and my movement falters. I don't think she's saying this deliberately to make me come. This is what she's imagining in her head, and it's all spilling out of her, like a cup running over. Like the screw that kept her wound up tight has been worked loose, letting her relax, uncensored, into what we're doing.

This next thrust I'm sure is my last, and I let out a long groan.

"Kate."

"God. Yes." Her hazy eyes lock on mine.

My lips smear across hers, eyes open and a hairsbreadth away. "I'm gonna come, Kate," I say, and her eyes widen as she moves against my fingers on her clit.

"So close," she gasps.

The ripples of her orgasm start all the way along my length, and her body convulses. I grit my teeth and withdraw for what surely, surely is the last time. As I push back in, my foreskin stretches back and works back over my tip, and, as all her spasms surround me, my own release barrels up. I gasp into her sweaty neck; the line that has been coiling inside me unwinding at a breakneck speed, flinging me into the crashing waves. My whole groin lights on fire as I shudder, shoulders jerking, and I hunch over, collapsing down, my cock pulsing … once … twice.

Again.

"Oh … h … h … h …"

Again.

I desperately suck air back into my lungs, mouth open, dry.

Again.

I brush my lips across her cheek, rub my nose into it, smelling lemons and almonds. Suddenly so sensitive, no way can I pull out. I lift up to see blonde eyelashes resting against bloodless cheeks, and concern burns through me.

"You okay?" My voice sounds like a rusty tractor starting and I clear my throat. No response. "Kate?"

Her lips curl up. *Settle down, Fabian.* One eye cracks open.

"Can't speak," she says.

"You just did," I say, grinning at her, and a huge smile ricochets across her face. Her hair is in some crazy halo around her head like a rat's nest on the pillow, and I feel stupidly, ridiculously proud. *This. This I can give her.*

"What are you doing to me?" she says, and I laugh at the wonder in her voice.

"Turning you on?" I say as I shift onto my elbows and cup her face in my hands.

"I've never had sex like that before," she says, and the pride turns into an all-encompassing furnace that reaches every part of my body. How could anyone keep their distance from this woman?

"Good."

"It certainly was. Again."

I laugh. "Oh God, Kate." I nuzzle her neck. "I think I'll need some recovery time."

She laughs and wraps her arms tight around me. I need to go and sort the condom, but I can't bring myself to do anything to dissipate the after-ache in my pelvis. She sighs and shudders under me, soft kisses starting under my ear.

"So good."

Her voice is sleepy, so I reach down, grab the base of the condom, and pull out, wincing and sitting back on my heels. Her eyes are closed against mottled, sweaty skin; traces of honey and oil all over her. *What handiwork.* Backing off the bed, I step into the bathroom and remove the rubber and dump it in the trash. I'd love a shower, but something in me doesn't want to wash any of this night away, so I move back to the bed and climb in beside her. Kate curls into me, and I stare at the ceiling where the clock is projecting 3 a.m. For once my mind is a still pool, no ripples disturbing the calm, and I let the silence of the night sweep me down.

*

My eyes blink open to find 6 a.m. projected on the same crumbling plaster. The vague tendrils of some erotic dream dance around my head, and I jerk up: My dick is buried in something hot and wet. I squint down to a blonde head of hair between my legs. I let out a long groan. Waking up like this has probably only happened to me once or twice in my life. *Fucking hell.* She smiles up at me in the dim light and licks my tip, sending shivers right up my body.

"You've had your recovery time now," she says.

# CHAPTER 16

## *Kate*

If I thought my performance couldn't get any worse in the ER, two weeks on from the wedding I know I'm mistaken. My mind is not on wounds and fractured bones; it's in a bed in Brooklyn, in a haze of inky patterns and dark, tangled hair. The minute my shift finishes, I push through the bodies on the subway and spend hours in Fabian's bed, lips and teeth on skin, gasping through the slow climb. I've never known anyone take time like Fabian takes time. He grabs me as soon as I enter the apartment, pins me down, pulls me back if I try to wander. I spent my day off giving him oral sex, bringing him to the brink time and time again: He was growling, tight and so angry, and came so hard at the end that I had the largest smile on my face that lasted the whole day.

Something is growing inside me, spreading through my veins. We have no time to go out, to do anything. We eat in bed, then start again. After the do-we-don't-we and the half-starts, we are both all in and I can't quite get my head around it. He's the most amazing man, considerate, kind, crazy. I want to dance down the street, throw my head back and laugh out loud, pin his hands to the wall and climb all over him.

Fabian feels bare to his core to me, and *now* I understand what was missing with David. The emotional honesty of this revealing all the fractures of the other. I didn't *know* David. The openness was all on my side. He never told me what he wanted. He held his secret life close, and as more conversations with him filter into my head, the more I think that he hid an awful lot more from me than I ever admitted. And not only me, other people too. Fabian doesn't tell me everything about his work, but about everything else he's clear and direct, emotions never far from the surface; and that is everything right now.

I get no reply when I buzz his door, so I hammer on it, looking down at the key in my hand that he gave me yesterday. I stand there for a minute. Two. A television plays somewhere downstairs, a crescendo of raised voices and then a door slams. I stare at the peeling gray paint as a spider crawls along the door jamb. He did say he'd be in. The key slots into the lock in a slow glide and I turn it, pushing the door open into silence.

"Fabian? Hello?"

I toe off my shoes and wander through the quiet apartment, sun filtering through closed blinds highlighting the dust curling through the air. His keys and wallet are on the counter in the kitchen as I pass. Darkness looms behind a crack in the door to the bedroom, and I hurry forward, pushing open the door into the dimly lit room. He's curled up on the bed fully clothed, boots on like he collapsed there. My heart stops.

"Fabian?"

In two steps I'm beside him, instinctively reaching to check his pulse, and a cold sweat washes over me when I feel it thumping away under my fingers. I sink down with a shaking hand. I'm already so attached to him that in a sharp moment I realize I'd be devastated if I came here and the situation was different.

Then he mumbles something incoherent, and I collapse back onto the bed eyes closed, sucking in a deep breath, staring at the high ceiling and willing my pulse to calm down. *Breathe in, breathe out.* Seconds tick by, and I check my hands, steadying now, tremors receding and order returning like birds lining up on a wire. I rub my face, turning over and curling around him. I don't know what to think about his drug-taking. I dispense enough drugs with strong side effects to know that this isn't a black-and-white thing. What's the difference between something that treats illness and something recreational? He likes to experiment, to live life on the edge. He's not an addict; the emergency department is full of them, and the difference is obvious. But by God, it's risky. And David tried to be someone else for me, and I don't want Fabian to do that.

The peace and quiet of the apartment sinks into my bones, and warmth pushes up as I drift. There is no pressure here, no expectations. Fabian never does that thing that so many people do—which is to expect you to be or do something other than what you are. He's here, being himself, doing his thing, and he's warm and safe. And I think, with sudden clarity, that I can keep him that way.

*

Someone's knocking on the door with a rhythmic tap-tap-tapping like the beat of a tune, and I'm trying to work out the rhythm, forcing my mind to concentrate. My eyes fly open to find Fabian dressed in a dark T-shirt in a black office chair in front of a bank of screens, long fingers flying over a keyboard. Tap, tap, tap. I grin, watching his hands: *programmer hands*. I blink the sleep out of my eyes, roll onto my back and stretch, and he wheels around.

My stomach sinks when I see his face. "What's up?"

He scrubs his hands over his face, mouth a flat line, eyes fixed on the corner window next to the bed. "I'm so sorry, Kate. I'm sorry you had to come in and find me like that. I don't want you to …"

He carries on staring into the distance, and I prop myself up on one arm, a blanket he must have put over me falling to my waist.

"Don't do that," I say.

"What?" He frowns somewhere over my left shoulder.

"Apologize. I like you the way you are. Don't adjust. I don't want you to feel you can't do things, or worse, that you need to hide them."

His mouth changes to an upward curve, eyes meeting mine for the first time, and he folds his arms over his chest as he leans back in his chair.

"Okay then. Fancy heading down to where the prostitutes hang around by the river and taking some drug I've never tried before?"

Is this a serious question? I shrug.

"I'm happy to go with you if you want my company."

His eyes rove over my face and my torso, and he smiles, shaking his head before coming over to the bed, pulling at the covers and climbing in beside me. *Such a cuddler.*

"You're a much better person than me," he mumbles into my hair as he curls around me.

I stiffen, turning over, but his eyes are closed. I hook my finger into the neck of his T-shirt, tugging.

"Hey you. No." I pull on his shirt again. "No, I'm not. You have a lot of qualities that I will never have."

"Such as?" His eyes snap open, fixed, intent.

"You're honest."

"Why wouldn't I be? I've got nothing to hide."

I laugh. "You do realize that most people don't think that way."

"Yeah, but …"

"You're warm, generous. You take risks with things I would never take."

He snorts. "I'm not sure that last one is such an amazing quality."

"Why is risk-taking a bad thing? Look at how cautious I am. And I've been like that all my life. My parents have been so desperate for none of us to mess up. Of course, Georgie decided to take their definition of messing up and turn it into an art form." I say the last bit half to myself.

Fabian's eyes narrow on me, and his gaze roams from the top of my head down to the cover.

"I'm not sure why I experiment with drugs. I've enough evidence of how bad it can be." He sighs and rolls onto his back as he stares at the ceiling. "I like the crazy wildness."

Here after so many weeks, I need to give this comment proper consideration, so I roll into his side wrapping my arm around his middle and

I lie there and listen to the whirr of the computer fans.

He tips his head to look down at me. “My father murdered my mother and went to prison for it.” And just like that his whole awful history with his father comes tumbling out.

When he finishes, I don’t know what to say. How terrible must it have been to be scared like that? To live like that?

“Perhaps you got used to the adrenaline kick when you were younger, the flight or fight, and it kept you safe, living on your wits. I mean people often repeat childhood patterns.”

He studies me for a long minute.

“I’ve never thought about it like that before.”

I prop myself on my elbow.

“Addiction killed my brother,” he says.

“But drugs are not like that for you?”

He shakes his head, but buzzing in the back of my mind are his trips to the ER, that he’s often *unconscious*.

“I was never as unhinged as Zach. Doesn’t mean I’m not messed up in a different way, though.”

He turns over toward me, sliding his hands down my back, pulling me down and right into him as he hardens between us. His eyelids droop and his mouth twists up at one corner.

“Stop distracting me with sex,” I say.

He groans. “I can’t lie in bed with you and not get hard, Kate—that’s not possible.”

My body hums. How can Fabian and I burn like this? Is this *all* we have? Once this burns out, where will we be? Ugh. I hate how I find grit among the pearls.

“You don’t seem to worry about anything,” I mumble into his chest.

He starts shaking, and I push back to catch his broad grin.

“I do worry about stuff, Kate, just different shit from other people. Sometimes I can’t stop my mind from spinning.”

He pulls me back into him, kissing my forehead, and I press in, heat popping through my pelvis. But before we're distracted, I want to make sure he understands.

"Don't hide your drug-taking from me, Fabian. I understand the desire to push yourself."

And maybe he'll recognize the dangers better in his own good time. Nobody's perfect.

"I'm not an addict."

"I know that. I know you like to experiment."

"Okay." His eyes narrow. "If I do anything you don't like, or you're too worried, you need to tell me."

My *I will* is cut off by his mouth on mine.

# CHAPTER 17

## *Fabian*

My handler, who's supposedly named Jeff, frowns when I hand the bound document over the table to him.

"Paper?" he says with a raised eyebrow. "I was expecting a USB stick."

I grin, shrugging. "Hard to hack into paper."

He laughs as he opens the first page and skims down the contents, then looks at me. "Anything you want to flag upfront?"

"Take a look through, then we can chat."

He nods and settles in to start reading. I check out everyone in the café one by one. I've already done this of course, but I've got time while he reads.

Out of the window, the midweek lunchtime crowd streams along the sidewalk. A man is standing shouting at a small boy who looks about ten years old. He's gesturing at the street full of cars, and something about how he's bent over to get right in the boy's face makes me want to curl up and die.

I can still feel the damp floorboards under my feet and see my father lurching through the door, beer belly hanging over his pants as he leaned against the wall in the hall trying to steady himself. That goddamn belt he used to take off and wrap around his fist was always there keeping his pants in place. I watched him piss himself in that doorway once, and he beat my mother so badly that night she couldn't speak for days. He shouted that it was all her fault even as she tried to help him. After he passed out, I tried to sort her face out, tried to persuade her to leave him. The hairs on the back of my neck stand up. I focus on the street again, but the father and the boy have gone.

Jeff flicks forward through the document and then back to where he was reading and looks up and says, "This is incredible."

I take a sip of coffee. "Yeah, I was surprised by how extensive it all was—the level of the bribes, how far into the political hierarchy it went."

He shakes his head. "No. Well, yes, that is surprising. But what I meant was, the information you've got is incredible. Dates, amounts, transactions, named people, you've tracked the money all the way through. There's just so much detail here." His eyes are narrowed and fixed on me. "They're going to be delighted with this."

I give him a small smile. "Good."

Jeff came to me via a hacker I've collaborated with on several projects, and who I trust not to land me in something questionable. The project sounded interesting enough, and the money was good.

He taps the paper in front of him. "We went through a number of people who all told us what we wanted was impossible."

"Yeah, you have to take quite a lot of risks trying to get into various systems."

He frowns. "Patience, too, I imagine."

This makes me laugh. "Sometimes months of it."

"And skill and experience." His eyes narrow again.

I don't want to tell him how I got all my experience hacking into banks, the National Archives, government databases and God knows where else.

"I've certainly dealt with a lot of different systems over the years."

"You're a very unusual man, Mr. Adramovich." He looks out of the window of the café at the stream of people heading along the street and purses his lips. "I'm delighted to have you on our side, and I hope we can continue this relationship."

I don't take sides, that's a dangerous game, but I'm happy to take on projects that are legit. And maybe he wouldn't say he wanted to work with me if he knew more about what I'd seen. Who talks about "sides" anyway? Spooks in suits, that's who: It's like some Cold War espionage nonsense. Don't they realize technology has changed all that?

I tilt my head diplomatically. "Of course. Let me know if you need anything more."

After I head out onto the street the warmth of a Manhattan June day burns into my back and I lift my face to the sky. I've been working on this goddamn thing for months. A huge wedge of money, too. Thank fuck.

I've tried to be everything my father isn't for so long: decent, straight with people. A good friend. A good man. I don't always manage it. Sometimes I feel like I'll explode with the effort. But here today, fighting bastards who are screwing over everyone and anyone on the side ... well, this makes it all worthwhile.

Parkour is what I need after this, burn off some energy. I take a deep breath, glance at my phone, and press Darren's number.

*

I clock the guy following me when I'm halfway toward Coney Island station to catch the F train back toward town after a drink with the parkour guys, and Jesus, he's not subtle. I'm exhausted, shaky, and in need of some food. *Goddammit.* I should have had something to eat in the bar. I scan the walls and the buildings, looking for a place to disappear, pulse thumping in my veins. Then I remember, the girders of the overpass all the way along the sidewalk by the station: I was thinking about the parkour possibilities when I came out here.

I slip behind a pillar and in seconds I'm up in the girders looking down on the sidewalk, waiting. I examine the cap pulled low over his face as he walks toward where I'm perched. He stops right under me, looking up and down the street. *Fucking perfect.* Too fucking stupid to look over his head. In a flash, I land on his back taking him down onto the sidewalk. I'm not a big guy but I know how to fight dirty. In seconds I have him immobilized, face down on the concrete.

"Why are you following me," I grit out.

"Hey, hey! My face! My face! No sweaty, guy. No sweaty! Know nothing! Know nothing!" he shouts, and I look over my shoulder, but no one is paying any attention. No backup just about to jump me.

I twist his arm a bit more. "Who's paying you?"

"Marty, Marty! I follow you. No harm! Yes, yes."

Who the fuck is Marty?

"Hey! Hey! No harm."

He is a goon, I can tell, no one gives up a name this fast, even if it isn't a real one, because I'm damn sure no real names are ever used when anything nefarious is going on.

"What did they ask you to do?" I hiss.

"I follow you. That's all! I promise. No threaten you! I good guy. Good guy."

Ha fucking ha.

"It's okay, it's okay." He writhes in my grip, and I wrench his arm higher, which earns me a howl. Keeping his arm twisted, I bend over to pat down his pockets, looking for something, anything, that might tell me more, but the world swims and then he moves suddenly, kicking out a leg that I manage to jump over, but my hand must slacken for a fraction of a second because he's out of my grasp and up and running and fuck I can run fast, but this guy … *Jesus Christ*. In seconds he's out in the street, racing between the cars and narrowly avoids getting ploughed by a taxi. A bus screeches to a halt with a blare of horns, and he disappears behind it and I'm seconds behind him but he's up the street veering off into a parking lot and I lose sight of him for a second. When I get through the parking lot to the street beyond, he's disappeared. *Goddammit.*

I stand in the street, watching, waiting, feeling sick. But I don't think he's going to appear from anywhere. I don't want to worry Janus, but I need to tell him about this. I pull out my phone and blow out a long shaky breath, suck another one back in and turn my phone over in my hand.

*What's Janus going to do?* The little voice in my head pipes up. Give me a lecture about security, no doubt. Mess around with some high-tech security system on my apartment that I could probably organize myself. Insist on a bodyguard: I don't want to put some ex-marine's life in danger. I study the quiet buildings in the street. Do I need to tell him? Why is being followed from parkour any different from someone turning up and asking questions in the first place? And I can look after myself—living on the street was way more dangerous than being followed by some idiot who gets noticed.

If this is those people that hacked into Janus's company, then they've worked out what I look like, but how? There's no pictures of me on the internet, I'm not anywhere. I've made sure of it. And I would have expected a group of hackers to be way more professional than this. Trailing after me on the street using some useless guy … maybe they're worried that Jo and I still have access to their system.

Whatever this is about, all this is just useless speculation. I clearly need to get my apartment secure. And maybe I'll do that before I say anything to Janus.

I turn around to head back toward the station, jumping over the low concrete wall of the parking lot but I'm feeling even more shaky now, and when I reach the avenue, the cars are swimming in and out. *What the hell's wrong with me?* I just need to sit down for a second or two. I move between the cars, a pain in my chest like someone's got it in a vice, and I sway into the hood of a car sitting in the traffic. The driver yells at me through the window. *So goddamn odd.* I slump down on the sidewalk and close my eyes, and the last thing I remember is a truck horn blaring right next to my head.

# CHAPTER 18

## *Kate*

When I see the body on the stretcher my heart goes into overload. Then someone shouts "Crashing!" and my body begins to shake. I'm light-headed. My limbs freeze. I'm mouthing words in my head that don't make it past my lips, but nobody is paying me any attention as the crash team swarms around. A resident I don't recognize starts chest compressions. Carol, one of the nurses, inserts a cannula in his arm with a steady hand as another couple of nurses work on his breathing and attach a bag valve mask, and Henry, another doctor, sticks pads to his chest. The attending, Neil, leans over him, blue scrubs already crumpled from a day of emergencies just like this one.

The beep of the defibrillator charging fills the room, and the call "Clear!" appears to come from nowhere as people straighten away from his body and everyone turns to watch the monitor. Sickness lurches through my stomach, and, almost in slow motion, word snippets start to bubble up in my head.

"I know the patient. He's been in before. He experiments with a mix of recreational drugs." My voice quavers, and Neil's gaze swings to mine and sweeps over me, eyes narrowing.

"That's all we need, some fucking weird drug combination," Neil mutters. "Okay, people! Suspected mixed overdose, unknown drugs. Carol! You're on notes and timing. Marcie!" he barks. "Did the EMS administer anything to the patient?"

"No, said he was drifting in and out of consciousness, wasn't making much sense," one of the nurses answers. "No information on whether the patient took anything himself."

"Let's move with the epinephrine. A mix of drugs. Fuck! Who's on toxicology today? I want them here now! Someone pull his records. We need to know what we're dealing with. Move. Move. Move."

"What about naloxone?" I say, still stuck to the floor, but blood starts to pump around my body, heart spinning fast. Books and articles swim before my eyes; all the reading I've been doing ever since that first, fateful, day. Neil's eyes narrow again.

"Yes. Why?" he barks.

"If he's used anything opioid-based, then it should help, and it won't cause issues if it's something else."

His gaze doesn't flicker. "Signs of an opioid overdose?"

"Pinprick pupils, unresponsive, a reduced respiratory rate or stopped altogether."

"Excellent. Marcie!" he shouts. "You heard that. I want IV naloxone, please! Fucking fast, right now!"

Carol says, "Two minutes," and the familiar beep fills the room again as Henry charges the defibrillator, and everyone shifts back as he shocks Fabian again.

"Come on, tell me what I'm dealing with," Neil says, leaning over, voice tight.

He spares no prisoners and he's an asshole a lot of the time, but I wouldn't want anyone else if I had an emergency. He paces and he fidgets, but everything moves like an express train when he's in Resus. His eyes haven't shifted from the body on the table as the resident steps back and restarts CPR.

"Alcohol?" the resident says.

I shake my head. "He's not much of a drinker. I read some research about cocaine being implicated in blood clots," I mumble, looking down at Fabian's inert body.

"What would we see if this was cocaine-related?" Neil asks.

"Hypertension and prolonged QRS." I glance at the trace. "We've not got that," I say quietly.

But Neil just nods at me. "Good. I like that we're reducing the options. We could easily have a clot for other reasons."

A clot. *Fuck.*

The call "Clear!" echoes through the room again, and everyone straightens away from Fabian again as Henry calls out, "Shocking on three: one, two, three."

"Come on, come on, you *asshole*," Neil mutters, examining the monitor.

The nurse, Marcie, appears at my side and presses the naloxone into my hand, and the words blur as I peer at the vial and show it to Neil, who nods, so she syringes it up and administers it via the IV in his arm. Fuck, I feel helpless.

"How many shocks?" Neil barks.

"Three," Carol says, her head bent over the recording she's keeping as we do this. Chances of success decrease with each attempt. I know it, and I don't want to know it.

"Clear!" Neil calls as the machine charges up. Everything stills, oxygen disappearing as we all study the trace.

"Come on!" Neil shouts. "You're too fucking young to go out. What have you taken, you asshole?"

I've heard him talk to comatose patients before, and I usually catch someone's eye and smile, but I can't take my eyes off Fabian's inert body. He says things to their face too, after whatever procedure he's done. My chest gets tight watching him, his desire for life, the sheer passion and effort. Thank God. I would love to be like him one day, but I'm just standing here, saying anything I can remember.

He's leaning over Fabian's body, and laughter bubbles up my throat and I clamp my hand over my mouth. Fuck.

"Any other ideas anyone?"

"I read something about flumazenil and benzodiazepines?" Henry says.

*No.* Neil shakes his head. "High chance of seizure. Mixed drugs. Too much of a risk," he says.

Silence. And still the trace on the monitor shows nothing but Fabian's heart vibrating in his chest.

"He's a friend, Neil," I blurt out, throat tightening as I wrap my numb arms around my body to try and wake them up.

Neil's eyebrows shoot up, gaze narrowing like he's seeing me as a person and not an intern for the first time since we arrived in Resus.

"Right then," he says and leans over Fabian's body, "we'll shock him again, and if it doesn't help …"

We all nearly jump out of our skin as Fabian twitches.

"Could be involuntary," he murmurs, leaning forward as Henry takes over the CPR from the resident, who shakes out his hands.

But no, suddenly the trace on the monitor starts to show an erratic heartbeat. Neil feels for a pulse, and then nods.

The room deflates like someone put a pin in a balloon. People start to smile. My hands are shaking, tremors moving up my arm to my torso. I stare at the smooth cream of the wall above all the machines. The nurses beaver around, and Neil and the resident examine the monitor as Fabian's heartbeat settles into a weak but identifiable rhythm.

"Good call on the drug-taking," the resident says, looking over at me.

I shake my head. There was no real skill involved in that.

"I want to review later," Neil growls, stripping off his gloves. "If he did that to himself, I'm going to kill him when he comes around."

Hot and cold sweat breaks out all over my body, and nausea bubbles up. I step out through the door and lurch against a wall, sinking to the floor and sticking my head between my knees. I really don't want to pass out here. I stare down at the concrete as a pair of feet appear next to mine.

"It's very different when it's someone you know, isn't it?" Neil says.

I look up at him. "I'm sorry I …"

But he waves a hand, cutting me off.

"I passed out when Daisy gave birth." He laughs mercilessly. "I was a wreck. The ob-gyn still gives me shit about it. You did well in there. Is he a close friend?"

What do I say about that? What is Fabian to me?

"He's best friends with my friend's boyfriend."

"Glad we saved him then." He smiles a crooked smile at me, then nods at the door to Resus. "Get his blood tests done and up to X-ray and talk to the cardiac team. I also want him monitored for withdrawal. Page me if his condition changes." And he is off, striding down the corridor. I swear he's whistling. Another patient, another day in the ER, and I tip my head back, staring at the strip lights on the ceiling. This place is zero to one hundred, black and white, life and death, in the blink of an eye. One minute you're dealing with a septic cut, the next moment someone is dead. Why is Neil so goddamn cheerful? Will I ever learn to ride this roller coaster, or will it chew me up in its wheels?

*

When I walk into the coronary care unit an hour later, Fabian is propped up in bed on his back, eyes closed, face gray, and my gaze moves to the monitors—the familiar peak and line of a normal trace. I unhook his chart from the end of the bed, and his eyes flick open. As he tries to struggle into more of a sitting position, I step forward to place my hand on his chest, and he places his hand on mine immediately, fingers tightening, and I sink down by his hip.

Fabian stares out of the window. "I don't know what happened to me."

Following his gaze, I take in the park, the East River, and the skyscrapers reaching up to the cloudless sky beyond. I swallow. "Your heart stopped, we …"

"I know. That doctor came in and gave me a lecture. Told me how many times you had to shock me." His jaw stretches, then pops. "But I've no idea why I was in that state."

"What do you mean?"

"I went to parkour with the guys, and then for a drink afterward. Then I started feeling really odd, and it just got worse and worse. I had to sit down. I think I must have passed out on the sidewalk."

"You didn't take anything?"

"No."

My heart clenches. "Are you sure?"

He frowns at me. "Kate. I'm not going to lie to you about something like that. I promised I won't hide stuff from you and I won't. I'm not that guy."

Okay then.

His jaw shifts like he's grinding grass in his molars. "I was followed."

"*What?* When?"

"After I left the bar and before I passed out. I've no idea who he was. I jumped him, and he didn't put up much of a fight. He was some goon, not great at the following gig. He got away from me, and I started to feel really odd and woke up here. The only thing I can think is that he put something in my drink at the bar." He lets out a long sigh. "Darren said someone was asking around about me at parkour, months ago."

My eyes widen. "Why didn't you say something? Do you know who it was?"
He grimaces. "No idea." Then a small smile twists his mouth. "You and I have had other things going on that seemed more important."

Oh God, the wedding and my awful family.

He must see something in my face because he squeezes my fingers. "I meant the nice things, Kate."

"But being *followed*, Fabian. Why would someone do that?"

He raises his eyebrows, clearly amused. "I can think of a lot of people I've annoyed. I just don't know how anyone would find out who I was from my hacking; I'm very, very careful. But this has to be something to do with the hack on Janus's company."

"Are you going to tell Janus?"

"God, I don't know." He blows out a long breath. "I've not forgiven myself for bringing that problem to his front door, and I really don't want to worry him. He's got enough on his plate. And what could he do anyway? Put a security system in my apartment. Which I can sort myself."

"God, Fabian, putting something in your drink, though ... that's pretty serious."

"I'll do some digging: online, on the street. At least I know what this guy looks like."

Some pressure sitting below my ribs eases. "Okay."

His mouth curls up at one corner. "Come here," he says, and I lean forward as he wraps his arms around me. The scent of hospital mingles with warm male, and something that's been frozen inside me since I saw who was on the stretcher starts to thaw. Without warning, a huge lump forms in my throat.

"I thought I'd lost you," I whisper into his collarbone above his green gown.

He groans. "Kate."

He tips his head down to look at me, and his hand comes up to brush over my cheek, pushing tears across my skin. I pull back and turn away, and he makes a small noise in the back of his throat.

"It was touch and go and …" I say.

"Whatever this is, I don't want to put you through something like this again. No more trips to the ER," he says, taking my chin and turning my head back to his, eyes soft like feathers.

His eyes roam over my face, and he rolls his lips together. "I love you, Kate," he says, and my breath disappears, the floodgates opening in earnest now as I collapse forward onto his chest.

"That bad, hunh? Thought as much." A smile threads through his voice, and I sit back laughing with a strangled huff, wiping at the mess on my cheeks and smearing wet everywhere.

I look at the curly hair and long nose, the scruff on his chin, those damn eyelashes. Air inflates my chest, and I spread my wings, wind rising under them.

"I love you too," I say, and his eyes widen and light dances over his face before he crinkles into a broad grin. He tips his head back, blinking at the ceiling and then his glassy eyes meet mine.

"No one has said those words to me before and meant them."

*What?* My stomach bottoms out as I swallow down the acid rising in the back of my throat. *No one?*

His fingers fidget with the weave on the taupe blanket on the bed.

"I'm not very good at choosing people to share my life with … They're damaged, I'm damaged. My family … Zach; it wasn't something that we did, say stuff like this. I'm not sure my parents even knew what love *meant*. Certainly, my dad … well, he didn't love *anyone*. My mom was terrified, and, looking back, she was checked out most of the time. My dad threatened to kill her if she made us 'soft,' as he called it. Which is ironic really, considering what he did. Zach and I were close, but we never said anything like that to each other."

I suck in an uneven breath. He didn't choose his family. "Perhaps I need to say it a lot more to compensate then." My smile wobbles.

He pulls me back into a tight hug, pressing shaky lips to my temple.

"You are the most wonderful woman, Kate. I'll do my best to deserve you."

I push back, straightening. "I don't want you to try to be or do anything." I'm determined to learn from my mistakes with David. Fabian doesn't have anything to live up to; I have all my own flaws. "You're an amazing guy. I'm lucky to have you."

He grins at me, shaking his head.

*

I'm called in to talk to Neil before I leave. Fabian is tucked up in the intensive care unit being monitored 24–7, staff peppering him with questions, much to his disgust. He is breathing, warm, talking, *alive*. Something in me is airy and light like I can scale mountains. The shock has receded like a tide, leaving behind a deep pool of calm. That monitor trace, having the courage to bring people back from the brink over and over again, saving someone's life even in the worst of circumstances. The ER is the sharp end of it: important, amazing.

When I come in, Neil stands up from where he's typing at his desk and gives me a half smile.

"How are you?"

As an intern, I'm guessing he's trying to look out for me.

I smile broadly at him. "I'm fine. Good even."

He nods at this. "I wasn't prying, Kate, but I happened to notice you through the door when you were talking to Mr. Adramovich. He looked like a bit more than a friend to me."

Heat creeps up my cheeks. Goddammit. But when I open my mouth to explain he shakes his head.

"It's fine, Kate. I didn't want to see you because I have a problem with it: Don't feel guilty. I just wanted to say that being clear about your relationship with a patient is important. It helps everyone involved enormously."

"I'm sorry. I should have … He's my, my … boyfriend."

The word "boyfriend" falls out of my mouth, rusty and old. It feels like a lie. Fabian is so much more to me than that. "I was just so shocked … I didn't know how to …"

Neil waves a hand. "This is not some disciplinary thing, or a reminder of proper procedure. God knows I'm not that guy." His gaze rests above my head. "I wanted to say that I'm glad you said that you knew him. In my past I … I should … I …" He clears his throat.

"I'm divorced now, Kate. But I had an affair while I was married. She was rushed into the ER, and I was there like you were today. I was resident, not long out of school, surrounded by the attending, more experienced residents, nurses …" He tails off and stares down at the papers strewn all over his desk. "I felt I couldn't say anything, that I had to keep it secret. She died, Kate, and I …"

His voice drops, and he walks over to the window to stare out at the road.

"I regret it to this day. I still feel like it was my fault, that we didn't try hard enough to save her, that the fact I didn't admit what she was to me meant I didn't care enough. I never got to say goodbye. I've never forgiven myself."

Oh God. I step forward and touch his arm. "I don't believe you didn't do enough. I'd love to be as talented as you are in Resus."

He laughs. "I wasn't when I started, believe you me. I spent the whole time in a panic, not knowing which way was up, convinced I was killing patients, that I didn't have what it took to be a doctor. Failing and flailing as I called it. I'd never failed at anything before."

It mirrors my thoughts so precisely that all I can do is stare at him.

"If I'd told the attending in charge, perhaps we would have tried more things. She might have made it."

I shake my head. "Don't torture yourself like that."

He smiles a sad smile at me. "Generally, I don't. It was a long time ago. I saw you today and … well, anyway, I didn't mean to burden you with all that. I wanted to tell you that saying what a patient means to you is the right thing to do. I would have felt terrible if we'd lost him and found out afterward that he was important to you. Losing anyone is sad, of course, but colleagues are particularly close to our hearts. That's just human nature."

I nod at him. He's right, and Fabian could be in here again. The thought makes cold shiver through me, and I cross my fingers behind my back.

"Thank you. I'll do that, I promise. I'm very close to him—'boyfriend' doesn't quite cut it actually." My voice shakes, but I'm being as honest as I can.

His face clears. "Good." Then he scowls, and some of the old Neil returns. "You're a great doctor, Kate. Don't ever forget it. I know you were struggling when you started, but it just took you longer than most to adjust, and everyone who works here knows what a huge adjustment the ER is. Being good at this is not all about tests, and you have a great heart. I'm sure you think you didn't help today, but the fact that you knew the patient's history was crucial. Now get your ass out of here. You're on an early shift tomorrow."

# CHAPTER 19

## *Kate*

Two weeks later and every day I seem to have a silly grin on my face. The I love yous have settled Fabian and me into a deeper place of slow hands and soft words. The heat of a hot Manhattan summer seeping into every pore and warming me from the inside out. Standing at the station on the ward, I study my phone: No proper messages from him since the day before yesterday, although I got a message saying "alive" with a winky smile this morning. I know he switches off like this; twenty-four-hour stints trying to crack something, grabbing an hour of sleep here and there. Still, a niggle works away at the back of my mind, and although his text was meant to reassure me, I've not seen him for two days.

I could go and surprise him. Curl around him instead of heading home. A bad traffic accident has kept us on our toes all through the Saturday nightshift, and we lost a young guy after battling to stop the bleeding and his body shutting down. We're all a bit antsy. Neil taps my arm as he comes up beside me to study a screen.

"Go," he says with a jerk of his head, and I look at the hard etches of his face, and I nod at him, swinging around and heading for the locker room to get out of my scrubs. Soon I'm on Henry Street, walking the blocks to Fabian's through deserted Sunday morning streets, the late June day not yet fully dialed up to temperature. I've no idea whether he will be up. He might be in bed, all skin and sleepy warmth, and my lips curl up.

I slot my key into the rusty old lock on his building, and wind up three flights of stairs. Then I'm outside his door and, as I open it, it all sounds so deadly quiet that I step silently over the shoes on the mat, pushing off my sneakers as my gaze is snagged by some small red trainers. I frown at the mess of dishes piled all over the kitchen counter—Fabian's usually pretty tidy for someone who doesn't care about his surroundings much. As I move through the apartment, the darkness wraps around me. The blinds are drawn down over the living-room windows, a duvet on the couch, empty food containers on the coffee table … The bedroom door is a dark crack in front of me, just like before. *No sound of tapping keys.*

Hand on the door, I push it open and make out Fabian stretched out in a jumble of blue covers, tattoos curling down, his arm flung over a pillow. But as I step forward, I realize it isn't a pillow at all: There's the shape of another body in the bed, and I can't move or drag my eyes away. As my eyes adjust to the gloom, ice drips through my veins. A woman, her black hair a tumbled mass next to his, is curled up under his outstretched arm. I step back, heart thumping so loudly I'm amazed no one can hear it, and a sharp pain pierces right through me, whipping my breath away and almost bending me double. Her thin arm is also thrown out in sleep. His arm pinning her, protective. Are they *naked*? My thoughts run around my head like a rat in a maze: a friend, a hookup, a prostitute, a … a … Something has my chest in a vice, and I gasp trying to suck in air, and the woman stirs. *Oh God.* I have to get out of here. If they wake up … I … I … I need to go right now. I turn, padding quickly down the corridor, fumbling with my shoes at the door. *Get out, Kate! Go! Go! Go!*

"Who's there?" The woman's voice calls, soft, sleepy.

*Get out!* I'm scrabbling into my shoes when she appears in a T-shirt in the bedroom doorway, a frown on her face.

"Who are you?" she says, voice sharpening. "What are you doing here?"

I want to ask her the exact same questions, but my brain is leaping around in my head dumping "Flee! Flee!" endorphins into my system. I can't suck enough air into my lungs. My sweaty hand slips over my laces, and I give up, thrusting my feet in and crushing the backs of the shoes.

As I reach for the door handle, she catches my arm.

"I said, who the fuck are you?" Her nails scratch my skin.

"Who are you?" I say.

"I'm his girlfriend," she says, eyes narrowing. "From college, we've been together years." A calm pride rings through her voice, and a knife reaches into my chest and slices into my heart. *Years?* My God. How can that be? All the time we've been together over the last month. Then I almost want to laugh at myself: *A month, Kate?* Seriously? My involvement with Fabian morphs before my eyes. And I said I love you after a *month.* Why did I believe him? Two years of David's warmth and I love you bullshit: This is just like finding that goddamn card in his pocket, except this time *she's* the one in the long-term relationship, *I'm* the bit on the side.

Her thick lashes and porcelain skin are surrounded by a huge array of black corkscrew curls, but under her T-shirt, which I recognize with a horrid jolt is one of Fabian's, she's thin and wasted and her jaw has a bitter jut to it like she's used to fighting. The "prostitutes from the river" comment floats into my head. Is she his drug pal? Something else? What do I *really* understand about his life around his drug experiments? Who he meets? What he buys? Nothing. A secret life, I almost groan at how gullible I am. She appears as mean as hell, and I'm not that girl—by God, I am *not* fighting her. I say the first thing that comes into my head.

"I'm his cleaner, but I don't want to disturb you. I'll come back." A lie, like so many others.

She studies me for a while, like she's trying to work out why I didn't tell her straight away, but her eyes grow hazy, like she can't quite keep a grasp on the conversation. She nods and turns to head back down the corridor.

"Sorry about the state of it." She waves a vague arm. "He's always been a messy fuck." And she disappears back into the bedroom, closing the door with a soft click.

I stare at the closed door. I must be a more convincing liar than I thought. All I can see is Fabian's body in the bed, and fire burns through my veins, sharp and hot: I want to go in and slap him, so hard. *He's* the most plausible cheat in the world. Love? What a joke. Sweat breaks out over my forehead: I'm going to be sick. I wrench open the door, thundering down the stairs and through the entrance as the contents of my stomach deposit onto the gray concrete. I lean weakly against the iron railings, wiping a shaking hand over my lips as I stare at the Brooklyn Bridge towering above me, the endless steel cables, cars zipping across the river. So much water and nothing to clean up this mess.

*

The bus lurches through the traffic, pulling out to a blare of horns right by my window. I close my eyes, suck a breath into tight lungs. People are resting against windows or glued to the screen on their phones. Travelling back to their homes like nothing is wrong. How many of these people are this shaky, this sick inside? I can still see her skinny legs heading away from me down the hallway, T-shirt covering her bottom, the vague and vacant look about her. I've come across those glazed eyes before in the ER: the Addict's Stare. A bitter laugh erupts out of my mouth, and the man next to me shifts in his seat. Great. Now I'm the maniac on the bus.

No surprise that Fabian's girlfriend would be into all that; of course she would appeal to him. She can't have been with him since college, though, can she? Janus would know about her, and I've seen Fabian a lot, I mean not every night, but perhaps she's some street girl he fits in between … I lean forward, pressing into my knees, and the guy beside me moves his legs into the aisle. How much do Janus and Jo really understand about his life around drugs? All the things we've done … how his arm was flung over her … Bile rises up my throat. To go through this again. To *see it* with my own eyes. *Stupid, stupid, Kate.* I dig my fingernails into my palm, the pain blunt and raw and so satisfying.

I've never been so glad to arrive at the red brick of our building on 22nd Street. I head up in the lift to the fourth floor, and quiet and dark washes over me when I open the door to the apartment and step inside. I blink around the small space, at the blinds down over the living-room windows, and I don't know what to do next, how to shut my thoughts off. The bedroom door clicks, and Liss appears, bleary-eyed.

"Just finished your shift?" she mumbles, and my eyes meet hers and I crumble, throat tightening and tears welling up. Her eyes widen as she hastens toward me, pulling me into a tight hug.

"My God, what's happened?" she says into my hair, arms wrapping around me. "Did you lose someone?"

She's talking about a patient of course, but I have lost somebody else.

"Fabian," I croak, and she pulls back, hands on my shoulders. Her face crumples, eyes filling as she searches mine.

"Oh my God, Kate. He *died*?"

She knows his history; I told her about his last admission. I shake my head at her, and her horrified expression morphs into relief.

"I found him in bed with … with …" I can hardly drag the words out. "Someone else."

Now her eyes really *do* go huge, and she presses a hand to her chest.

"*What?*" Her voice cracks like a starter pistol. "No way, Kate."

I collapse onto the couch, pulling my knees up into my body, and she flops down next to me, hand on my arm.

"She was skinny, all this wild dark hair." I make an arc over my head. Why am I telling her this?

"But he … I don't understand. What happened?"

I try to recount my visit to his apartment, sitting back and taking deep gulping breaths. She's quiet, eyes fixed on me, occasionally interjecting with exclamations of "No" and, eventually, "That fucker!"

"I can't believe it." She shakes her head and stares at the Turkish rug at our feet. Out of the window, the buildings loom up across the street. It is unreal. My eyes tighten, more tears spilling over, and I flap my hands, putting them down on my legs to try to calm myself. Then I'm up and pacing across to our small, open-plan kitchen.

"Goddammit, how could he do that?"

Acid bubbles in the back of my throat. "I'm going to be sick." And I shoot into the bathroom, skidding on my knees in my haste to reach the toilet. Liss follows me in and sinks down, holding my hair back and stroking my back. It's like some awful echo of Javier's wedding. I turn my head, and she makes a face at me as sobs roll through my body and tears track down my cheeks.

"How could he do that? How could he sleep with someone else?" I choke out.

"I'm so sorry, Kate. I feel so useless. What can I do?"

Closing my eyes, I say, "You're good, you're here."

"Alcohol? Distraction?"

I want to curl into a ball.

"Bed." And pulling myself up from the cold tiled floor, I stagger down the hall into my bedroom and collapse onto the soft white duvet. Liss appears minutes later, a bucket in her hand, her face pursed in worry.

"I've got a lecture this morning, but I don't like leaving you. I can—"

I shake my head at her.

"I'll be fine. I'm exhausted and I worked all night. I'll be better once I've slept."

It's a lie. I don't think I'll sleep at all.

# CHAPTER 20

## *Fabian*

A clatter in the kitchen wakes me, and I squint at the blue bedcovers, the dim light coming from around the door. *Nadine.* I roll onto my back and stare at the cracks in the plaster over my head, then the room lightens as the door swings open, and she appears with a cup of coffee in her hand as she wanders over to place it on my nightstand. A sigh bubbles up my throat from nowhere when I notice she's wearing one of my T-shirts. She's been here for two nights when I said one, and she needs to leave today. I'll have a fight on my hands; she's mean when she's crossed.

She turns away, but not before her hungry gaze rakes over my body. I'm half-covered in sheets, but she's well aware that I'm naked. Wincing, I try to pull a blanket farther over me. She's in here, and I don't know where she got my T-shirt from. This is all wrong.

"Oh, your cleaner came around, said she'd come back," she calls at me over her shoulder as she heads out the bedroom door.

I frown and blink at the ceiling. *What?* What cleaner?

Before I can think better of it, I'm flinging the covers back and placing my feet on the floor, bending down to grab some clothes.

"The cleaner?" I call after her.

Her head pops back around the door, and I clutch at my jeans to cover myself, but her eyes travel all over what she can see.

"Blonde? Sleek-looking bitch? She let herself in." Her eyes narrow on me as I stare at her, pulse thumping like a drumbeat in my neck. *Kate?* Kate was here?

Oh.

Fuck.

Oh no, no, no.

Bile burns up the back of my throat. No. No. *What was I thinking?* I open my mouth to ask something, anything, but pull myself up short with a shaky breath.

I've not talked to Kate about my past history because what happened with Nadine at college makes me look like an idiot. *Stupid, stupid, stupid.* I drag a T-shirt over my head before I glance at Nadine again, only to discover her eyes are narrowed on me. She's mean and she's a liar. I don't want her to know about my relationship with Kate. I take a calming breath. If I want to find out what went down this morning, I need to be careful how I play this.

"Oh yeah, Tuesday," I say, staring at the floor and dropping my hands between my knees as if I've forgotten all about the cleaner and the day she comes. Fuck. *Kate found her here and left.* I try and tamp down the nausea, making my voice sound normal. Nadine's eyes drift sideways when I look back at her, and she nods before heading out of my room. I hastily thrust my legs into my jeans and shrug them on, following her to the living area.

"Is she coming back to clean up?" I say as casually as I can, starting to gather the plates lying on every surface, letting my hair fall forward so she can't see my face.

She sinks onto the couch and waves a limp hand. "Don't tidy up, babe; we'll just make it messy again."

*We'll* make it messy? I grind my teeth. I'm tempted to tell her about the house I grew up in: the huge piles of things dumped all over, gathering in corners. One side of the living room was piled high with junk and left to rot for years and years. How my mom ripped the carpets up when they got so matted with dirt you couldn't make out their original color or pattern, and we lived on dirty floorboards. My favorite things, important things, lost forever, destroyed. I suck in a deep breath. *Focus.*

"Is she coming round later?"

"Yeah. Yeah. She said she'd come back. Asked me who I was." Nadine gives a throaty laugh, and something black and slick slithers up my throat. Alarm bells are ringing loud and insistently.

I pick up some dirty mugs, smile like I'm relaxed and don't care. This is the only way I'll get even the approximate truth out of her: She's a junkie, she doesn't know fact from fiction half the time.

"What did you say to that?" I say, taking the greasy plates to the kitchen and staring at the mess on the counter—not an inch of space anywhere.

She sticks her head around the wall that divides the kitchen from the lounge. "I told her I was your girlfriend. Since college." She grins at me. "Kind of true, right?" Her head tips to one side.

And God, this is worse. So much worse. My brain is screaming now. Fucking hell, I want to rip my hair out. I have to find Kate and explain.

"Were you dressed like that?" I say, smiling, trying to make sure I'm not baring my teeth at her.

"Yeah," she says with a shrug.

Oh God, Kate saw her in my T-shirt? *Holy shit.*

"She opened the door to the bedroom. I think it woke me up."

*What?*

"The bedroom door?" Why would that wake her up? Nadine's sleeping on the couch. Kate would have walked passed her to reach my room.

Her eyes slide sideways, and something crosses her face and I've seen this look a million times before. She's fucking lying.

"Yeah, I just heard a noise, you know?" Her voice grows vague, and she gestures toward the couch. I study her gaunt face for a beat. Why is she making stuff up? Fuck. What the hell happened between her and Kate? Surely, if there'd been an argument, I'd have woken up?

"What time did she come by?" I say.

Her face has shifted into that deliberately vacant stare she has. Damn. "Oh, no idea, babe. A couple of hours ago. Maybe?"

She came by after her shift finished. I stack the plates on the counter. I'm not going to get any more out of Nadine, and if I push, she'll give me a whole pack of nonsense. I head to the bedroom and grab my phone. When I come out, she's got the television on.

"I'm going out to get a coffee. Clean this shit up, yeah?"

She pouts, eyes drifting back to the screen. "My coffee's not good enough for you?" she says.

I wave a nonchalant hand at her. I can be vague too when I want to be. "Yeah, yeah. Just tidy up."

The door slams behind me as I head down the stairs to the street. I press call as soon as I'm on the sidewalk, but the phone just rings and rings in my hand, so I hang up and try again. Four, five times. No response. Her voice makes a shiver run down my spine.

"*Hey, this is Kate. Sorry I can't talk right now. Please leave a message after the beep.*"

What do I say here? How do I explain?

"Kate. It's Fabian. Call me."

Then I send a text:

Ring me back. It's urgent.

# CHAPTER 21

## *Kate*

A woman in a long black coat is chasing me, and the green hedges of the maze bend and sway as I turn left, then right, wind whipping down the narrow alleyways as I fight to stay upright. I round another corner, and a flash of light appears up ahead, and I turn and glance quickly behind me. She's close now, and ragged breathing fills my ears. *Follow the light.* The beam bobs, moving on, and I race toward it, chest tight. My heart lifts as it gets closer—someone is holding it! Then a claw lands on my arm, and I twist around and she's right there, all black hair and snarling rotten teeth. I keel over backward into the soft earth and I'm falling, sinking. Oh God, I'm going too far, into the ground, and I scrabble at the sides to climb out, but she laughs as soil starts pouring down on top of me.

My eyes snap open to lines of slats on blue blinds. *My bedroom.* I roll onto my back, heart still hammering. It was her, my God. It was her. I press my hand to my chest, blinking. The image of them in bed together tightens my throat. Could this be any worse? Unless he was married and had kids—the bastard. This is the end. I'm going to tattoo it on my body somewhere so I don't forget, maybe my hand so I remind myself every damn day. *No sexy bad boys.* I laugh, trying to choke it all down. What will it take to get through this? The months of avoiding David, the fact that I was still affected by it two years later. I turn my head. My backpack is sitting on the floor by the bed, and my phone is plugged in on the nightstand, a note from Liss propped up next to it. She must have come in with everything after I dropped off.

*"Gone to work. Call me when you wake up."*

I gasp as I register the number of missed calls and texts, all from Fabian. My finger hovers over the texting icon—do I want to read all his crappy justifications? His lovely "girlfriend" will have no doubt mentioned that his "cleaner" called by. He must know I walked in on them. What could he say? I wish I'd taken a picture—I could send it to him as a card with "GOODBYE" scratched over it.

The sheer quantity of messages is like déjà vu, though; this is exactly what happened with David after I told him it was over. He kept calling and sending things, and I read them all and it made it a hundred times worse. I know what I need to do. I grit my teeth, clicking through the menu for the delete button, watching them all disappear. I'm not reading them. I'm not listening to them. Then I remove Fabian's contact details and all his texts, going right back to day one. At one point I looked back through David's messages, and the warmth and love in them ate away at me for over a year. It was a special kind of torture. No. No. Not doing that again. All gone.

I stare down at my phone: Jo is top of my call list, and on impulse I press the button. She answers after two rings with a sharp. "Kate!" And I deduce immediately that Liss has talked to her. "Come to my office."

"You know?"

"Liss called me, but she didn't give me details. Come here, Kate, please."

I want to see her. I want her soothing words and warm hugs.

"Tell me I'm not an idiot for making the same mistake twice," I whisper.

"Jesus, of course not!"

"You got the only good one," I say, and why did I say that? But Janus is

Fabian's best buddy, and I can't understand why guys don't ever see this kind of behavior as an indication that their friend is an asshole. Do I think Fabian is a jerk? Goddammit, I don't. I pinch the skin on the inside of my arm, hard. Wake up, Kate! I should hate him, the lying, cheating …

"He has his moments," Jo drily interrupts my mental tirade. "He can be a real jackass too."

I laugh at this. Somehow Jo always manages to say the right thing.

"But maybe not finding him in bed with someone else," I say, and she groans.

"Seriously, you have to come here to tell me this whole thing. I am not doing this over the phone. Janus is going to tear him apart."

"I'm on my way," I say, climbing out of bed with a deep breath. I need to cry on her shoulder and have her build me back up again.

# CHAPTER 22

## *Fabian*

I glance at the sky, then the time on the screen. Fuck. 6 p.m. I've rung Kate about a hundred times, sent text after text, phone glued to my hand all day. Around 2 p.m., I went to her apartment, figuring she'd be up after her night shift. I called, buzzed on her door, hung around for a couple of hours. She should have *been* there. Where the *fuck* is she?

A hurricane is building somewhere deep in my body. Even Nadine has stopped coming into the bedroom on some pretext or other, as my responses to her guileless questions about how to work the oven or her phone get more and more explosive. My hand drums on the desk as I watch the test code I'm running—the number of errors is higher than the last time I tested it. My face goes into my hands. Everything is going backward, like a rope slipping through a ratchet. I make some stupid, too-generous decision and someone exploits it. I punch my knuckles into the side of the desk, hard, shaking them out to relieve the pain.

When I said Nadine could stay for a night, I gave her two rules: It was one night only, and she couldn't interrupt me. So, when she opens the door again, something hot and dark settles over me.

"Do you want me to make something to eat?" she says, words tumbling out in a rush.

I stare at her. I ought to go back and hang around at Kate's for longer. She'll have to come home eventually. But I need to get Nadine out of my apartment first.

"You're leaving today, yeah?"

"Faaaaab." It comes out on a long whine. "I've got nowhere else to go."

I've not been concentrating on the problem of Nadine today, and I inwardly curse.

"The deal was one night."

"You've got lots of space, though, babe. I'll behave. I promise, Fab." She walks toward me, wheedling, and I hold up my hands as hers reach out.

"No, Nadine, that was the agreement."

"I won't do drugs or anything." She shakes her head, and how often did I hear that *exact* sentence coming out of her mouth when we were at college? Nothing has changed for her, and when she contacted me, I really hoped it had. I examine her drawn face, her skinny arms, and my stomach hollows out.

"I don't want to physically throw you out, but I will," I say.

Her wheedling instantly switches. "You're a fucking bastard, you are. After all we shared, you're throwing me out on the street. You don't know what it's like. You can't kick me out tonight."

I shake my head at her. This game … she turns on a dime, every damn time. She played this card yesterday evening, and I shouldn't have waited until six today to start this conversation. I gave in yesterday because, fuck it all, I *do* know what sleeping out is like.

She drops her head, dark hair falling around her face, and this is so similar to when Zach stayed here that my whole body wants to cave in. I let out a long, controlled breath. She needs some fucking help. And then my chest expands, I'm an idiot. I know people out there. *Steve.* I can find her a place in a woman's refuge.

"I'll find you a bed for tonight. I'm friends with someone who works in a shelter."

Her jaw drops, and she folds her arms. "No way in hell, babe! Those places are awful—you've no idea."

"Actually, I do," I mutter. Zach died in my third year, not long after I'd extricated myself from her and her bullshit, and I don't want to tell her any more about what happened to him or what I did afterward; it'll only give her more ammunition, more things to exploit.

I pull my phone from my pocket, and Steve's voice is warm and happy on the other end of the line. He's like a soothing balm after the day I've had. God love these people who take care of the homeless in this city. He was a godsend through my many months of trying to find Zach and then living on the street, and I've helped him out many times with the shelter's computers. He tells me returning the favor is long overdue. Nadine listens, mouth pinched, her black beady eyes fixed on my face.

When I thank him and hang up, she calls me a "fucking asshole who's no friend at all" and flounces off to the kitchen and starts banging pots around. I don't care. She's taken advantage of me too many times for me to feel sorry for her. Why did I even take her in in the first place? I guess part of me was curious to see if she'd managed to sort herself out, but it was also because my annoyance with her had faded. I'd forgotten what she'd put me through, and my sympathy for her and her situation bubbled up again. *This time when I help it will make a difference.* I must stop listening to that voice in my head.

So … now all I need to do is get her out of the apartment—

Thud!

Thud!

Thud!

A heavy fist lands on the door, and I stand stock-still for a second before stepping silently into the corridor, prickles running down my spine. Dammit, my alarm security people aren't coming until next week: Could someone have found me here already? *I've been careful.* The slimy guy on the sidewalk pops into my head. *Goddammit.*

Nadine appears behind me. I shake my head, pressing my finger to my lips, walking silently up to the door and peering through the peephole …

Janus's messy head of hair is bent forward, and my body deflates like someone took a pin out of it. And I'm so pleased to see him. Today has been so shit. I wrench open the door with a grin on my face.

"Fucker," I say to him, but he doesn't smile and his face turns stony when Nadine appears at my side and winds an arm around my waist. Frowning at her, I shift away, but her mouth twists coyly, and she wraps a long tendril of hair around her finger. Janus lived through everything that happened with her at college, and Nadine would be at the top of his shit list.

"Hi, Janus," she says breathlessly, and my stomach curls inward.

He doesn't say anything to her and looks at me, tightness around his eyes and in the thin line of his mouth. I'm in a world of trouble, and I probably deserve to be.

"Let's talk," he says through clenched teeth, gesturing at me to come out of the apartment. I'm going to get a lecture. Janus does being disappointed in people like no one else I know, and I hate being in his bad books. I ram my feet into my boots as Nadine hangs on the door.

"I'll make us something to eat," she calls after me as I thump down the stairs, and I shake my head at her. I think I'm going to have to physically remove her from my apartment.

As soon as we are on the street, Janus turns, red-faced. "What the *fuck* are you doing?" The words explode out of him like he can't contain them in his body for another minute. My head jerks back at his ferocious scowl.

"What do you mean?"

"You're back with *Nadine*?"

Ice runs through my veins. "What are you talking about? No, of course not. Fuck! What do you take me for?"

"Then what the hell is she doing in your apartment?" He flaps his hand at my waist where she curled an arm around me. "Winding her tentacles around you?"

The traffic is thumping over the bridge, and I sigh and run my fingers through my hair, gesturing at him to walk toward the coffee shop.

"She called me and asked for a place to stay two days ago."

"Man, what are you *doing*? You cannot go back there again. Don't you remember how difficult it was to remove her from your life last time? My *God*, Fab."

His face is red, and his shoulders are hunched over, and I come to a halt on the sidewalk and hold up a placating hand. Sweat is prickling my neck, making the thin cotton of my T-shirt stick to my skin. I don't need Janus losing his shit. I shove my hands deep into my pockets: To stop them shaking or to make sure I don't punch him, I'm not sure.

"For God's sake! I agreed she'd stay one night. No more," I say through gritted teeth. "She called me late in the day, and she was desperate."

Janus makes a face. He understands Nadine's schemes better than anyone, but dammit all to hell, I know them too. I wish he trusted me more. He blinks to the side and takes a deep breath.

I put a hand on his arm. "Look, I know her ploys. I can handle her. I've already found her an alternative place to stay. I just …"

"Fuck, Fabian. Kate—she's the best thing that's ever happened to you and …"

How does he know where my head's been all day? "What about Kate? I've been trying to find her and talk to her all day and …"

"I think you're way beyond talking," Janus mutters, staring down at the cracks and weeds in the sidewalk.

*What?* I stare at him open-mouthed. Words bubble up as a hot mist grows in my head.

"What do you mean?"

"She came here this morning," he says.

I gape at him. "I know she did. How the hell …?" Then I realize. "You've fucking *seen* her? Fuck. That." I grab him by his T-shirt. "Where the fuck is she?" I shout. "She's not been answering any of my calls. I've been waiting outside her goddamn apartment." The concern that's been growing all day morphs into a tiger with claws and thrashing feet. My insides are being torn to pieces. "What did she say to you?"

He lets out a long groan and holds up his hands.

"Calm down. Calm down," he says, prizing my fingers off his top. "She came to Jo's office. She's really fucking upset, Fabian. I haven't spoken to her. Jo told me that Kate had found you with somebody else. Little did I realize it was Nadine."

My feet pace across the gray concrete as I jump around the sidewalk. I can't stay still.

My words come out sharp and jerky. "I'm not with *someone else*. Nadine talked to her when I was sleeping. I don't know what she said. Kate pretended to be my cleaner. I've no idea why."

Janus rolls his eyes. "You know what Nadine is like, that's a crapshoot. She'll have said all sorts of shit to her. Have you told Kate about Nadine?"

"Fuck no. You think I'm sullying what we have with that car crash?"

Janus groans. "Man, that is one of the stupidest things I think I've heard you say."

"What the hell do you know about it? You and Jo weren't exactly models of clear communication. We're new! You don't risk shit early on if it's good, do you?" I tip back my head, groaning. "Why didn't she try and talk to me? Why didn't she demand an explanation? God, if I'd met a guy in her apartment, I'd be shouting the place down."

"Yeah, if you'd found that fucker David staying with her, you'd have killed him."

My body goes rigid, black clouds descending over my head.

"Who's the fuck's David?" I say, and Janus stares at me.

"Her ex."

Of course, she has an ex. Kate hasn't shared with me either? Oh, the fucking irony.

And what he's said, about not liking someone else being with Kate … the sting is sharp and brutal. Why am I helping Nadine? Why am I doing any of this?

I turn around and slam my head into the concrete front of the building next to us.

# CHAPTER 23

## *Kate*

A couple of loud shouts echo down the corridor, and I hear running feet, so I smile at the patient with the bad leg wound I've spent half an hour stitching up.

"Just another day in the ER," I say as I get up from my chair. "Drunk people are the worst. Let me check that I don't need to do anything." And I stick my head out the curtains. My eyes move to the reception area, and someone in scrubs steps aside, and then I see him. *Oh God.*

"Sorry, I ..." I flap my hand at the man on the bed and step out of the cubicle.

Fabian's reeling around with something in his hand, and my feet take me toward the main desk, toward him. As soon as his eyes lock on mine, it's like being plugged into a thousand-volt socket. A hundred emotions wash across his face in one look: pleading, anger, desperation.

"Why won't you fucking *talk* to me?" he shouts.

Several eyes turn to look at me, wide with horror. Out of the corner of my eye, I see a doctor skid to a halt beyond reception, and Chris, an ER resident, comes up behind me. Erica, the nurse who's trying to calm Fabian down, glances over her shoulder at me and shifts to one side. Another staff member whose name I don't know is crouched down below the front desk on the phone like she's calling the cops. I wouldn't blame her: He's dirty and disheveled and has a large scrape on his forehead. Drugs? Weapons? I peer at his hand again. *What is he holding?*

I shake my head at him, and he steps toward me. At my back, Chris shifts closer.

"Please, Kate, I need to talk to you. I want to explain," he says, and my eyes track down his body and my heart constricts in my chest. My God, this man, this damaged, amazing man. But I don't want the excuses and everything I know that goes with that.

"It's better this way, Fabian." My voice shakes. I can't look at him.

The doctor by the desk steps forward and raises a placating hand.

"Sir ..." he starts, and Fabian swings his arm and then I realize what's in his hand: a long shard of glass. It misses the doctor by inches. Oh Christ.

"Keep away from me," he shouts. "I just want to speak to her."

"Jesus, Fabian," I say. "What are you doing?"

"You're not going to give me a chance here, Kate? After everything?" And the pain in his voice pierces right through me. "I'm not even worth a conversation? Five minutes of your time?"

*Oh God.*

"You'll listen to me if I do this," he says, and I stare at him in horror as he runs the piece of glass down the artery in his arm.

"Oh shit!" Chris says behind me as blood spurts out of Fabian's vein and starts bubbling out from beneath his skin. He didn't just do that, did he?

"You going to talk to me or watch me bleed to death? How long have I got, Kate?" he taunts as red streams pour down over his wrist and onto the floor. The whole place has come to a standstill, frozen in time.

And then he sways, and three of us lunge forward, grabbing his arm, hands frantic. Before I know what's happening, we have him on the ground, pinned. Someone thrusts a tourniquet in my hand. My hands slip with the blood, a fumbling, shaking blur in front of my face. It's everywhere, and I'm used to bleeding, but Jesus, it soaks into the knees of my scrubs and seeps onto the tiles, sliding under our feet.

But somewhere at the back of my mind is a drumbeat: arm, Velcro, tighten, distal pulse. A switch has flipped. The man on the floor is a patient to save, not the man I am angry with, the man I could strangle with my own bare hands, the man who has left me wrecked. His face is right there, dark stubble and circles under his eyes as I concentrate on his arm, tightening and tightening the windlass, stains collecting in the dry skin of my fingers and the edges of my nails. Red smears everywhere. His eyes drift across my face as his eyelids flutter down. A tight band wraps around my chest.

"Come on, come on." I'm not sure whether I'm asking Fabian to hang on or the other doctors to hurry up or the bleeding to stop. Chris is trying to get a line in his other arm, shouting for someone to call the blood bank.

"What's your blood type," Chris says.

"He's been admitted before, it'll be on the system," I say.

"I love you, Kate," Fabian slurs, and in the blink of an eye I'm pulled out of medical mode and back into reality. My heart is like horses' hooves thundering closer and closer. After all the agony of the last fourteen hours, he *loves* me?

Chris gapes at me before focusing back on Fabian, who mumbles something as his eyes droop. I grab his chin, and his eyelids flutter.

"Two units of packed red blood cells to Resus, right now!" Chris shouts. "Step on it!"

"You didn't have to do this, why did you do this? I'll talk to you, you nut." I hear urgent feet in the corridor, the bed rattling toward us.

Vacancy is stealing his focus. "Just wanted to make sure," he slurs as his eyes finally close.

# CHAPTER 24

## *Fabian*

My eyes flutter open to white-and-green walls. *Fucking hell.* Someone chuckles from next to my bed, and my head jerks to discover Janus in ripped denim shorts and a light-blue vest, one leg resting across his knee.

"Why did she call you?" I say, my voice like sandpaper. "I'm so fucking mortified."

He laughs. "Oh, come on, when have I not been there for your most spectacular incidents? Apparently, you slashed an artery open and declared undying love to her in her place of work," he says, grinning from ear to ear, and I try to shift, to move my hand, but nothing happens, and I look down to find it wrapped like a mummy, fingers protruding slightly from the end. My arm must weigh a hundred kilos.

A sharp pain shoots through my shoulder. Wires and tubes have me linked to what appears to be every machine known to humankind.

"The staff are besides themselves," he continues. "They've never had anything so exciting happen here, and that is saying something given this is the emergency department. Mind you, I think your woman is pretty embarrassed about the whole thing. She's been dragged in to speak to the head of the hospital, the head of the ED, her rotation program director …"

"Fuck." My hand curls into a fist, and I tip my head back on the pillow. "She wouldn't fucking talk to me."

"Couldn't you have done a poem and flowers like a normal guy?"

That's absurd: Who does that kind of low-maintenance crap?

"Not my style," I say, and he snorts.

"Not sure I can stomach all the drama that's going to unfold between you and Kate if this relationship carries on." And I glance at him to see a smile playing around his mouth.

"I don't think you need to be too worried about that. What with Nadine and this"—I try and lift my arm—"she'll probably never speak to me again."

Janus leans forward, eyes narrowing. "I think you'll find that she likes the craziness. She doesn't want a regular guy; she wants you." His lips curve up in a smug smile, and I rub my hand up and down the blue hospital blanket covering my thigh. Does she? Even after all this?

"Bullshit," I say.

He shakes his head, and I stare at the machine closest to me. If I rip the sensors off my chest, will it … and without any warning my stomach goes into freefall.

"I've got no money to pay for this," I groan, trying to sit up, but Janus waves his hand at me.

"Don't be a fucking idiot. What do you think's been happening with all these hospital visits? You're covered."

What the fuck? "I don't want handouts from you."

"You're on my company's health insurance policy."

"What? Since when?"

"About three months ago, when I realized how often you were going into the ER. We can't have something happening to you." He pats my leg.

"Stop patronizing me." I try to put my head in my hands, but I can't move my arm. "Another fucking thing I owe you."

Janus rolls his eyes. "I'm bored with this conversation. You owe *me*? You remember that small incident of you saving my business?"

"I think you'll find I caused that," I mumble.

A voice picks up outside the door, and I catch a glimpse of Kate through the clear glass circle. She's nodding, talking to someone, and my whole body tightens as I watch her blonde hair gleaming under the lights. I'm desperate to see her and dreading it at the same time. Is she going to kick me to the curb, finally fed up with my crazy decisions and less than balanced behavior? As she opens the door and studies me, her eyes are guarded. She doesn't *look* furious, but she doesn't look as though she's exactly feeling warm and cuddly either. Black clouds settle around me. Janus stands, grins at us both.

"Give him hell, Kate," he says, leaning in to kiss her cheek before sauntering out the door. I want to flip him the bird, but weakness is stealing through my body, and I lean back into the pillows and close my eyes.

When I open my eyes again, I find her looking at the record on my clipboard. "Are you mad with me?"

She inclines her head.

"Will you talk to me?"

She nods, and clearly this is all I'm going to get, so I take a deep breath and shut my eyes again.

"Her name is Nadine. We met in college. When we first hooked up, she was fun, wild; we had a few crazy nights together, which were …" I screw my face up, I want to be honest, but I'm not sure by how much. "The truth is they were thrilling, but I realized that what for me was a game, a bit of a laugh, for her … well … drugs were her whole life."

When I open my eyes, Kate's face still has a neutral holding pattern expression that I can't read.

"I've no idea what she said to you, but you probably view my lifestyle and think I'm crazy, but I'm not. I experiment and my interests are eclectic, but I'm all right up here." I lift my undamaged arm to tap my head. "Nadine *isn't* right. When I first met her, she was crazier than I was, and she dared me to do all kinds of mad, impulsive things. I was young, thrilled to have found somebody who seemed to get where I was coming from. After a while, I became aware that she wasn't what she seemed, that she'd used tricks like this before to hook herself into guys."

How do I explain this? "I took more and more risks. Things spiraled downward. She was high a lot of the time, and underneath the crazy girl exterior there was depression and neediness. She was heavily dependent on drugs, *dealt* them too, and I got wise to it, although like most addicts, she hid it well. It took me a long time to cotton on to what was going on. She was crafty, so good at pretending." I run my good hand over my hair and inhale deeply.

"She'd been chucked out of colleges and jobs, drifting from one thing to the next, in all sorts of trouble with the police, and other people you don't want to be in trouble with. She sold sex to escape from some of her problems. I think she looked at me and saw a way out, someone who was prepared to help and not fuck her over. She never understood that she got screwed over because *she* screwed people over. I felt responsible and she exploited that, told me I was her last hope. Extracting myself seemed impossible, and I ended up staying with her and trying to sort her out. God, I tried so hard." I scan Kate's face: She's not meeting my eyes.

"I knew that she manipulated me. I wasn't stupid. But I didn't mind. I wanted to help, and I felt sorry for her. She was an addict like Zach, and it was a path I could have so easily been on myself. Even if I couldn't turn him around, perhaps I could save *her*. I don't know … She was desperate to hang on to me, desperate to pretend. And I was naïve. But she didn't really want to change, and I couldn't do it for her. She tried to commit suicide when I left her."

Maybe telling Kate all this will kill everything we have, but I've watched too often how lies play out, and I should have been honest before now.

"After the overdose, she was hospitalized. I didn't go and see her, and I'm still ashamed of that, but I knew …" I draw in a sharp breath. "I couldn't be sucked into her craziness any longer. I had to protect myself. I'm not proud of it. I abandoned her."

"You sound like you did a lot." Kate's voice is a calm well of stillness.

I did, but I will never feel I did enough for Nadine, and maybe I let her stay with me because of that. But there is no rationality in any of this, so I nod, and my chest eases slightly. Kate is still here and talking to me: That's a good sign, right?

"She contacted me three weeks ago and said she was in a ton of trouble and needed somewhere off-grid to camp down. She said she tracked me down through some old college friends. I was surprised and relieved to hear she was still alive, and I still felt guilty. But I refused to have her in my apartment. I knew what would happen. Then, two nights ago, she turned up on my doorstep, and she was so wobbly and ill, I gave in, said she could stay for one night. That's all it was meant to be: one night."

"One night with you …" Kate croaks.

"She's very manipulative, and I'm sure she thought this would be her route to stepping back into things with me. I was crystal clear that I was giving her shelter and nothing else, but obviously Nadine doesn't work that way …"

"So you slept with her."

"*What?* No! Of course, I didn't sleep with her, Kate, I …"

"When I came to your apartment, she was in bed with you."

My body floods with ice. "*What?*"

"She was tucked under your arm like …" Her voice breaks, and I reach for her hand, but she moves away.

Sickness curls in my belly. I grip the soft blue blanket covering my legs. *This* is why she hasn't responded to any of my messages?

"Like it was me." It comes out whispered, hoarse, like Kate is only just holding it all together.

"No, no, no."

This can't be right. I open and close my fist on the covers trying to remember that night in bed. I settled down late, left some code running overnight. It was late, and I was exhausted. Spots dance in front of my eyes. How on *earth* did she end up in there with me?

"Nothing happened with Nadine, Kate."

I've been stone-cold sober the whole time she's been there. Fucking hell. Did she do something to me? Sweat trickles down my neck, and words rush up and out my mouth in a torrent.

"I've no idea how she got in my bed. Honest to God. I was crystal clear she was sleeping on the couch. I did not … I would never … not after you and I … You know how we are, Kate … I wouldn't do that …" I stare past her shoulder. "She must have climbed in there after I went to sleep. Fuck, that's the only thing I can think of." The desire for honesty jumbles all my words. "She tried to persuade me into having sex with her, and I told her there was no way that was going to happen. She wasn't happy."

Kate winces.

"I'm trying to be honest. Shit. This is not what it seems."

I rub my hand up and down my thigh, and this time she puts a hand on my arm.

"Why didn't you tell me about her? I came to see you because I hadn't heard from you and … and …" She swallows. "I found you …"

I'm crumbling inside.

"We're so new, Kate, and it was so special … it *is* so special with us. This was supposed to be one night. I didn't want to bring all my past bad decisions into our relationship." I run my hand over my face. "I'm mortified about the whole thing with her—how I got sucked in, the fact that I left her. Her tactics are always the same, and I should have known what she'd try and do, so now I'm ashamed all over again. It must have been terrible to see us like that. It wasn't what it looked like, I swear, Kate. I don't know why my arm was over her. Maybe I thought it was you in my bed."

Now I'm wincing, and I glance at her to find she's chewing her lip.

"After I saw you …" She swallows. "… together, she came after me, asked me who I was, told me she was your girlfriend, that you'd been with her since college. It just seemed so plausible that I was some bit on the side …"

I'm already shaking my head. "How can you *think* that after how good it's been? You've been with me most nights! That's insane."

I reach for her hand, but she dodges me again. "I don't know what to think anymore."

I beckon her with my hand. "Kate." But she steps farther back. "You know," I say, pressing my hand to my heart. "You know how it feels in here. Do you think I would do anything to jeopardize this? Every time we're together, I'm lit up inside. I've never felt like this."

She turns her head away and closes her eyes, and numbness invades my chest. Her face is pale and her mouth a straight line, milky lashes a ghost against her cheeks.

"Ask Janus," I mutter. "Ask him what Nadine was like, what I did, whether what I've told you is true. I would never get back together with her, Kate. You know what we have." I gesture between the two of us, then look up at the ceiling. How can I convince her?

"I was with Nadine for three years, all told. It took me a year to understand, and two years to extract myself. You've no idea how relieved I was when our relationship finally ended. She got chucked out of NYU, but she hung around with the crowd anyway, ingratiating herself with anyone who would give her a bed. Eventually, she disappeared, and that was like a get out-of-jail-free card, but I was also worried that she'd spiral down into something worse. So, I did a bit of research and I found out she'd taken up with a guy from a biker gang. And that was the end of it. I'd not heard from her until three weeks ago."

"Okay."

That isn't saying anything.

"What do you mean, okay?"

She takes a deep breath and meets my eyes, steady, calm.

"Just that. Okay. I'll think about what you've said to me. I'll talk to Janus."

The hollow feeling in my stomach hasn't gone away. "Where does that leave us?"

"I don't know, Fabian. I just don't know."

# CHAPTER 25

## *Kate*

Every day something arrives for me, sometimes two things, either at my work, in the mail or some kind of delivery. A card is in the apartment letterbox every morning—a goddamn card!—some of them he's made himself, and those ones are terrible. Yesterday's read:

*Roses are red*
*Violets are blue*
*You're the one for me*
*And I'm the one for you.*

I laughed. My God, so bad. And Fabian has never appeared to be *that* guy, the guy who would orchestrate something like this. Liss always wants to see what he's sent and what the card says, no matter how crude or personal. She gives me raised eyebrows when there's sexual innuendo, and I get that: I have never been *that girl*. White-hot passion and I are strange bedfellows. The first couple of days she collected the mail because I didn't realize what was coming, and she peered over my shoulder as I went scarlet, but as soon as it was clear these things were going to turn up every day, there's been no refusing her.

On the third day, a huge bunch of red roses arrived at the ER. It was such a classic romance thing that I wanted to text him: "Really? Flowers? What's happened to you?"

But, of course, I couldn't. And what I secretly loved about the roses was I think he was saying that he could be the kind of guy that had romantic gestures in his playbook.

Of course, the ER is in uproar with all this. Fabian slashing his arm, then this. There is no greater topic of discussion. The number of times I've interrupted a conversation where all I catch is some murmur about roses and romance, before it all goes quiet. I can't tell them I found him in bed with another woman because my life would be discussed all over the hospital.

I caught two residents discussing it yesterday, and I growled at them about going back to talking about medicine and saving patients. They just laughed at me and told me they were enjoying my love life, and by the way, when was I going to forgive him? One of them even had the nerve to say that slashing a vein was an impressive feat. *Seriously?*

And I've talked to Janus. He was great, as he always is, goddammit. He didn't try and plead Fabian's case or even take his side. He told me what happened with Nadine at college, and I don't think he's lying or even supporting his friend; our conversation didn't have that veneer. Everything Fabian told me stacks up. Janus did tell me that Fabian would never go there again, and given what I know about their relationship now, I can see that. Janus said he hoped we worked it out and that he thought what we had was "worth it." Whatever that means. But I'm struggling to put aside the image I have of them together, and my own crazy idea is to talk to Nadine and work out for myself what she's capable of. How much of a car crash would that be? And anyway, how would I find her?

So, when I round the corridor from a consulting room and see her standing at reception, seven days into my deliveries from Fabian, I stop dead. She's waving her hands haphazardly at a nurse, and, taking a deep breath, I walk slowly down the hallway toward her. The desire to dive into the nearest room is enormous, and, as if she's registered that someone is watching her, she turns and her mouth twists up in a sneer. The assessment I made in the first few seconds of meeting her feels spot-on: She's as mean as all hell. How has she found me here?

"I don't take kindly to being lied to, bitch," she says, hand landing on her hip.

"Hello, Nadine," I say, eyes narrowing. *She's on something.* And I switch modes, ticking off the details—dilated pupils, slightly slurred speech—and any emotion I might have felt seeing her here disappears behind a curtain. My eyes flick to the receptionist, Dawn, widening my eyes, and she nods almost imperceptibly at me, before getting up from her seat to go and find assistance. My eyes drift back toward Nadine to find her smirking.

"You might think you're with him, but he's not yours," she says.

I watch Dawn's back as she heads up the corridor; I hope she didn't hear that. But I've no time to think about how this is happening *yet again* in my place of work. I step back and to the side, gesturing to Nadine to move into a room I know is empty, but she squints at me aggressively and doesn't budge from reception, chin jutting out like she's expecting a response. Nothing bubbles up.

She's the one who made me back away from Fabian but seeing her here isn't exciting any wild feelings. *Fabian is right.* I know what we have: something deep and warm that goes down to my bones. My heart expands until it feels like it's filling my ribcage.

"How did you find me here? That's clever of you," I say. Flattery has worked in the past with the drug addicts that come into the ER.

She smiles smugly at me, like the cat that got the cream, and my heart sinks. If she's been an addict a long time, then she'll have seen every trick in the book.

"Fabian always underestimates me, like you are right now. He thinks I'm high all the time." She cackles loudly, and several people turn around. "He figures I can't concentrate, that I don't realize what he's doing." She leans forward. "He left me alone in his apartment enough times for me to do some digging."

Alarm bells ring in my head. Fabian's paranoid, and she's a loose cannon. She could exploit her access to Fabian in return for drugs. My blood runs cold. Maybe she's found a way into his computer system: God knows what she could have gotten her hands on.

"Did you study computer science too?" I say.

She snorts at me. "If you think he does anything interesting messing around on those machines, you're an idiot, girl."

How little she knows him.

"It didn't take a fancy degree to work out who you were, where you worked." She wags her finger at me and cackles again. "Fabian had your picture in his phone and everything."

I hope she's had no deeper thought than finding his contacts, who he texts.

I switch tactics. "The problem is, Nadine, you lied to Fabian, and he doesn't like being lied to."

She waves a hand dismissively. "Guys are easy to manipulate, especially him. He enjoys sex, a lot of it, and I know how he likes it. It was good to do it again with him after all this time. He takes care of a girl in bed. I hope you don't mind sharing."

Her lip curls at me. Oh God, the reminder that she's been with him in the same way as me makes me feel like I've swallowed acid. Did he take his time with her too? Ugh. I suck in air through my teeth, that image of her tucked under Fabian's arm is like having little daggers stuck into my skin all over my body. I glance over her shoulder to find several people watching us, riveted. *Jesus.*

I take a deep breath and shake my head at her. "Still lying, Nadine."

"I'm not fucking lying, you bitch. He's mine. He'll always be mine. He takes me back every time I turn up on his doorstep."

"You haven't been with him for over ten years," I say, making an approximate guess.

"He's still mine." She folds her arms over her chest.

I wonder if she even grasps how much time has passed since they were at college together, how much she's confirming with this conversation.

"He does things with me he'd never do with anyone else, things no one else would do with him," she says.

My stomach churns. Do I need to listen to any more of her taunts? Dammit, I want one last attempt to get information out of her.

"Why did you sneak into his bed?"

Her whole face hardens. "Is that what he said? He's a liar."

"Either he's lying or you are. What's more likely in this scenario?"

Her brow furrows as she tilts her head to one side, eyes losing focus. What has she taken? *And Kate, honey, this little chat is getting you nowhere.* She's not the problem here, my problem lies elsewhere: in my terror of making a mistake once and repeating it.

"I have no idea why you're here," I say.

"I know who you are, where you are." She points a shaking finger at me. "You stay away from him."

A laugh forces itself up. After all the stuff I've been bombarded with this week, I don't think I've got much say in it. If she had any sort of relationship with him, she wouldn't be here confronting me. I should stop messing around and trust what he told me.

"Thanks for the memo," I say. "Bye."

I turn around, intending to head back to my patient, but Neil is standing behind the desk bent over studying something, and I know he's heard every word. My face burns as I straighten my scrubs. Jesus, does my love life have to be waved in front of my colleagues like a red flag at every available opportunity? A clawing hand lands on my arm.

"Didn't you hear what I said?" she hisses, and I see Neil stiffen, lift his head.

"Yeah, I did. Problem is, Nadine, I don't think this is down to you or me."

I pull back and turn, heading off up the corridor, and type out the first text I've sent Fabian since he slashed his vein in front of me:

Thanks for the flowers.

As I look back over my shoulder, Neil has come out from behind reception and has a firm hold on Nadine's arm and is gesturing toward the door.

"I'll get you, you bitch!" she shouts. "Watch your back."

*

I focus down on my phone. The typing icon appears, disappears, then starts again. Once I'm round the nearest corner, I lean against the wall and stare down at it. *Get on with it already!* Is he sitting in his apartment feeling the same thing? My lips curl up. I've been on radio silence this past week, but my God I need to tell him what Nadine said about accessing his stuff.

Eventually, a text comes through:

I can't think of anything clever to say to that, and all I'm doing is typing cheesy replies, so here goes: I'm glad you liked them.

The cards are nice too.

I love you, Kate.

My breath stops at this, staring at the words on my screen. Distant voices echo down the hallway from reception, the department phone ringing. What do I say?

I need to talk to you. Nadine turned up at work today.

Within seconds, my phone rings in my hand. This time, I pick up.

"Kate." His voice is all growing urgency. "What the hell happened?"

"I'm still in the ER," I say, looking around at the empty corridor. I open the nearest door and step into a consulting room. "My life is like a soap opera. You've no idea how riveted my colleagues are by all this."

He lets out a huff of breath. "You sound cheery considering Nadine visited you." A smile twists his voice, but then his tone tightens like a vice when he says, "What happened, Kate?"

"She told me to stay away from you, that you were hers. That you'd had sex with her."

A muffled thud reverberates on the other end, like he threw something, possibly his phone. There's a loud rustling, then he growls, "Fucking hell! It's not true, not one word of it. I've not seen her in over ten years. That's such utter bullshit."

"She said she did things with you that no one else would do with you."

"I can't imagine what that would be," he says sarcastically. "I did a lot of dumb shit with her. Did she say what? Drugs maybe?"

*I didn't even think of that.* I gape at the bed in the consultation room. I interpreted what she said as a sex thing, but Fabian's first thought is somewhere else. My God. My thoughts are so skewed.

He sighs. "We did stupid stuff like you do when you're young. Mistakes I never want to repeat. She OD'd once by mistake. I never want to relive that fucking experience."

He's looking for the truth in her words where there is none. But what she said niggles away at me like an old injury, and this has been eating away at me for two years.

"Did you do things with her sexually that"—I pull my courage out of my boots—"that you don't do with me?"

"What the hell, Kate? What kind of question is that? You want a comparison? We're talking ten years ago here."

"I just … I want an honest answer. A guy I went out with"—this is not the time to tell him the whole history here—"David, went to a prostitute because he said there were things he did with her he couldn't ask me for … He said it like it was a given. I know I'm uptight, I …"

"Jesus Christ, Kate. If he did that, then he's a fucking asshole. We have an amazing time in bed. I would ask you for anything I'd want, and I do, Kate. I do all sorts of stuff with you, and you do things to me that make me … Goddammit! How can you even be asking this? I'm hard all the time thinking about the sex we have. I can't concentrate on my work. My brain's so useless I'm a danger to myself. Seriously? I've never had anyone like you in my bed. You're a tiger under those blue scrubs."

The warm lava coursing through my veins bursts out in a laugh. I love talking to him like this: I ask him a question, and he answers it. He more than answers it.

"Just thinking about it is …" he grumbles at me. "Come over. I want you here. I need to torture you a bit more to remind you." I can hear his smile and the catch in his breath, the hope that he can persuade me that all this will be fine.

"Maybe I'll do that to you," I say, smiling, and he groans.

And heat takes over the lightness that has been building ever since I saw Nadine in reception. His skin, his intense concentration … I'm not imagining how good this is.

"We need to have a chat about this David guy." His voice is dust and rust, and guilt invades. I have my own explaining to do.

"I know."

Ugh. I remember the other reason I called him.

"Nadine knew where I worked because she got into your phone. She told me she'd accessed some stuff in your apartment, she didn't say what."

"What? Fuck." His words crack out, followed by a long groan which sounds like … "Goddammit. I let her just walk in here. I'm a fucking idiot. I'm normally so paranoid as well."

Another thump lands like a hand or a head slamming against something. "How many problems have I created by giving her a place to stay? Jesus. Did she say anything about what she'd looked at?"

"Your phone. I asked her if she knew how to program, and she said you did 'nothing interesting on your machines.'"

His steps vibrate across the wooden floor. "Ha! That's funny. I should have known she'd pull some shit like that. I'd be very surprised if she got into my computers, but I'll check what she's accessed. You can't do anything on my devices without leaving a blindingly obvious trail."

I let out a long breath and close my eyes as I sag into the wall. We both have history, exes. He was trying to help her.

"I'm sorry if I overreacted," I say.

"What? No! What the hell, Kate? Come over after your shift, come straight from work." Urgency curls through his voice.

I've missed going to his apartment, missed him.

"Okay."

# CHAPTER 26

## *Fabian*

A loud beeping wakes me, and I stare at the spines of the books on the nightstand. I hear a soft "Shit" as the door clicks closed. *Kate.* My head is filled with cotton wool, and I peer at the time on the ceiling: 8 a.m.

"Put zero-six-seven-nine into the keypad!" I shout. And there's some rustling and beeps and then the noise switches off.

After tossing and turning for hours, I got up to code at 3 a.m., my arm throbbing. I hitch myself up, trying to prop up against the pillow, and the door cracks open and I see her hesitant face, followed by wide eyes: Whether because of the alarm, because I'm in bed or because I'm naked, I've no idea.

"Hey," I say softly.

She pads over to the bed. "You sorted the alarm. Did you ever find out anything about that guy who followed you?"

"I've been a bit caught up with other events." I give her a half smile, and when she scowls at me, I raise a weak hand. "Nothing's happened since then, and there's no evidence anyone knows where I live. I'm tracking the messaging on the hackers' systems." I shrug. "I don't know what more I can do. Maybe I'm being blasé but …"

She's quiet for a few minutes, and I squeeze her hand. "I don't want to tell Janus; he's done more than enough for me. I'll do some more asking around on the street, see if anyone knows anything."

"Sounds good." She smiles as she scans my face. "Rough night?"

Do I look that bad? My eyebrows come together.

"I've had a stressful few days. The woman I'm in love with wouldn't speak to me, and I slashed my arm in some crazy attempt to win her back."

She grins at me, sinking onto the side of the mattress, and I shift over to make space for her.

"Talking of your arm, how is it?"

That's all she's going to give me? My frown deepens, but she ignores my scowling face and naked chest and stretches out my elbow. Damn. She's such a doctor. Pains shoot up to my shoulder, and I wince as her eyes narrow.

"Is it sore? Have you been back to the hospital to get it checked?"

"I don't have an outstanding record with those places."

Starting to unwrap the bandage, she purses her lips at me.

"Don't look at me like that," I say.

This gets me a smile. "I'd have thought with your contacts you'd have industrial-strength pain relief on tap."

"Funnily enough, they don't sell much of that stuff on the street; too easy to buy through the standard routes." I focus on my arm, stretched out on the blue covers, and my voice cracks. "And I promised this girl I know that I wouldn't experiment so much."

She frowns as she unwinds the stretchy cotton. "I also said I didn't want you to change, just not kill yourself."

We both look at the red welt on my arm at the same time, and an irrepressible grin breaks out on Kate's face.

"Not doing so brilliantly on that front, am I?" I say, starting to laugh, and her smile morphs into a giggle and suddenly my chest fills with air.

She looks down, examining my skin, and I tip my head back against the pillows and close my eyes. The building's unusually quiet, dim light seeping around the blinds, the computer fans humming. For the first time in a week, I'm not twisted up inside.

"Was there any problem with the computers? Did Nadine …?"

My eyes pop open. Having that name in this room when I've only just got Kate back in it feels like blasphemy. I press my fingers to her lips, shaking my head.

"She'd only been in my phone."

Her face clears as she nods.

"I'm sorry I doubted you," she says, studying the wound.

My mouth goes slack. What a generous thing to say. Are all doctors this amazing or is it just Kate? Her head is bent, blonde strands curling around her cheeks as she assesses the stitches in my arm.

"God. You do not need to apologize to me, Kate. I'm the one … I'm the one who fucked up here." I stumble over my words.

She shakes her head at me.

She's decided to trust me in this? Believe what I told her? I mean, of the three of us at college, I was *never* the trustworthy one; that's Adam or Janus. I'm the sketchy guy doing crazy shit. The back of my throat is scratchy. I tip my head back onto the pillows again, eyes watery, and a wave of weakness washes over me. This is important, this … this … whatever this light-as-air feeling is. Some age-long weight, that has been living in my skin for as long as I can remember, is slowly being scrubbed away.

She rubs a warm thumb over my stitches, oblivious to my meltdown.

"This has healed nicely. We should take these out."

She stands and heads into the kitchen, and I close my eyes again, listening to her rummaging through the cupboards, water running.

"Fabian?"

I raise my head, and she's got a bowl of soapy water, a pair of scissors, a wad of cotton wool, and a tube of ointment in her hands. She shifts the books to place what she's holding on the nightstand, and I smile at the warmth in her eyes. Then she leans down, her face moving toward mine. *A kiss.*

"If you ever slash your arm like that again, I'm leaving you to bleed out," she says against my mouth, and I cough up a rusty laugh. She's so close, blonde lashes and clear white around her eyes, smelling like summer and raspberries. Her lips are soft and warm.

"You wouldn't talk to me," I say, pulling back. As if that justifies anything.

"I would have talked to you eventually." Her eyes scan mine. "I'm serious, Fabian: You could have died if we'd made one mistake with you. Impaired hand movement, nerve damage. I know you want to live life on the edge, but there's testing your limits and there's idiocy. Slashing an artery …" She takes a shaky inhale as she sinks down again at my hip. "It was shocking, seeing her in your bed. I needed to get to a place where I felt ready to speak to you."

"I'm a lunatic. I'm sorry."

She nods at me. "I'm sorry too. Sorry I didn't talk to you."

We stare at each other as the water gurgles in the pipes through the building.

"Talk to me about what happened with this David guy."

She groans and rolls her lips together, but I squeeze her hand, and she nods, taking a deep breath.

"We were together for two years in college, engaged actually, so … yeah."

*Engaged?* My stomach turns over. Holy shit.

She shakes her head. "He was *such* a charmer, a real master at reading people and giving them what they wanted. But it took me a while to realize that. I found out he used prostitutes in the most prosaic way possible: There was a card in the pocket of his jeans that I was putting into the wash with some of my clothes. I rang the number on the card." Kate looks down at her nails. "I didn't know what to say, so I just pretended to be his personal assistant, arranging a time for him. She asked me if I wanted the 'stuff he'd had before,' and I was so horrified I just said yes. I wanted to ask how many times he'd been in the past and what this 'stuff' was, but I couldn't find the courage."

She glances at my face, like she doesn't know how much to tell me, but fuck I want to know everything about this asshole and what he did. Sympathy burns through me. "Understandable," I say, and she takes a sharp inhale.

"I just couldn't believe it, you know? I mean we were really close, like you and me." She gestures back and forward between us, and then she winces as I close my eyes, pain sharp in my chest. "I wanted there to be some silly explanation, like it was for his dad, but I knew as soon as I handed the card to him that he knew what it was and what it meant. He was so angry with himself. He said he had a death wish to fuck up everything good in his life."

A long groan leaks out of me. I don't want there to be any parallels with my behavior and this David guy, but the idea of doing something that fucks everything up … that feels so familiar, *goddammit.*

"I even felt sorry for him." She laughs. "Sorry that he'd been found out. That's crazy."

I shake my head, jaw cracking with the effort of not punching the nearest wall. "It's not crazy, Kate, when you care about someone." I try and swallow it all down. "It's part of why I helped Nadine. When you're a loyal person and you've been close to someone, it's incredibly hard to turn your back on them, no matter how badly they behave."

She blinks at me, eyes watery. "I asked him why he'd done it, and I remember this so clearly, he said, 'You're not going to like what I'm going to say, but I need to be honest.' You see, he was always saying stuff like that." She breathes in deeply and bends her head, staring at the covers, so I squeeze her hand and she looks up at me. "I just don't know if he ever was honest with me," she whispers.

I shake my head. I'd bet my ass he was *never* fucking honest with her.

"He told me that he'd used prostitutes all his life. His dad, too, and it was his dad who took him the first time, when he was *fifteen*. God, I felt so sick. He said it was like gambling: exciting and addictive, the unknown, the thrill. He swore that this was the first time since he'd met me that he'd been, but I knew from what she'd asked me on the phone that he was lying."

That fucking slimeball!

"But being the stupid little analyst that I am I wanted to understand what he got from it that I didn't give him, so I asked if it was better than sex with me."

Oh my God. And she thinks she lacks courage? "It's not stupid, Kate. I think that's the first question any sensible person would want to ask, but they're probably not brave enough to fucking ask it."

Her eyes shoot to mine, and I squeeze her hand.

"Did he tell you?"

She shakes her head. "He said that they did things that he wouldn't, couldn't, ask me to do."

"Figures. These are the kinds of guys that get girls to do sick things."

She stares at me. "Holy shit. You think?"

"I know."

Then her eyes narrow on me. "What do you mean, you know? Have you ever done that?"

Is she fucking kidding? "Asked for sick things?" I am fucking offended.

"No! Used a prostitute."

*Calm down, Fabian.* "Only once and I wasn't exactly a willing participant." I fill her in on the day I lost my phone and the girls by the river. "But I've met a lot of these girls. They're often drug addicts, and the sick guys take advantage of that." I don't know what to tell her here—they're so much part of the drug world. "When I was out looking for Zach, I'd often see some guy turn up in a car that I'd know was as sick as fuck, and sometimes I'd give the girls money so they didn't have to do whatever his sick thing was. It was probably the wrong thing to do, but if I didn't do it, they would come back with bruises all over their bodies or worse. Steve at the shelter would find a doctor to fix them up and I'd pay." I shake my head.

"We've had a few girls like that turn up in the ER."

I close my eyes. "Fuck, it makes my blood boil."

"David said he wasn't a cheat," Kate says suddenly, and a sharp laugh hurtles out of my mouth.

"This guy, Kate, he sounds like a monumental asshole."

"I couldn't bring myself to ask any more and find out what they did with him," she whispers.

"Probably just as well. You could have been scarred for life." I shake my head. "He would never have told you."

She stares at me. "I've never thought of it like this. I've just regretted not asking him every day, wishing I was braver. The idea that I didn't do what he wanted …" She shakes her head. "And now you're saying … It's not about me at all, is it?" She gives a harsh laugh. "It's about the fact that he likes sick stuff, and he can only get that in one place. He wouldn't have asked *anyone*—I mean anyone he was in a relationship with—for it." She clenches her fists. "And he kept telling me how much he loved me and how sorry he was. Oh my God."

"Jesus, Kate, the nerve of this prick!" I growl. "Just tell me where he is so I can go and rip his head off."

She laughs at me. "You are not going to pick a fight with David."

"I'd fucking like to."

She shakes her head at me. "For so long I've hated that I got it so wrong. He bombarded me afterward—notes, flowers, reminders of things that were special to us."

My God, the echoes of what I did with her are almost obscene. "You are not to blame."

She laughs out loud. "He still calls me sometimes."

And I narrow my eyes on her. "You are fucking kidding me. Next time he calls, I'm fucking speaking to him."

She looks down at her hands. "I could have so easily ended up married to him. I think I had a lucky escape. God, I was so easily fooled."

I don't want her to feel that way, but I get it. "You and me both. But maybe these are the important experiences, the ones that teach you something valuable about people and what you want." I stare off out the window. "But I … I have had to apologize to you too many fucking times, my crazy behavior … Am I really any better? I …"

She snorts. "You are nothing like David. Trust me. He was a master manipulator, and I just don't think you do that."

She's right. I don't. And she's here. She's sitting on my bed. Talking. I run my finger down her arm, lace my fingers through hers.

"You really take care of other people," she says.

What? My breath stalls as I stare at her. *I love you so fucking much.*

She squeezes my hand before pulling back and reaching for the soapy water, cleaning my wound and smearing the ointment up and down it. She digs a bandage out of the pocket of her scrubs and starts wrapping it around and around.

She's clearly trying to draw an end to talking about David. For her or for me? Either way, I'm going to let her have that.

"You're a badass doctor."

"I'm wrapping a bandage around your arm."

"What? So, is that like doctoring 101?"

She pauses. "I'll want you to give me space sometimes."

I nod at this. I need time to process too. "I'll give you time, Kate, but you need to talk to me: shout, scream, whatever it is. Don't disappear. Tell me you're taking a breather, not walking away forever. I just felt …"

She nods, hair slipping forward from its mooring behind her ear, and I push a strand out of her face and tuck it back.

"I get it, Fabian. It's a deal."

"I don't want anything sitting between us."

She finishes wrapping the bandage, securing the end in that complicated way only medical staff seem to be able to do.

I trail my hand down her arm, sliding my fingers back through hers, and she considers our joined hands, swallowing.

"You don't have to keep apologizing. You're forgiven. You might have to burn those sheets, though." She tips her head down to the bedcovers, and I laugh at how extreme that sounds.

"I'll set fire to the bed too if you like," I say, and she smiles.

"I think that's a little over the top." Looking around the room, she gives a little shiver. "I just don't want to see the covers …"

I can't even think how I'd be if I'd seen her with someone else in bed. The thought curdles like sour milk in my gut. I want to reassure her with my hands and my mouth, spend all day and night worshipping her body, but except for that kiss, she's not leaning into me, like she's not staying. I'm not sure why.

"Are you sleeping here tonight?"

She shakes her head.

"Is it the covers? The bed? Me?"

She shakes her head again, like she doesn't trust herself to speak. "I just need to take it one step at a time."

What the fuck does that mean?

# CHAPTER 27

## *Fabian*

Bloomingdale's is dead at 7 p.m. on a hot Tuesday evening in July, and the sales assistants are chatting quietly while surreptitiously staring at me out of the corner of their eyes. I glance down at my roughed-up shorts, faded T-shirt, and bandaged arm: I'll bet they don't get many customers that want to buy a bed and look like me at this time of night. It's like a morgue in here, and the staff look about ready to be in one too.

After Kate left, I forced down painkillers and slept as they kicked in, waking late, scarfing down leftovers that were floating around on the kitchen counter. Then I came straight here having decided, with the conversation about bedcovers, that Kate and I need a bed that is ours. Never mind the sheets, I am replacing the whole thing, and I want something really fucking special. I wander around between the beds, lying down on two or three, and they're all so comfortable I think I might never leave this department. My own bed dates back to when I first moved into the apartment after college, and it sags, forcing you to roll toward the middle.

As I round a corner into another section, I'm suddenly standing in front of a wooden four-poster bed with curtains in a white gauze material that cover the top and sweep the floor. Ha! This is way better than a dozen roses, right? And, my God, it's even got red petals strewn across the covers and pillows, all artfully arranged like in a show house. The idea of laying Kate down on this … I fling myself down and close my eyes, sinking into the soft cushions and quiet, drifting away on the thought of lying next to her and turning over to …

"Pretty good, isn't it?" A voice interrupts my fantasy.

My eyes fly open to find a round gray-haired lady with twinkling eyes leaning over me like a bird looking at a worm. I grin up at her and she says, "Don't smile at me like that, young man, I might be tempted to jump on there with you."

I sit up on the edge, laughing. She's dressed in a smart black outfit: She's a member of staff.

"How much is it?"

She names a figure that would make even Janus's eyes water, but the money for Jeff's project in South Africa has just come in. I'm not at all sure about that job if I'm honest. The money was too good, and the evidence was almost too convenient. I've done no work for weeks, and I need to do some more of my own digging into it. Whatever. I've got the money now, and although I know I should use it to pay off some of the debts that sit like dark clouds on the horizon, I'm nowhere near that sensible.

"It's handmade in Connecticut, solid oak. They put a plaque on the base of the bed in brass with your name on it."

"Sounds amazing," I say. "How long would it take?"

"Twelve weeks," she says, and I make a face.

I look at the bed and smooth my hands over the soft cotton.

"I kind of need it today," I say, and her painted eyebrows shoot up. I give her what I hope is my best persuasive grin. "It's a special occasion. Could I buy this one?"

She laughs. "Well, I don't know that we could …"

"I need to apologize to a special lady."

I give her the rough lowdown of the apology I need to make and why. Her eyes grow round.

"Anyway," I conclude, "I have to find something to give to her by tomorrow." I want more from Kate than a chaste kiss and a taking-her-time message.

She stares over toward the central payment desk as if she's trying to decide something, probably working out her commission. "Let me go and find out," she says.

She talks to an older guy at the counter gesturing toward me and the bed. He shakes his head, but she carries on waving her hand, and I can't help smiling: I told the perfect saleslady the ideal story. In five minutes, she's back.

"We can sell you this one, and we'll give you 10 percent off with it being ex-display, but of course we can't do a plaque."

She's a genius, and I've even wangled a discount. I don't care about some crazy nameplate; all I can think about is what Kate will say when she sees it. However, I'm not so flush with money that I'm not going to push and see what else she'll give me.

"Make it fifteen and you have yourself a deal," I say, and she narrows her eyes at me and holds up her hands, but then she weaves her way through the beds to discuss my proposal with her manager.

Another couple of minutes go by while I lie back on the covers, then she appears again and says, "Twelve and a half percent is our best offer."

So, I smile and give her my credit card, hoping like fuck the thing got paid off. Then I root around in my pocket and pull out my phone to call the one guy I know who can sort this for me.

"Seamus?" I say to the man who answers, my Mr. Fixit. There's nothing Seamus can't get done in Manhattan, and I pay him in kind with his clients who want some difficult computer problem sorted.

"I need a couple of guys who can dismantle a bed and install it in my apartment by tomorrow night."

A loud laugh bounces back down the line.

"Where the fuck are you?"

"Bloomingdale's."

There's a long-suffering sigh on the other end. "Text me the details."

# CHAPTER 28

## *Kate*

July passes in a sparkling blur, like sunlight dancing on water. I head to Fabian's or he comes to mine, and we potter around the kitchen together, shoveling in food and trying to sleep. He won't wear anything in bed, and most nights I find it impossible not to put my hands on his body, running my fingers over the lines and patterns, as he watches me with serious gray eyes that grow increasingly heated. I never thought I'd be insatiable, and Fabian always wants to take his time. I'm so sleep-deprived I don't know how I'm standing up and making sense in the ER, but something has clicked over like the cog of a well-oiled wheel. I'm not confident, but perhaps I'm getting used to the ebb and flow. Either way, the chaos and responsibility don't make my stomach churn in quite the same way they did when I first started.

What with the arm slashing and the roses, I'm now something of a celebrity at Bellevue, or as much as you can be in a hospital where people are heroes every day. When I turn up in people's offices for advice, I get a smile of recognition and a generous amount of medical explanation. I'm no longer some lowly new intern, I'm the one with the crazy but romantic boyfriend, and this gets me nods in corridors and smiles everywhere. What happened to quiet Dr. Dull? Before Fabian, this would all have made me mutter under my breath about concentrating on the job, but now I like the fact that people know who I am, that they stop and talk, that they're happy to answer my questions.

The bed, my God, the bed! The day after I went to his apartment to check on his arm, he growled at me down the phone to come over, clearly keen to end whatever time he thought I was taking with him. There's something heartwarming about the way he pushes through obstacles and refuses to stand still. He blindfolded me the minute I arrived, despite my protests and jokes about sexual things we hadn't tried yet. He told me to stop being such a doctor and questioning everything. Then he led me into his bedroom, squeezing my shoulders and weaving his hand through mine before standing behind me, body pressed all the way down my back, chin on my shoulder. When he took off my blindfold, I don't think I'd seen anything quite so beautiful … all that white gauze and the wood. When he grunted, "This is yours," in my ear, I turned around and grabbed his T-shirt, pulling him onto the covers with me. Then I did other delicious things to him, and that was the end of that.

The honeyed wood of the floor glows in the afternoon sunlight, and my eyes droop as I curl up into Fabian's heat on the couch, joints aching. His chest underneath my head is rising and falling, in and out, and everything goes hazy around the edges. We're like some old couple sleeping during the day. When I wake, I'm stretched out and covered by a blanket. I can hear keys tap-tapping away in the next room. I straighten my legs, joints complaining. The throw smells of man and soap, and I press it to my nose and inhale. How sweetly he takes care of me! I've fallen asleep here every day this week; maybe it's my shifts moving between days and nights.

I stand and stretch, heading into the bedroom, and Fabian stops typing, swiveling around in his chair to grin at me.

My jaw cracks as I yawn. "Have I been out long?"

He studies the clock on his screen, frowning. "About four hours actually."

Jesus. "I need to track my sleep better. I think you're keeping me awake too long at night."

"I'm keeping *you* awake?" His face curls into a smirk, and he's thinking about last night when I woke him up by taking his cock—which I happened to find erect under the sheets—into my mouth.

"You need to stop sleeping naked," I say.

This gets me a husky laugh. "You know it's a ploy, right? To get the kind of thing you did to me last night."

I grin and scrape my palms down my face. "Is it too early to go to bed?"

He waves his hand. "Do you want me to take my clothes off right now or …"

Collapsing face down onto the bed, I mumble into the covers. "No sex tonight. I need to catch up on my sleep."

Footsteps pad over to where I'm sprawled on the new navy bedlinen. Despite him insisting that this bed is mine, and mine alone, I've told him it belongs to both of us. I turn my head sideways to stare at the white curtains tied back at the corners of the frame.

The bed shifts as he walks onto it on his knees, and a long finger finds the dip of my neck under my hair and trails right the way down my spine. Again and again. Then he moves my hair and kisses my nape, teeth testing my skin, shifting my T-shirt with his nose to nibble a bit farther down. I shift against the seam of my sweatpants, muscles tightening, and curl my hands into fists.

"Aren't you tired?" I ask.

He laughs at this, collapsing down next to me. "Exhausted actually." His eyes dance. "But I've got this amazing woman in my bed at the moment … she's insatiable." He rolls onto his back, eyes closed.

"Insatiable, huh?"

His eyes crinkle at the corners, and it gives me goosebumps. This is so good. Certainly the hands on bodies bit, but also this easy conversation that warms the coldest, most mistrustful, parts inside. Fabian doesn't ask or expect me to be anything I don't want to be.

He twists into me, sniffing my hair. "I love waking up with your mouth on my cock, Kate. I'm right there with you."

His hand is already on my behind, long fingers splaying over the curve, the tips rubbing along the crease. I groan. I remember the color high on his cheeks in the dim light this morning, his flushed length in between my lips, the way his eyes screwed up and his head tipped back as he came. I move my hips under his hand, and he shifts closer, erection pressing into me, fingers tightening into a hard grip. A hand slides up to drag my gray sweatpants down my legs, and he lets out a long groan when he sees my black, stretchy boy shorts. Are *they* sexy? They cover everything up. I wiggle my hips.

"Why do you like this underwear?"

He gives a croaky laugh, warm hand spanning my ass. "Okay, I need to show you," he says as he tips off the bed. *He's taking a photo?*

I prop myself up on my arms, turning my head. "What are you … ?"

But he lies on top of me, heavy and hot, and shoves his phone in front of my face. I look at the picture, and—oh my God!—my underwear is halfway up my backside. Wiggling, I stretch my hand to pull the material back down to cover my butt, but he grabs my arm.

"What? They look terrible, my cheeks are sticking out and …"

"No, Kate, no," he says as he shifts half off me, sliding a warm hand up my thigh and inside the leg of my shorts, long fingers cradling me and squeezing.

He nuzzles into my neck, mumbling. "You know nothing about men. Your butt, Kate, oh God …" He gives me another squeeze. "… and half hanging out, it looks …"

He moves his hand out of my briefs to trace the curve of my backside on the screen. I stare at it, then turn to peer sideways at him resting his chin on my shoulder, his mouth a sensuous rough line. He's rubbing his erection into me, and I don't think he realizes he's doing it. Slickness builds between my legs.

"Look at this," he whispers, still tracing the curve on the photo like a road on a treasure map.

Dropping the phone on the sheets, he shifts backward, straddling the tops of my thighs. He pushes a hot hand up into my underwear, taking his weight on the other hand while he leans his hips into mine.

"Can I come all over this?" he whispers. "So fucking sexy, Kate."

Long fingers pull my shorts half down, and he works his teeth along the skin he's bared before peeling them off, kissing my ass. He stands and unzips and drops his jeans, and as I turn my head, I'm just in time to see him strip his T-shirt off. I scan over the hard nipples, the map of muscles curling around his thin torso, the scripts that curl out from his shoulder and over his pectoral muscles and disappear by his hip into his tight black boxers. Will I ever want to stop looking at this?

Grinning, he dips his head down to drag my eyes up to his face, then he hooks his fingers into the band of his underpants, lifting them away from his waist, and I roll onto my back. The outline of his cock is hard beneath the thin cotton, and he slides both his hands under the material, stroking himself. Crooking my finger at him gets me a laugh as he walks toward me on his knees on the bed. When he's close, I stroke him over the fabric.

"I love watching you do things to me," he grunts, watching me rub my thumb across the top of his still-concealed cock, feather-light, teasing. Eyes darken like a hurricane, and my breathing stutters as twitches dance across his skin, his face shifting to tight craving. This is the transformation I like best on him. The one only I get to see—the stark seriousness, how bleak his face becomes, his jaw tightening as need builds. I shift, slippery between my legs, and he gives me a predatory, turned-on smile—all teeth and growling—and I like this expression, too—another one that belongs to me.

"When you start to move around," he says, "you get this look on your face…"

I stare up at him, lips parting, and he leans forward to rub a soft kiss over them, groaning as I tighten my hand on his length.

"What look?"

"Turned-on Kate." He rubs his nose against my cheek, inhaling. "It's all for me," he whispers, and the echo of my own thoughts has me melting into the bed, shivering as his hand skates up my leg. He pauses, long fingers curling up over my thigh, thumb stroking the crease so close to where I'm hot and tight. Little rivulets of pleasure radiate outward as I bite down on my bottom lip.

"Please, Fabian," I whisper, and he smiles that strained smile again, moving his finger to brush the edges of my sex; still not delving down to where my skin will be pink and slippery and my hand fumbles on his cock. Tingling runs through my pelvis as he pulses under my hand, an unreal groan moving through his body as he glances down at our hands and then shifts back on his knees, and I pout, but a small smile is playing around the corner of his mouth. He slides his hand into his boxers and takes himself in hand.

"Let me see." The words barely make it out, but all they get is a shake of his head.

"Do you want what's under here, Kate?"

"Oh God," I groan.

He looks down at what he can see under the fabric but I can't, stroking himself before leaning forward to put his open mouth on mine.

"I'm dark red and wet and ready for you, Kate," he mumbles against my lips, and I close my eyes to stop myself from ripping those boxers off his very sexy hips.

"I want you in my mouth," I say. And oh! Where does this woman come from when we have sex? Fabian gets the sex witch with her runaway mouth out of the box to run wild for a couple of hours before I shut her away and sit on the lid. I say the most outrageous things to him sometimes, and it just seems to encourage him to say the most outrageous things back. I'm safe here. Outrage is encouraged, welcomed even.

"Let me see you play with yourself," I mumble against his lips, and he pulls back again, shuffling onto his knees between my legs before pulling his boxers down and moving to take them off. His cock sticks straight out, flushed and swollen, and he takes it in hand giving it one or two rough strokes, releasing a hoarse chuckle as he bends to kiss me again.

"Is it fascinating, Kate?"

"Yes." I've been staring, clearly.

He sits back, head bowed, and runs a teasing finger over his tip to the underside where his foreskin joins and back again. Back and forward. His chest tightens, abs jumping. Bending my legs, I rub my feet up and down his calves and he gives me a half smile, eyes dark and droopy, before he strokes himself a few more times, letting out a long groan as his head tips back. The muscles stand out on his throat, nipples hard, his right pec tensed with the grip he has, and I lever up, hands skimming up the inside of his thighs, stroking the soft skin between his legs. His gaze drops to meet mine.

"Were you serious about tasting me?" he growls.

Shifting onto my knees on the bed and pushing his hand out of the way, I bend down and take him in my mouth, licking the tip as salt explodes on my tongue. I rub across the sensitive nerves, and a rumble starts low somewhere in his body, and I smirk up at him, but his face is tight and dangerous as he slides a hand in my hair.

"Behave."

I seal my lips around the head, suckling, and his hand tightens as he tries to push his hips forward. I close my teeth around his length, gently holding him so he can't thrust, and he sucks in a jagged breath.

"*Kate*."

My teeth scrape softly over him as I pull off him and straighten, and he lets out a disbelieving hiss. Normally, I'm happy for him to take over, but this time I want something different.

"I want this my way," I say.

Dark eyes hold mine as the distant grumbling of the streets washes in. The pianist upstairs is practicing some complicated tune I don't recognize. He grinds his teeth, heat climbing up his face from a vein throbbing in his neck.

"I want to give you pleasure, my way. I don't want you to take over," I say.

I want him to trust *me*.

His hand grips my jaw, almost hurting me, then he inclines his head in acquiescence. "But you're only allowed so much teasing, Kate."

I run my knuckles gently down either side of his cock. This earns me a growl, so I bend down to take him in my mouth, sucking on the red tip, and my eyes are fixed on his face as he struggles to let me take control, to not thrust. Every so often his pelvis moves before he applies the brakes with a shudder. Adrenaline leaks into my body and, after one jerk forward when he stutters and manages to stop, I take him all the way to the back of my throat and the noise he makes when I do this is ungodly. He seems to lose it: Hands invade my hair, not taking over exactly, but his hips shift frantically from side to side, tremors running up his legs, which slide out as I reach behind to stroke his balls and the skin behind. The muscles in his abdomen tighten under my hands and down his thighs. *My God.*

"Fuuuuuck. Jesus. Fuuuuck!" The words rip out like he's close to disaster.

Sliding all the way down and back, I swirl my tongue around his tip, playing with his foreskin. I can taste how much he's leaking, and I rub the sensitive bit under the head, pulling his skin down with my fist.

"Oh, Oh. Oh. Fuck. I can't …"

"I'm …"

"Jesus Christ."

My hips shift to try and relieve my own ache, slipperiness making my thighs wet.

"Kate. I'm …"

I test my teeth on him, sucking hard, and he lets out a loud shout, pushing roughly forward. Pulses move down his cock as he spills over my tongue. Sweat makes my hands slide on his hips as his body jerks several times with aftershocks, chest heaving and gasping for air. He falls onto his hands over where I'm crouched, propping himself up on the bed, whole body shaking. I give him a few more experimental licks, and he shudders, groaning, before collapsing sideways onto the sheets next to me and letting out a long moan, arm over his eyes. A smug grin stretches my mouth as I take in his splayed body: I am stupidly, ridiculously proud. Shifting around, I collapse down beside him.

"Sorry," he mumbles, arm still over his face, and I laugh out loud.

# CHAPTER 29

## *Kate*

A day later the message "When did I last see you?" pops into the WhatsApp group I share with Liss that usually just says things like "Buy tampons" or "Landlord says there's a leak on the 15th floor."

I look up, but everything's quiet in the ward, and I place my thumbs on the phone. Hmmm.

Hello, lovely friend.

My God, she's alive, hang on, I have to call the missing person's helpline back.

We were in the apartment last week, Liss.

Yeah—a week ago!—you missed my PMS week. I had no one to drink wine and rage with.

Oh shit, I'm a bad friend. We've dealt with our PMS together for a long time, and ever since we started sharing the apartment our periods would turn up at around the same time, so we've been downing bottles of wine and getting drunk and testy together for years.

I'm sorry!

Hope Fabian enjoyed your company last week. :-)

I shake my head.

Be great to see you.

Yeah, when?

Tomorrow? I'm on an early shift. You fancy a pizza and wine evening?

Sounds perfect.

*

I stare at the two blue lines on the stick in front of me. That's impossible. We've not used condoms for a while, but I've been on the shot forever, so there's just no chance. I delve into the package shaking my head—I'll use the other stick. A tremor in my hand makes me fumble as I try and pull the other package out of the box, and I stop and stare at the back of the toilet door. I only did this because Liss said that thing about PMS, and I couldn't remember when I'd last had my period. Maybe I won't think about this now. Maybe I'll check tomorrow. Can I keep calm until tomorrow? No, no I can't.

I pull the second stick out. Thoughts buzz through my head like wasps: my internship, Fabian … fuck, my parents. My gut roils—they will flip. Despite how uptight my parents are and our sometimes shaky relationship, my mom has nurtured me through this doctor's career I'm aiming for. She's so invested in what I'm doing, so proud I'm following in her footsteps: God knows how she'll take something like this. I am not the child who does this kind of thing, who messes up their lives with a mistake. My stomach turns sour. I don't want to think of this as a mistake. No child should start their lives that way. This is how my parents think, for God's sake. *Child*. Jesus.

I press my hand to my stomach. Am I really viewing this stick in my hand as a child? Is this real? There's no thought in my head that I might get rid of it, and I suck in a sharp breath: This is a shock but I'm not desperately searching for the nearest exit. I'm … I'm … My God, Fabian! I've no idea how he'll react to something like this; we've been so busy enjoying each other's company that we've hardly talked about what we want for the future, how we feel about this sort of thing.

I look down at my shaking hands, and I bury my head in them. I've got to talk to someone. It has to be him. There's no one else I can tell, no one else who should be the first person to hear about this. I look at the unused stick in my hand and shove it back in my bag. The two blue lines on the other stick look like an accusation, but something warm burns through me nonetheless. I put it in my bag and stand up, pulling up my pants and heading out of the stall to stare at the white-faced, blonde-haired woman in the mirror, giving myself a half-assed smile and a ridiculous thumbs-up before washing my hands and stepping out into the corridor.

The rest of my shift is a blur of nameless faces and reassurance. I'm so distracted imagining small children with dark tumbling curls that I take all the easy cases; it's a dreadful move and one I wouldn't normally do, but I'm staring at walls and patients' bodies like I don't know what I'm looking at and making no sense of anything anyone tells me. It's all I can do to fix broken bones and administer drugs, as long as someone else makes the decision about which drug and how much.

By the time I leave, my whole body feels like I've been through a car crusher. The hot weather, the grumpy New Yorkers, the guy who shouts at me for taking up too much of his seat on the bus … it all slips off my shoulders like butter. I'm moving underwater, unable to connect properly with anyone. I just need to get to his apartment.

I take a deep breath when I arrive at his door, and everything swings sharply into focus again: I'm here, this is it. My key in the lock, the worn stairs to his apartment, the gray battered door; breathe in, breathe out. I open the door to the familiar tap-tap of keys, which stops as soon as I tap the code into the keypad. Then he appears in the bedroom doorway, and I can't help the smile that breaks out when I see his tousled hair and clothes that look like he picked them up from where he left them last night on the floor. He grimaces.

"Let me shower," he says, running a hand down at his crumpled T-shirt, and I laugh. He's been lost in whatever he's been doing all day. My eyes scan the tousled curls and scruff on his chin, and I take a few short steps over to him, wrapping myself around his warm body. He feels like home.

"You okay?" he mumbles into my hair.

My stomach is an echoing cavern. It's now or never.

"I've got some news," I say.

"Good or bad?" he says, and I step back to rub my hands over my face. I want to see *his* face when I say this.

"Kate?" he says, taking my hands away from my face. His legs are bent so he's at my level, and I meet his steady gaze.

"Not sure."

"Okay," he says slowly, a small frown creeping over his forehead.

There is no easy and slow way to get into this. I suck in a breath. Breathe in, breathe out.

"I'm pregnant."

His eyes go wide. "*What?*" His voice is an incredulous crack. "Are you kidding me?"

His arms drop and then shoot up to wrap around me, picking me up and swinging me around. My breath is crushed out of my chest as he spins.

"You're serious?" He's loud now, right in my ear.

It's all I can do to hang on and nod my head where it's pressed to the prickle of his chin.

He puts me down then grabs my face in a frenzy and kisses my eyelashes, my cheeks, my mouth.

"Oh my God!" He spins away from me, raking his hands through his hair before bending over double like he can't breathe, and I stretch out my hand. Maybe I misinterpreted his early reaction, and he's shocked in a bad way rather than a good one.

"Fabian?" I say, my voice a strange wobble.

He turns back to look up at me with the widest grin, and all the tension seeps out of my body. My lips curve up.

He straightens again and takes my hands, looking at my fingers as if he's counting them, as if he can't believe what he's seeing. He seems almost dazed.

"I can't believe it. I just can't believe it. Jesus Christ. You're sure?"

I nod. "The test sticks aren't often wrong, but we should get a test at a hospital to check." I hesitate for a second. "You seem really pleased?" The words spin out as a rough croak, and his face changes when I say this—some emotion I don't recognize tracking across his features.

"Fuck yeah!" he hoots, spinning away laughing with a crazy cackle, hands running through his hair. "I can't fucking believe this. Goddamn! I'm going to be a dad!" He shouts the last bit up at the cracked ceiling over our heads.

Then he turns to look at me and steps back taking my face in my hands, frowning. "Are *you* pleased? I mean, it's really bad timing for you, isn't it?" His face creases in concern. "Shit. I didn't think about that." He chews his cheek. But I almost don't care what he says now because with this whole reaction there's no question that he wants me, wants this child, like our commitment to each other is a given. It's not a question of if we'd ever do this, but when.

"I almost don't want to talk about the problems now," I mumble. "It seems wrong."

He nods like he understands. "Yeah, I just want to experience the thrill of it. Are you happy?" His face has lapsed into worry, and I smile at him. I want to go back to his earlier, more honest, reaction.

"I think? I'm worried about everything. I was worried about what you'd think."

His eyebrows rise at me. "God, why? I can't think of anything better than being a dad." He grins a heart-stopping smile at me.

"But we're so new and ..."

"Yeah, but we know, right?" He gestures between us. "There's no one else for me, Kate. You're it."

I feel a lump start in the back of my throat, and I think he sees my eyes start to become glassy because he pulls me into a tight hug.

"Don't worry about it. I'll do all the childcare. You can finish your residency and everything you need to do. We'll make it work."

My God, that offer came so fast. He's just instantly taking care of it all, taking care of me. And he's completely misinterpreting my tears, and it just makes me cry more. Taking my face in his hands, he wipes the tears away with his thumbs.

"What?"

I shake my head at him. "It's not that. It's *you*."

"Me?"

"What you just said."

"What did I just say?"

"That I'm it for you." I gulp the words out through a hiccup, and he laughs, pulling me into a tight hug. Lifting me off the floor and swinging me around again.

"Well, you are," he says, breath warm against my ear.

"You're it for me too," I mumble into his shoulder.

He stops and pulls back. "Yeah?" His voice is quiet and scratchy, like he's fighting a lump in *his* throat. But it's a question too. Maybe he's never been anyone's "it." He's given in relationships and never got much back in return. I want to change all that.

I lean in and kiss his lips. "There's no doubt about that. You're wonderful."

He looks at me with wide eyes like he can't believe I just said that.

# CHAPTER 30

## *Kate*

Two weeks of August leak away in a daze of sick people, sick mornings, and hot nights. Fabian and I agree we're not telling anyone until I'm twelve weeks along, and the scan at the ob-gyn's office has confirmed I'm about eleven weeks now. Eleven weeks! Lying on the bed while the doctor ran the ultrasound over my stomach, I could see the tiny heartbeat thumping out like a drumbeat, and it was all I could do to fight down the tears when Fabian's hand gripped mine so tightly as he leaned forward to peer at the screen. Then he stood with his hands on his hips and lectured me about finishing my residency and about him looking after the baby, and he's right, but I also don't want to miss the first few years of our son or daughter's life. What has my life become, talking about these kinds of things with him? Oh, and morning sickness? Ugh. It deserves all the swearwords I've ever known. Every day it burns through my stomach, and I'm shoveling packets of crackers down to keep it at bay, and thank God nobody at work has noticed.

I'm desperate to share with Jo and Liss … Georgie too. At the moment, it's my thrilling secret, the calm before I have to face the reality of what this all means—how difficult life will become. But after another week goes by, I'm close to exploding. It's not been easy hiding things, and when Jo calls to suggest we all meet in the McNally coffee shop for our usual catchup, it feels like I can't *not* tell them. I need to build up to other people's reactions; the very idea of telling my parents gives me stomach cramps.

I spot Jo's red hair bent next to Liss's dark curls as I weave through the tables toward them in our little sanctuary.

"It's so good to see you guys," I say on a warm exhale when I reach their table and they both look up.

"Are you ever at our apartment?" Liss tuts at me with a broad grin.

Heat creeps up my cheeks: I go days without talking to her when I'm at Fabian's.

"I'm a crappy friend."

But she just shakes her head, still smiling. "You're spending every night being shagged senseless by the hottest man on the planet. You know I can't believe that good-girl, hardworking Kate ended up with a guy like that. That deliciously dangerous vibe, and all those tattoo scripts …" She fans herself with her hand. "You're going to have to tell us some day about where they all go, i*n detail.*"

I laugh at her emphasis.

"Preferably with photographs." She pauses and leans forward. "Naked photographs."

"You're incorrigible." I look down at my hands for a minute, and then I look up to see them both smiling at me like a couple of happy chipmunks and my throat gets tight as I wave my hand at them.

"Actually, I've got some news."

Jo's face morphs into a delighted grin. "A crazy proposal?" she says.

"A crazy pregnancy." It just bursts out of me, and their faces shift in the blink of an eye. There's a long, long pause.

"Holy shit," Liss says, mouth gaping. "Seriously?"

But Jo launches herself onto me, pulling me into the tightest hug before leaning back to look at me.

"My God, Kate, are you pleased?"

I bury my face in my hands. "Oh God, I am. It's crazy and so much the wrong time and not planned"—I suck in a deep breath—"but …" I place my hand on my stomach. "I just keep imagining a little boy with serious gray eyes and dark curls."

"Oh my God!" Jo says, pulling me into a hug again.

Liss launches herself at me too, until we're all in a heap on a chair, mumbling and laughing. The couple at the next table stare over at us.

"Oh my God, I can't believe it," Liss says, as they both sink back down. "Our first pregnancy. Can I touch?"

"What?" I say. "You know it's tiny right now."

She snorts, slapping my arm as she puts her hand on my stomach. "I'm sure it's not. And stop being such a doctor. Let me absorb this."

"What did Fabian say? I presume you told him first."

I groan. "It's such a bad time to do this, and I was terrified … I mean I *am* terrified really … but he was *so* delighted. I just … it made it all … all fine; better than fine, actually. Good. Exciting. He's so thrilled."

"Oh God, he really is the best man on the planet," Liss grumbles. "You know I hate you right now. And you." She points at Jo.

Jo just makes a face, and Liss sticks her tongue out at her. "What are you going to do about work?"

"Fabian says he's going to look after him or her, that I can carry on. I don't know how that will work exactly … but he's determined to do it. Really up for it actually." I groan. "This is such a bad time. I've got over three years of my residency left to do."

Jo looks at her hands. "There's no good time. Janus and I have talked about how we might manage something like this, but even being in the same country at the moment is a challenge. It's probably going to be busier when you finish. I think it's amazing that Fabian wants to do that. So many guys just back off …"

I look at her for a beat: She's never mentioned this before.

"Is he going to stop …?" Liss is looking down at her hands, and I know immediately what she's asking.

"The last time he was admitted to hospital he said he wouldn't get admitted again." I blow out a long breath. "I don't know."

I can't pretend that this isn't bubbling away under everything else, but I don't want to put any dampers on this baby. Am I burying my head in the sand? Yes, but there are so many other things to worry about that it feels like anything else would make the whole Jenga pile topple over.

"I'm trying to take it one step at a time. Pushing him in one direction or another might change who he is, and I like who he is. I don't expect him to give up the experimenting: I don't even know that I want him to. Maybe he can do that when I'm looking after the baby or something."

This sounds sketchy even to my ears, and I squint at them, trying to work out my feelings. "I've never minded that he does it. I'm sure he's planning to work it out when the baby's here and he understands better what we can and can't do."

They're both staring at me, and my heart sinks. I get that this is a big question mark. Fabian's not someone who screams "reliable" as a first descriptor, but he stood up to my dad and Javier at the wedding and looked after me when I was sick. He wants to do the right thing, and I hope this won't change who he is, or worse, that he'll hate giving up things for our child, or just spiral down into … into … what? Experimenting is his coping mechanism. Maybe he'll end up giving up everything while I'm not giving up anything? The thought makes a shiver run down my spine.

Jo licks her lips. "Has he told Janus?"

I shake my head, and Jo purses her lips.

"It'll be difficult to keep this a secret from him."

"I'll tell him to talk to him," I say.

Worry seems to burrow under my skin. The logistics of how we are going to make this work seem impossible. Jo pats my hand.

"You were happy when you came in here, and now we've made you worry. We're crap friends. You can't control this, and there's so much you don't know yet."

"Sorry," Liss says. "I'm honestly thrilled for you."

I get it, we're all worriers really, and we chew over things for each other. It's one of the reasons we've held together for so long. I knew they'd hone in on the one thing I was trying to suppress but worrying about anyway.

"We really shouldn't be worrying about Fabian; he's a really good guy," Jo says.

# CHAPTER 31

## *Kate*

My mother grimaces, face tight, and I stare down at my feet. I've waited until twelve weeks, but what made me think telling them this early was a good idea?

"You … you're *pregnant*?"

I wasn't expecting joy exactly, but I wasn't expecting a white face and horror either.

"It's that guy, isn't it?" my father barks out. "This is so fucking typical of guys like him."

He throws his hands up and paces over to the window looking out at the perfectly landscaped lawns close to the house. I've not heard my father swear like this before; he's always so upright and correct. "Not a responsible bone in his body—" He draws in a sharp breath.

"I think I bear some of the responsibility too," I interrupt before he can get into one of his cold dismissals and says more things about Fabian that we can't get over.

"Kate, how *could* you?" my mother says, and I hate the sharp disappointment in her voice. "You've just started your residency. How could you do this? It's so *irresponsible*. I thought we'd brought you up better than that. Where is your judgment? I just can't understand how you could have got pregnant. It's not like birth control is difficult."

Ever the doctor. My God. I look at the perfect silk cream curtains, the huge patterned Turkish rug, and settle on the cat sitting peacefully on the end of the couch, oblivious.

"I was on birth control," I say, pulling my breath up from deep in my body.

"Well, we need to get this sorted out," my father says briskly as my mother opens her mouth to say more. "Ivan will sort her out."

Ivan's a doctor friend of theirs, I think.

"Sort me out?" I say, cold fingers of dread rippling through me. He's talking about his grandchild here.

"Well, you can't be thinking of keeping it," he says, like it's obvious. "Someone like that guy ..." He swallows like he can hardly bring himself to say Fabian's name.

"Fabian," I interrupt tightly.

"He won't stick by you, Kate. That isn't how men like him operate. He has no proper job, clearly takes drugs. I mean just look at his behavior at Javier's wedding."

You mean that dreadful behavior where he told the truth, I don't say. I'm gripping the edge of their perfect blue couch leaving imprints that I know my mother will smooth out as soon as I leave. Are they really suggesting ...? I shake my head. There's no point in a tit for tat. They have judged Fabian, written him off, when he's responsible and kind, generous too. Every day he's working on trying to get to the truth, exposing corruption and duplicity, in his small way trying to change the world, but they have a particular worldview, and it would be stupid to fight right now; that's not why I came here. My head throbs; I wasn't expecting a positive conversation, but I didn't think they'd be quite as bad as this. I thought I could talk them round.

"Let me get this right? You're suggesting I have an abortion?"

"Well, you can't be thinking of keeping it?" my mother says, voice rising, as though it's a foregone conclusion.

"This is your *grandchild*."

"Don't be ridiculous, Kate," she says on a snap. "As you well know, it's tiny at this stage." She frowns at me, neck stretched forward like a peacock, and it's a cold echo of what I said to Liss.

"I mean just look at this." My father waves his arm around. "Why isn't he here, with you, having this conversation with us? It's just typical of guys like him. Anything difficult and you can't see them for dust."

He does stuff that's way more difficult than this every damn day of his life. He never shies away from "difficult." The words rush up my throat, and I choke them back down.

"I persuaded him not to come."

Was that wise? Should he have been here and heard this, no matter what the fallout? I thought I could handle my parents on their own, but seeing their tight faces and the cold hard reality of what they are, I have to admit that a hand to hold would have been nice. Fabian's a wild experimenter, and because of that I'm not asking him to step up, but we're in this together, and I've no evidence he wouldn't take on the responsibility. Ugh. Maybe I've got some of the same prejudices that my parents have.

"I'm glad I persuaded him not to come. Not in a million years would I want him to hear your condemnation of him, when he's a good guy."

My fingers curl into my palms. Why am I sitting here and listening to their prejudices? I could walk out now. I need to think about the life growing inside me and do what's best for us. Warmth steals through my blood. *My family with Fabian.*

"You're deluded," my father growls. "By no stretch of the imagination, Kate, is he a good guy." His lip curls, eyes narrowing. "I've had him investigated."

I'm stare at him, frozen. "Investigated?" My mother nods, lips curving up, her gaze darting to my father.

"After the wedding when he was clearly drunk and threw those ridiculous accusations at me, I thought I should look into who was hanging around with my daughter. Well, I'll have you know he's a crook, Kate, he's on the wrong side of the law. He's not a 'programmer,' as he liked to describe it. This information is buried deep, but my investigator is a very clever guy." He wags his finger at me. "You can't hide this stuff from people who know what they're doing on the internet these days. He's done work for the Russians, illegal work, work that is treasonable, work that goes against everything this country stands for. He's the worst kind of person … unpatriotic!"

I almost laugh at the relish in his voice, as though he thinks he could find out anything about Fabian that Fabian wouldn't want him to know. As though I wouldn't know what he does. Fabian has told me what he's doing, despite a less-than-stellar upbringing when he probably should have learned never to trust anyone. How has he done that? Could I throw off the grip of my parents? What he puts his body through—it's like he's punishing himself. And there's no way he's done anything illegal with the Russians. He's way too cautious about getting on anyone's radar, he hides everything he's done, and he's certainly good enough to easily dodge anyone my father might employ to find out about him. Jo told me what he did to help sort a hack on Janus's company.

"I know what he does, Dad," I say, exhaling and leaning forward to rest my elbows on my knees.

"Well, you're even more stupid than I thought getting involved with someone like that. It's like that damn art student all over again."

"Euan. His name was Euan. Also a good guy," I say, eyeing my father's flushed face. A bitter aftertaste fills my mouth.

"Fabian knows exactly what you've done, Dad. He can pretty much hack into anywhere." I see something flash across my father's face before he tucks it away. Dammit, I probably shouldn't have said that.

"I don't think that this is getting us anywhere," my mother says, shifting in her seat and smoothing a hand down her pants, as if she can smooth over that episode as well as this one. "Let's get Kate booked in to see Ivan, and then this whole sorry episode will be sorted out."

*Sorry episode? What?*

"I'm not seeing Ivan."

A frown skates across her perfectly symmetrical eyebrows. "What do you mean you're not seeing him? He's the best person for this, Kate. I really wouldn't recommend anyone else."

The automatic assumption that I'm not keeping this baby makes my stomach lurch. Enough is enough.

"I'm not having an abortion."

"Of course, you have to have an abortion, Kate! Everything you've worked for will go down the drain. You can't look after a small baby and finish your residency; the shifts just don't work that way. The hospital, being on call"—she shakes her head—"it's just not practical. It's not even possible."

"It's fine. Fabian is going to look after the baby while I finish."

My father snorts. "Well, if you think he's going to be reliable enough to do that you're more delusional than I thought."

"How long have you known him?" my mother asks, and the hair lifts on the nape of my neck. *Not long enough for you*, I think, as her eyes scan my face before she looks down and examines her nails, then purses her lips as she stares out of the window.

Tod's right, she *is* a robot, and something much worse I can't even bring myself to think about. I lift my chin, and my mother's eyes narrow.

"It's ridiculous," she snaps. "It's bad enough having one daughter who makes terrible decisions. We're not picking up the pieces when he messes up, Kate, I'm telling you that now. If you decide to go ahead with this, then you're on your own."

How many times have they issued ultimatums like this? The ultimatums that always got me to knuckle under and do what they wanted; the ones that Georgie always did the opposite to. God, I wish she was here right now. She'd stand next to me and tell them to fuck off, tell them how appalling they are, tell them all about what the lack of support does to you as their daughter.

"Fine. I'm on my own then." I stand up. I'm done with this conversation, done with being manipulated.

My mother's eyebrows rise up before she carefully masks her expression. My father's face goes even redder, and his chin juts out belligerently. He was probably expecting me to be obedient like I always am, but something about being with Fabian, watching his balls-to-the-wall approach to life, has made it sink into my subconscious that I need to take some risks, and disobeying my parents when I'm a full-grown woman is not the biggest crime in the world.

"Be warned, Kate, we're not helping you out," he spits.

I look steadily at him. "When did you start to think that threatening your children was a good idea?" I say, and I'm actually really curious.

"When they started messing up their lives."

"Messing up what *you* think their lives should be you mean. I'm quite happy with my life and my decisions. I'm very happy about this baby, and if you were any kind of parents at all, you'd support me in the choices I make. This is your grandchild, and you're talking about disposing of him or her like, like …"

My mother holds up her hand. "That's enough. I think we've all said our piece now. It's not a person yet, Kate, as you well know." She looks at me, and I see something wash through her eyes, something I've never wanted to see aimed at me. "I'm really disappointed in you, Kate," she finally says.

"Me too," I say, feeling the tremor in my hand as I push it into the pocket of my jeans. "I'm disappointed in both of you."

And I walk out the door.

# CHAPTER 32

## *Kate*

The tremor in my hand has advanced to a full-on shake by the time I get in the car. It's only with difficulty that I turn the ignition on to get the aircon going, hand slipping as I pull my phone from my bag. There's only one person who will understand what just happened, who's been on the receiving end of so many of these conversations, who never got a penny from my parents. As the ringtone echoes through the car speakers, I stare out of the window across the perfectly manicured lawns toward the cream-and-taupe façade of the fake Colonial building I grew up in.

"Hello? Kate?"

"Georgie," I groan. "Can you talk?"

"Of course! How did it go with the dragons?"

The tears tighten my eyes, gathering in the corners. And I turn the ignition another notch, starting the engine and inching forward down the long drive.

"It was awful," I choke out. "They just assumed I was having an abortion, like it was a foregone conclusion. Dad"—I swallow—"hired a PI to dig up dirt on Fabian."

Georgie gives a chortled laugh of glee, and something about it makes my chest ease. This is why I called her—she knows them so precisely and she just doesn't care.

"Oh my God, he is *such* an asshole! He was really pissed about what Fabian said to him at the wedding. I bet he's been plotting his revenge ever since. Yuck. I think he does that with everyone we go out with. He had Brad investigated too. Did you knuckle under like you normally do?"

I turn out of the driveway onto the long road that leads out of their gated community. I'm not offended by this, not even a little. We all know the roles we play. Georgie has told me how my obedience allowed her to be more of a rebel, that she relished the heat of their focus and their anger. She's hated them for a long time, what they did to her, how it's made her always question her own motives—whether she's doing something to rebel against them or conform—and I know it messes with her head.

"Jesus, no way! I want it so much, G."

And ice bites into my skin. I do. I really do. Despite all the problems, the worry about my career, whether I can hack all the pressure, the idea of Fabian and I having a child together fills me with white heat and sunshine. Like an extension of the lightness that invades me every time I'm with him. Watching his face deep in thought about some problem, watching his eyes flick over the code rolling down his screen, watching his long fingers that do delicious things to my body or tap a rhythm against the desktop as he waits for code to compile.

"Well, I'm impressed, sis. Despite the fact you were the good kid and I wasn't, you've no idea how much I hated watching them manipulate you into their agenda. I wish I'd been there to see this."

I laugh at this. "And my God, I wanted you there."

"Nah, I would have been too cross and waded in. I bet you did it in your own calm way. I bet you took them apart with medical precision."

"Not exactly. I think Mom's the expert there. She kept talking about how the baby 'wasn't a person.'"

Georgie gives a hoarse laugh. "Oh God, as if anyone could really think that about something so emotional. She's like a fucking robot. That calm logic thing she does? I could never deal with it. The only way I could escape the pressure she put on me to conform is to use no logic at all."

Those were her tactics? Georgie and Mom always butted heads, whereas Mom and I often seemed to see things in a similar fashion. I used to wonder about Georgie's wild arguments and flying off the handle. They were a ploy she used to escape the control?

"I didn't realize you did that deliberately."

"I'm not sure I understood that that was what I was doing when I was younger; it was just how I used to escape from all the things they tried to get me to do. I've only realized it recently." She pauses. "What are you going to do about the parents?"

A large splat of rain lands on the windscreen, followed by another, and I peer upward at the darkening sky. I take a deep breath. I'm pregnant. I'm their daughter. Their behavior on that basis alone was unforgivable. I'm generally a peacemaker, but it will take a long time to repair the wounds of that last conversation.

"Nothing, absolutely nothing. I'm ignoring any calls or other methods of communication. They said they were disappointed in me, and I told them they weren't as disappointed as I was. When this baby is born, they are going to have to suck up to me something rotten if they want to see their grandchild."

Georgie laughs. "You're a tiger under that compliant behavior. They owe you a fucking apology, Kate."

That's what I called her for, and the tension seeps out of me with the idea that I'm not being a difficult child or making a terrible mistake.

"I'm not holding my breath for that, but watch this space."

# CHAPTER 33

## *Kate*

"My father has been digging into you," I say quietly into the warm patterned skin of Fabian's back in bed later.

From what Jo has told me, I think anyone would have a hard time tracking Fabian, but the words "work that is treasonable" keep popping into my head, niggling away, like my dad knew it would. The manipulative bastard. I don't know much about what Fabian does, although I think he's been nothing but honest with me.

Fabian sighs. "I know he has."

My heart lifts at this simple statement.

"You do?"

"He used a useless investigator to do it too," Fabian rumbles on as if I haven't spoken. "I made sure he found some nonsense information that was supposedly difficult to access. What did he tell you?"

His bedroom is cool and dark, dim light filtering around the side of the blinds, and he rolls onto his back and tucks me into him as I fill him in on everything my father said—omitting the part where he said he was a loser.

Fabian snorts. "He's an asshole saying shit like that to you, Kate."

"Have you done work for the Russians?" I ask.

He pauses for far too long and sighs.

"The honest answer is that as far as I'm aware I haven't. It's complicated, difficult to ascertain who's behind attempts at security, who's working for who. Mind you, if I can't ascertain it, there's no way your dad could, or that idiot he had working for him. A lot of the things I do are unbelievably trivial—who's behind a virus, that kind of thing—but I'm not going to pretend to you, what I'm doing is often illegal, so I guess I have to have my own code about what's right and wrong. I used to be very idealistic when I was younger: I was always trying to do the right thing, fighting for a just cause. But who knows what's right? You wouldn't believe who's behind the spread of some information. I got interested in how much supposedly independent sources are manipulated years ago and gathered a trail of evidence on it. I eventually gave it to a consortium of newspapers."

"The Newssource papers?" I say, propping myself on my elbow to look at him properly. "The big exposé in *World* magazine?" My hand stills where I've been tracing the tattoos on his chest. There was *so* much press coverage of that.

"Yeah, well … I was just trying to change the world one chink at a time." His voice is dry, self-depreciating as if amused by his own folly. *He* was behind that? I splay my hand on his chest. It was *huge* news.

"But that was that group …" I wave my arm around.

He chuckles. "Yeah. They fronted it."

I examine the wry curve of his lips, the scruff on his chin, how he's smiling at me. The cool air of the old air conditioning system makes my skin prickle, the warmth of his body where I'm pressing into his side. *My God.*

"I like it that you did that."

He closes his eyes, all traces of a smile disappearing. "Don't try and make me into a good guy here, Kate. I'm not. In some ways, your dad isn't wrong. I've done all sorts of dubious stuff for people that I either thought was the right thing at the time or when I just desperately needed the money. There's a lot of things I'm not proud of. I can tell you the bad stuff if you like. I'm a threat to some people. I know too much about people who don't want me to know that stuff." He squints at me. "That information about your dad's company at the wedding. I didn't deliberately dig into your dad, Kate. I only did that with Javier. I've been working on tracking illegal deals and payments to politicians in South Africa for almost a year now. I've recently handed over all the work I've been doing, but it was such a complicated web of lies, and Xeracorp kept coming up, and when I looked at your dad's profile before the wedding, I realized he was a director there."

"*What?*"

"I was genuinely trying to warn him."

"Oh my God! What is my dad doing? Why would he get involved in something like that?"

"There's a lot of corruption in parts of Africa, in some places business is just done that way, but … yeah … what Xeracorp is doing is way beyond that." His face tightens as he looks distantly at the ceiling. "I need to think about moving. The work I'm doing, being followed, and that hack into Janus's systems earlier this year. I'm pretty sure no one knows where I live, but with this baby coming …"

*Who? What? Why?* First things first, Kate.

"You're moving?"

And he laughs turning into me, burying his face in my hair, inhaling deeply like he wants to suck me into him.

"Yeah. Well … we'll both be moving soon anyway, into an apartment together," he mumbles into my neck.

My breath stalls. "Are you asking me to move in with you?" Talk about a shift in conversation. I can hear the rising note in my voice, and my face breaks into a giddy smile, my dad's manipulation and bad decisions swept away like leaves. *Living with Fabian?* I press my hands into his lower back as he shifts into me, taking my face in his hands and brushing warm lips over mine.

"Of course. What were you thinking we'd be doing? I want all of you. All of him." He slides his hand down over my belly lingering there before sliding lower. His touch is feather light over my folds, and even though we made love about an hour ago my body is hot and charged with his fingers moving on where I'm still sensitive. He groans.

"All this wetness, I have to put my mouth on it," he says as he moves down, putting his mouth on me before I can get a coherent thought in my head. What was that conversation we just had? Is he changing the subject? And did we just agree we were going to live together?

"*Her*, you mean," I gasp out.

His tongue is wet and soft, and I can feel my muscles pull up inside as he rubs the tip across my clit, my legs sliding wider as he growls, raising his head.

"It's a boy," he says before putting his mouth back on me, and I pull air into my struggling lungs. "I could do this all day," he mumbles into my skin.

My mind feels like it's stretching out to catch snippets of conversation. "No-o-o-o objection … h-here to that idea." The words come out in a long blur.

He lifts himself back, a smile playing around his mouth, and I feel him part me with a warm thumb as his other hand skates up my thigh. His thumb brushes my nub, gently rubbing before bending to place his mouth on top, moving his tongue and fingers on me at the same time. The wet slipperiness makes my chest arch. His lifts his head, dark lashes narrowed, watching my breasts as I move, mouth fixing into a hard, flat line. My breasts are aching, and I slide my hands over my stomach and up as he watches me cup the sensitive skin, feeling the tips harden even more under my hands.

"Fuck, Kate." He pulls himself up onto his knees, mouth shiny and wet. My eyes drift lower, snagging on the tattoos and down to where his cock is dark and erect, sexual tension radiating off him in waves.

He takes hold of my hands and pins them on either side of my head. "What am I going to do to you today?" He bends down and kisses my stomach. "Are you okay with this?"

I laugh. He's been more careful with me the last few weeks when we've had sex, and I can't say I like it. He's never been rough, but he used to flip me over, put me where he wanted me.

"Don't be careful with me. He's snugged up tight inside, you can't harm him unless you do something drastic."

"You said *him*."

I laugh, pushing against his hands. But he keeps me pinned as he inspects me.

"Tying you up, that's what I think I'll do."

I blink at him. I wasn't expecting that.

# CHAPTER 34

## *Kate*

September burns by in a blur of a waning Manhattan summer, and one night late in the month I wake in knowing immediately that something has disturbed me. I blink into the darkness, listening. The room dips as I make out the fuzzy shadows of the window and my chair, whispers of a dream, of a tattooed man, still dancing through my brain. I hold my breath, but apart from a car on the road outside, it's completely quiet. I shift slightly and something feels off—there's some damp sweat and stickiness—and as I turn over, my stomach clenches. I frown, leaning up to switch on the bedside light as I throw back the covers. I look down, and oh my God, there's the blood on my crotch, bright red on my pajamas and the sheet. I place trembling fingers on the fabric, trying to … oh God. I lift my hips, looking at the mattress. That's not just a little, is it? I squeeze my eyes shut. *It's blood, Kate. You see it every damn day.*

I stick out a shaky hand and grab my phone from the nightstand, pressing Fabian's number.

"'lo."

"Fabian." My voice comes out so goddamn shaky.

"Kate! Are you okay? It's 3 a.m."

"I don't know, I don't … I'm bleeding."

"*Bleeding?*"

My chest constricts. *He was so delighted.* "The baby, I think I'm … "

He lets out shaky breath that tickles my ear, and I hear rustling as he says, "Fuck, Kate, hold on. Hold on. Oh Christ. I'll come straight over."

He hangs up on me.

I stare at my phone for a beat. I should call my ob-gyn, but I'll just get the out-of-hours service and what will they suggest? Probably going to the ER, and at least I know the people at Bellevue. And if something is wrong … shit, I know all the things that can go wrong. Nope, I'm not risking this. I press the buttons with trembling fingers for 911, looking at the blood caked on one nail. The lady asks me questions about where I am and how much blood. "I'm a medical intern," I say, even though she doesn't ask. "It's a decent amount." *Blood always looks worse than it is.* "Someone will be with you right away," she says. "Stay on the line."

"Liss, Liss!" I shout.

I pause, pulling in a shaky breath, but the only sound is the distant rumble of a car and the woman at 911 talking to the ambulance center. Liss won't wake up with me calling. Fumbling with the phone again, I tell the 911 lady I'm hanging up to call my roommate and I'll call straight back. I press Liss's number, and it rings and rings in my ear before she answers groggily.

"Kate?" she sounds confused, not surprisingly. I'm in the next room and I'm calling her.

"I'm bleeding, Liss."

"Shit! Where are you?"

"I'm in my bedroom. I thought the phone was the best way to wake you up."

"Yeah. Shit." I hear rustling down the phone, and then her door opens in the apartment, soft feet padding along the corridor to my room. Then she appears, red T-shirt and black curls in a wild disarray, and I slump backward onto my pillows, throat tightening as I take in her sleepy concern. Her eyes widen as she takes in my pajamas and the bed.

"Oh, shit, Kate, is it bad? What can I do?"

"I don't know how bad yet." *Calm*. It could just be a small bleed.

"I'll call an ambulance." Her gaze moves to the phone in her hand.

"I've done it, but I need to call them back." I press the button again.

"Shit, but you're good." She grins at me, and it brings an answering one to my face as my eyes nip in at the sides, watering. *Friends*. Holy crap, how glad am I to have these people. I put my hand on my stomach. I wanted this so much and … I blink and blink and blink.

Liss sits quietly while I explain the situation to the operator again and she checks her records. "They're not far away now," she says.

"Have you called Fabian?" Liss says when I finish talking.

I nod. "Can you get me a pad? I want you to take my blood pressure. There's a blood pressure monitor in the cupboard under the sink in there."

She turns on her heel and trots off obediently into the bathroom, and another cramp takes hold. *I don't like the feel of that*. All my panicky patients where it turned out to be nothing … the lovely old Jewish guy flapping his hands in the ER yesterday. I need to be more sympathetic.

"It's very unlikely I'll pass out, but if I do, you need to do the talking for me, tell them I'm pregnant, get them to scan me."

The buzzer in the apartment sounds loud in the quiet, making us both jump. "That'll be them."

"Shit. Do you want me to come with you to hospital?" Liss says.

"Yes. Oh God yes. Do you mind?"

"Not at all. I'll fling some clothes on."

She races to the buzzer and tells the night doorman to let them up, and it feels like only minutes later I'm talking to a very nice paramedic who's delighted I'm an intern; and it feels normal and almost light-hearted as he teases me about not being certified yet, and am I sure I know what I'm doing? God, he's good at his job. After a series of questions which I know are all correct, a spasm grabs me across my back and abdomen and I gasp and double over, grabbing on to his shoulder for support.

"Okay, Kate," he says. "Just hold on there. We're going to get you to hospital right away."

And the second guy is there, and they're helping me onto a stretcher, Liss buzzing around, now fully dressed and gathering up things we might need. Within minutes we are in the ambulance, red light flashing over the small window as we bump through the empty streets. *Breathe in, breathe out. Breathe in, breathe out.* Nausea catches the back of my throat, and I'm breathing too fast; it's making me light-headed. The prickle behind my eyes intensifies. There's something about this situation, my mind skittering toward losing the baby and away again, and I rub my hand over my stomach in silent apology.

Liss must see something in my face because she grabs my hand. "You okay?"

My smile wobbles, and I nod as tears leak out unbidden over my cheeks.

"Yeah, you look okay. What a stupid question. Do you think you're losing it?"

I nod again, unable to articulate a single word, and she leans right over the stretcher and pulls me into a hug. She holds me so tightly but so carefully that I want her to do that forever, breathe in her soft smell of peaches and disappear into her, emerge into a velvety, sweeter world. The cotton of her T-shirt is soft beneath my hands, and I can feel her breath on my neck and the thrum of her pulse and the hard body from all her running; the sheer life of Liss coursing out of her and through us both.

"Have I told you how much I love you?" I say.

I feel her laugh through my body.

"Stop being sentimental. You'll scare me into thinking you're dying, and then there'll be no stopping my panic," she mumbles into my ear.

My mouth curls up, and the tears recede. Right on, Liss, you're a badass in an emergency situation. Maybe I'll try that line on my patients next time. Fabian, oh Fabian. *I'm so sorry.*

As if she can read my mind, Liss pulls back, eyes roaming my face. "Where's Fabian headed?"

I hand her my phone and lie back and close my eyes. "Can you call him? Tell him to go to Bellevue."

I need to hold on here: I think I'm losing the baby, but I've seen enough emergencies to know that it's never clear cut; bleeds happen all the time.

The arrival at hospital and the chat with the doctor passes in a blur, and of course there's no issues here. I've met the doctor on duty before, and if she's surprised by the pregnancy, she says nothing. Just pats my hand and tells me about her own three miscarriages and her three strapping teenage boys as she examines me and asks me how far along I am. And I choke out, "Sixteen weeks," and start crying again, tears leaking out all over the bed and the pillow. She squeezes my hand as Liss hugs me, and tells me what I already know: that they need to do blood tests and a scan and she wants to keep an eye on me. And I'm warm with the idea of being here and in her hands. This job. One day I want to be a doctor like this.

As she pats my hand, she tells me quietly that, given the quantity of blood, she suspects that I'm losing the baby, but she doesn't think there's anything worse going on. And in that moment, I'm standing next to her in my white coat, watching the words coming out of her mouth, another smiling doctor discussing someone else's pregnancy.

In the middle of all this, Fabian arrives with his hair in a wild halo around his head, clothes askew. He sits on my bed as Liss stands to the side listening to the doctor, and tears well up in his eyes as he listens too. Liss frowns at the pair of us then decides loudly that what this situation needs is good coffee. I close my eyes. Fabian's warm deep voice asking questions sends a thrill of reassurance through me.

But, of course, there's no reassurance here. When she scans, there's no heartbeat and Fabian's face crumples as he buries his head in his hands. I can't believe I'm losing it so late on the chances are …

But the doctor just says she's admitting me, that the fetus should pass naturally, but she can give me something to speed up the process if we need it.

"Josh," Fabian says, head snapping up as his Adam's apple bobs. "We called him Josh."

We did?

The doctor nods. “Of course. Josh,” she says.

And twenty-four hours later we’re asked whether we want to see him. It feels like a big question, but Fabian says yes before I can stop him, and we’re given a small bundle wrapped in a white muslin cloth. He’s tiny and perfect, and my whole chest feels like it’s trapped in a vice as I stare at the small pink and blue bundle and then at Fabian blinking. Hard lines are etched in his face.

*He was ours.* “Josh.” I swallow.

Then Fabian kisses me on the forehead, pulls me into him, and tells me that it’s all going to be okay.

# CHAPTER 35

## *Kate*

But a week later everything is very far from okay. I hear the music thumping as I approach Fabian's building, and I press my hands together to stop them shaking. Every night I've come here and it's been the same, like he's checked out. When I wake in the night, I find him sitting in the dark, drunk. He's been taking drugs too. As I walk up the stairs in the building, the music gets louder and louder, and a door opens on the second-floor landing, a red-faced man bristling in front of me.

"I've told him to turn that goddamn music down!" he spits in my face. "Turn that fucking noise off."

Two people died on me today, one of them in his teens. So, I just nod and carry on walking up the stone stairs, the man's voice echoing off the concrete walls behind me.

"I'm calling the cops!" he shouts. *Oh God, that's all I need.*

When I reach the third floor, it feels like the walls are vibrating. Another door opens on the landing, the lady's face set in a harsh frown.

"I'll turn it off," I say. "I'm sorry."

The apartment door isn't even shut when I get to it, and when I push it open, Fabian is there in the lounge dressed only in tracksuit pants, eyes closed, shouting the words to the song at the top of his voice. I look down at my phone, open up the app and turn the music off. The silence seems to echo as Fabian swings around.

"Hey! Whatchadoing? I'm singing!" he says, flinging his arms wide and beaming.

It's been the same every evening I've come here this week.

"Yeah, and every neighbor in the building can hear it and they all talked to me about it on the way up here."

"Killjoys," he mumbles, reeling toward the couch and picking up his phone. In two presses, the music starts thumping out again.

"This is the best bit! *And now …*" he sings loudly, "*we are …*" I can hardly hear what he's singing.

I tap my screen to turn the music off again. "Fab. Fab! We can't have the music on this loud. Put your headphones on!"

"Let's partayyyyyy!" he shouts, taking my hands and swinging them out to the side and around pulling me into him and dragging me in a waltz around the lounge.

And it would be funny if I wasn't bone tired. If I hadn't been looking after people all day. If I didn't feel like *I* needed to be looked after.

"Fab …"

"Don't be miserable, Kate! We're young and in the best city in the world!"

I bite the inside of my cheek as my stomach grumbles.

"I'm going to order something to eat. Have you eaten anything?"

"Na, I'm good! I'm gooooood!"

When did he eat last? But half an hour later when the delivery guy arrives, Fabian's passed out on the couch. I eat my food, shower, and pay a couple of bills online, and when I'm ready for bed, I sit on the cushion next to his hip examining his pale gray face. *What do I do with you now?* I take hold of his wrist and take his pulse. It's fast but not unreasonably so: I wonder what he took. Perhaps leaving him to sleep it off here is the best approach.

*

I wake up to a loud crash, and I shoot out of bed, heart racing. But as I listen, I hear feet shuffling around and a muttered curse. When I peer into the lounge, Fabian is on his feet, swaying. He blinks at me confused and then smiles a checked-out, predatory smile. Then his eyes roll and he lurches. And I try to catch him as he falls, but he comes down hard, lying on the floor groaning as I drop down beside him.

"Are you okay?" I look at his ribs, pronounced against his pale skin. "God, you're wasting away." I don't know if I'm talking to myself or him.

"Oh God, my arm," he says as his eyes roll.

"Fab, Fab." I push at him to try to examine the side of his body where he hit the floor. He feels so light as I roll him onto his back. How much weight is he losing? He grunts. "Did you eat yesterday?"

"He was so tiny," he mumbles, and my heart squeezes.

I smooth his hair back from his face. "I know that, honey."

"Blue. He was blue. Perfect like a little blue bird."

My throat tightens. I don't want to relive this. It was bad enough seeing him once, stroking his soft transparent skin as tears rolled down my cheeks.

"Fab, I can't …"

"Why aren't you more upset? You're going in to work and …"

"I'm just trying to get through one day at a time. I have to work. I can't afford another problem with the hospital."

"Ice queen Kate," he mumbles, and I stare at him, a sharp pain piercing my ribs and taking my breath away.

"What?"

"You box up your emotions like a robot. One compartment for people dying, one for your family. Cling-clang, shut the box, all sorted."

Does he know what he's saying? "This is what you think of me?" He doesn't answer. "Would it be better if I was spaced out and taking drugs?"

Nothing. I look at the side of his head. There's a bruise coming up on his temple.

"At least you'd be happy," he mutters.

*Happy?* Red-hot lava bubbles up inside me. "So, getting out of your head every night is the solution?"

He scowls at me. "It's better than trying to pretend it didn't happen, to tough it out."

"I'm not pretending it didn't happen! And I'm not the one who's in the ER every few weeks."

"Doctors. Always so clinical."

This time the pain takes hold of everything inside me.

"Shit, Kate, I'm sorry." He shakes his head and tries to push himself up, tries to kiss me. "I shouldn't have said that."

And it all rises up inside me like a wave. "But you're thinking it? Is this how you're going to deal with everything? Every time something goes wrong, I'm going to have weeks, maybe months, of helping you pick up the pieces? What about me? I'm helping *you*, picking up *your* pieces. Two people died on me today, one of them was in their teens, somebody's son." My hand lands on my chest. "I spent time talking to them today, honoring *their* child. Who looks out for me? Just because I'm quiet about it doesn't mean I feel Josh dying any less deeply. This is how you see me? You're just self-absorbed and self-indulgent and taking me along for the ride."

He's staring at me eyes barely focusing, and I can't take everything that's rising up inside me any longer. My life feels like a forest fire has swept through it ever since I met him, razing everything I ever thought I knew about myself to the ground. And I'm up and out the door before he can say anything worse.

# CHAPTER 36

## *Kate*

I close the door to the apartment and lean against it, sweat making my clothes stick to my body.

"Hey," Liss says, face appearing around her bedroom door.

"Hey," I growl.

She raises an eyebrow. "What's up? I thought you were staying at Fabian's tonight?"

I shake my head, throat tightening. And she narrows her eyes and walks across the floor to me.

"How was he? Are you okay?"

"He was high as a kite and we had an argument and he just … he said the most god-awful things to me."

She tips back frowning. "What did he say?"

"He called me 'ice queen Kate.' Said that I boxed my emotions up like a robot."

She grimaces and then looks off to the side. "I think I need a drink to hear about this."

She heads into the kitchen, pulls out two tumblers and the gin, and pours a generous measure. She waves the bottle at me, and I nod, coming to stand next to her.

"About twice what you put in yours," I say, peering into her glass.

"That bad, hunh? Tell me what happened."

We settle on the couch, and I give her a blow-by-blow account of finding him in the apartment, the loud music, and the angry neighbors. "All the shit I'm carrying, dealing with those irate people after a day of working in the ER. I just feel like I've got all this weight, and he's doing nothing for me. I *miscarried.* And even though my doctor brain knows rationally that this happens a lot and often happens for a reason, I got used to the idea of being pregnant. I wanted to meet Josh and …" Tears fill my eyes, and she leans forward and pulls me into a warm hug.

"I know, honey, and I'm so sorry you lost him."

"He had a big go at me for 'toughing it out.'" I make air quotes. "Whatever that means. So, I sarcastically said, 'I'm not that one who's in the ER every few weeks.' Then he said I was so clinical, like a doctor."

She eyes me quietly. "Which is how you're trained to be? No?"

I blow out a long breath. "He wasn't making a positive comment."

"Yeah, I get that. Honey, you're both devastated, dealing with it in your own ways." She pats my hand. "Tearing each other apart because you deal with it differently isn't helping anyone."

"I don't think getting high is a way of dealing with anything, more like burying your head in the sand."

She purses her lips. "You know I love you dearly—" she begins.

I groan.

"… I'm just going to play devil's advocate and put this out there, okay. You do close down when something bad happens, and I get that, Kate. I've met your parents, and I know what they're like, and I understand that survival for you when you were younger was to close it down. You weren't a let-it-all-hang-loose person, or even a stand-and-fight person, and it's not wrong, you just need to recognize that that's what you do, and get Fabian to understand it too."

I scowl at her, swilling my ice and getting up for a refill from the kitchen. Liss's glass is still half full.

I head back to the couch and flop down beside her.

"He sent you roses and poems and bought you a bed. He's just a man of extremes," she adds.

"You can say that again."

"He wanted a family, didn't he?"

I hate the hope this ignites in my chest. "Yes," I growl and study the herbs now wilting on our windowsill overlooking 22nd Street.

"Honey, he might mess things up every now and again, but I don't think he's an asshole."

"But am I going to deal with him falling apart for the rest of my life?"

"What makes you think he's falling apart?"

I pick at a nail on my hand. "I don't know. How do I know this isn't the start of some downward spiral?"

"Has he ever fallen apart?"

"He slashed his arm open in the hospital," I mutter.

She laughs. "I think that was a bit of Fabian extreme behavior to get you back. I mean, *really* fallen apart?"

I roll my eyes. I think about how he got into college, how he confronted Dad and Javier at the wedding, about what he survived and how he's still standing, about the way he talks to me about my work. *His confidence in me.*

Liss sighs. "At some point you have to trust people. I think you've got a decision to make. Do you trust him enough to believe he'll come through this?"

Do I? Am I the one that can't give trust here? I take a large gulp of my drink, and fizz shoots up my nose I try and inhale, making it worse, and bend over my knees as my throat closes. Liss thumps me on the back, and I wave my hand at her.

"Handsome charming men are the worst," she says, and I can hear the smile in her voice.

I start to wheeze-laugh.

Liss squeezes my arm. "Talk to him, Kate." She leans against the back of the couch, and I turn my head to look at her turning her glass around in her hand. "He was prepared to change his life radically to fit around having a child. He gave up a lot of what held him together. It all matters so much to him; *you* matter so much to him. I think he's allowed a little meltdown over this, don't you?"

I can still see the joy on his face when I told him I was pregnant ... I can replay the conversation about moving from the apartment he's lived in ever since he came to New York.

"I lost Josh too. Aren't I allowed a meltdown too?" I say defiantly.

"Maybe you are; maybe that's what he's trying to say to you. Maybe he wants you to lean on him a little, to let go a little with him."

I stare into my now empty glass. I'm not used to sharing my feelings with other people, but maybe he isn't either. Ugh. It's just so hard to break the tendency to guard myself, even a little.

Tomorrow. I'll let him sleep it all off and talk to him tomorrow.

# CHAPTER 37

## *Fabian*

When I come to, I'm lying on some dirty worn-out mattress in an old building. I blink up at the holes in the ceiling: I remember some girl offering me a bottle of vodka and staggering along a street supported on someone's shoulder. I turn my head on the mattress, and right enough there's a body buried in a sleeping bag. *Nothing happened.* I'm fully clothed, cold seeping in through the holes in the windows, rubble on the floor, plaster and wood and graffiti everywhere. *A squat.* I sit up on the edge of the mattress How did I get here? How many days have gone by? An image of a lifeless tiny body pops into my head, and I groan. Is this how the slide down into oblivion happens, one awful incident that sends you down a track of no return? Is this what happened to Zach? Looking for something, anything that would help him cope with things he kept seeing in his head? Probably our father. My chest aches.

Josh seems to live in my bones. This past week all I could hear from the park across the road were the shrieks and laughter of children playing, and I wanted to lean out of the window and shout at them to shut the fuck up.

I don't think I've seen Kate for days, and I scrabble in my pockets for my phone, but come up empty. Fuck, maybe I didn't bring it out with me. But that's a good thing: People will steal it in a second if you're out of it. Every day I see the pain etched in Kate's face, grooves around her mouth getting deeper, and I don't know what to do about it, how to help. Will she implode eventually if she can't let it all out?

The need to pee pulls at me, and I drag myself up as the room swims. God, when did I last eat? I stumble over the rubble and past a guy curled on another mattress out into what passes as a corridor. I can see down through holes in the floor, and even though I do parkour I don't like the feel of this two-storey building. The wood creaks as I head down the stairs. Where the fuck am I? Images of last night flip through my head. I think I fell over at some point, and I rub my temple and the pain that shoots through my head takes me by surprise. An image of Kate bent over me suddenly pops up, and I stop walking. Kate was here? I stare at the decaying brickwork.

My bladder aches, and I pull my cock out and pee out of a window that's missing on the stairwell. The relief makes me light-headed, and I steady myself with my hand against the frame.

"Hey! No urinating in the building!" a voice shouts, and I freeze, tucking myself away then looking around. Where did that come from?

I move down the stairs, and through a gap in the wall, a guy with a thick neck and colorful tattoos is sitting by a drum with a kettle over a fire. "There's a bucket in each room, your responsibility to empty it into the outhouse over there." He gestures toward a ramshackle hut standing on an area of muddy ground.

Fuck. I don't want to rub the long-termers up the wrong way. "No problem, sorry about that." He inclines his head, and I look around, trying to get my bearings, Brooklyn I think, then look back at the guy poking the fire under the kettle. "How long have you lived here?" I ask.

"About ten years." He jerks his chin up.

And I examine his face. "Have we met before? I had a brother, Zach ..." I wave my arm around. "I don't remember him here but ..."

He raises his eyebrows. "I remember Zach. Crazy guy he was. Bad addict. Stole shit like they all do. He talked about a brother. You were in a circus, yeah?"

I laugh. "Only if he was high. Parkour maybe?"

He nods. "Parkour." He looks off out over the water. "I remember some crazy fucking videos," he mutters, eyes roaming over my face intently.

And I examine him back. My God, he looks beaten down. How much does this kind of life leave a toll? It's not freedom, it's attrition, it's years and years of fighting against the system. And for better or for worse, I think of my warm apartment: I know I'm part of the system, not part of the community trying to fight for a space to live in.

"You want a coffee?"

I grin at him. "That would be amazing."

He disappears into his phone, and I sink down onto an old camping chair. A couple of guys appear, and I chat to them as we share coffee and a packet of Oreos. One of them is young—I suspect a runaway who shouldn't be here—but he talks about how he's an alternative artist and musician and his enthusiasm to show me his art burns away some of my cynicism. The other young guy is quiet, nervous, and I wonder what his story is, how long he's been here.

And the reality of their life bites into me more as they talk. I've moved on from this, in fact, so long ago. It feels like I've hung around the fringes forever with my experimenting and my hacking, but I know deep down that I don't belong here and that I have the ability with Kate to let it go forever, to step into a warmer, securer place, to stop messing up my money and living on the fringes.

Eventually, I get up and give them a wave. "I need to be off," I say. "Thanks for the coffee," and I head off over the waste ground toward a road I hope leads down into Brooklyn.

I don't know what causes me to glance behind, but the quiet young guy has got up and followed me, and I stop and wait for him. He grimaces when he reaches me.

"You okay?" I ask, and he tilts his head at me as I look at his narrowed eyes.

His face is almost shimmering in the sunlight. I stare off toward the squat, and the drum has disappeared from view, just a wreck of ground and wild grasses growing everywhere.

"I'm good," he says softly, still watching me. Why is he looking at me like that? And when I reach out to touch his arm, suddenly I feel something strange take me over. My head wooly and dislocated, the horizon swimming.

The guy's face washes in and out. "You're Fabian, aren't you?"

I frown at him. I don't remember telling them my name.

I don't see the blade that pierces my side. I just feel an excruciating pain that washes through my body. And my hand locks around his wrist, his face looming over me as I stare up at the stubble on his chin. "You should keep your nose out of other people's business," he whispers, "keep your nose out of South Africa." And his feet blur as he walks away from me. I watch him wipe the blade on the grass—my blood. And I think about Kate and Josh's little lifeless body, and how much I wanted to look after her, as I go down on my knees. I have no ability to defend myself or run away, and he's back now and his foot comes up and he kicks me in the face. Pain sears through my head before everything goes black.

# CHAPTER 38

## *Kate*

The apartment seems eerily quiet when I arrive and head through to the bedroom: The room is dark but the bed is empty. I move back through to the lounge. Fabian's phone is sitting on the coffee table, and I pick it up and tap in his security code. My message from last night saying I was heading here after work and another one from this morning saying, "*I'm coming over,*" are the last ones there, unread. I walk slowly into the kitchen. It's exactly how it was when I left it, my dishes still in the sink.

On impulse I pull my phone out of my pocket and press Jo's number.

"Hey," she says.

"Did Fabian crash at yours last night?"

"No, why?"

"I don't know." I look at the food crusting on the dishes. "I'm at Fabian's and he's not here."

"Is that unusual?"

"Maybe not. He's probably out on a run, clearing his head."

"What do you mean, clearing his head?"

I give her a blow-by-blow account of how I found him high as a kite with the door open and our argument. "I came back this morning to talk to him, but he's not here and his apartment …" I stare around the kitchen again. "It's like he didn't touch anything after I left."

"What's that?" I hear Janus's voice in the background.

"Kate's at Fabian's, and he's not there. Hang on, I'll put you on speaker," Jo says, as she talks him through what I've just told her.

There's a loud rustle on the line.

"Do you think he went on a bender?" Janus echoes through the speaker, warm voice reassuring in my ear and so like Fabian's.

God, maybe those people that followed him came back and … "Maybe, but I'm in the apartment and everything's here, his phone, everything."

"He's not just popped out for some milk? Or parkour? He can be out for hours, can't he?"

"Yeah." But … "Without his phone?" I swallow. "Janus, a couple of months ago he was followed and drugged on the street."

"You *what*? *Drugged?* Are you *kidding* me? How?"

"It was in June. Months ago. After parkour. He went for a drink with Darren and someone followed him when he left the bar. He started feeling really odd and thought maybe the guy had slipped something in his drink. So, he got an alarm installed and said he was watching the messages of those hackers that attacked your company. He said that he didn't think anyone knew where he lived."

"Followed. *Fucking hell!* The crazy shit. Why didn't he tell me?"

"He didn't want to worry you. I'm sorry, Janus. Tell me what to do."

He blows out a long breath. "I can't believe that happened and he didn't tell me. Jesus Christ. What was he *thinking*?" I can hear him pacing over the floor through the line, the urgency in his voice when he says, "The alarm: was it on when you got there?"

"No."

"Is there any sign of anything unusual?"

"Like what?"

"A struggle?"

Good point. "No."

"The door's not busted in? No damage?"

"No." I move up the hallway and examine the door lock. It looks much like it always does.

"Have a look around, see if you can see anything that's missing, but don't disturb anything. We're coming over."

When Janus arrives, concern is etched into his face. Once he's inside the door, he looks around like he's expecting Fabian to materialize from somewhere. Then he starts walking through the apartment.

"And it was all just like this? Yeah?"

"Yes, except I've found his two other phones."

Janus's eyes swing to mine. "How many has he got?"

"Three, I think. An ordinary one. A secret one, and a burner."

Janus lets out a long whistle. "Three phones!"

Jo shakes her head. "Why wouldn't you take a phone with you?"

"Maybe he didn't have time?" Janus mumbles. "It's really odd. Why wasn't the alarm set if he went out this morning?"

"Unless he was too spaced out and forgot to put the alarm on last night and then someone turned up who was a threat," I say.

"The door's not damaged, though: He wouldn't open it," Janus points out.

"Okay, okay. Let's be logical here and try and rule things out," Jo says. "What are our options? He went out for milk, he's out doing parkour or running, he's been kidnapped by these people whoever they are, he's on the run, he's passed out somewhere, he's fallen in the river, committed suicide, got hit by a car."

My chest feels like someone has it in a vice, and my eyes fill with tears.

Jo makes a face. "Oh God, I'm sorry, honey. I shouldn't have said all that." She steps into me and pulls me into a warm hug.

"I can't lose him too," I mumble into her jacket.

"Have you checked the ER?" she says, and I pull back.

"Goddammit!" She's right. The most likely explanation is always the simplest one. And if he took some more drugs … I fumble in my pocket for my phone with shaking hands.

"I'll check his phones and see if I can find a number for that guy we met, Darren, see if he's out with anyone." Jo says.

Twenty minutes later, we've a big fat zero.

"Darren's organizing the guys to go out and check their usual places. He said some of them weren't the safest for a person on their own, but also that he didn't think it was likely that Fabian would go there alone," Jo says.

"What was he like when you left him, Kate?"

"High as a kite."

"Fuck, that's not good. I thought he'd packed that shit in?"

I scrub my hand over my face. "The baby, I think he …"

"Yeah, yeah, that's enough to send anyone off the rails. A bender's got to be the most logical explanation. It's just not likely that the Russians who hacked into my company would turn up after so many months." He pats my arm. "He'll be passed out somewhere."

And I nod at him. Is he just being hopeful? But he could be right—all those times I've seen him sleeping it off in the apartment. It's the most likely explanation, but my God, he's not always been safe doing that.

"We need to know where he goes to get the particular drugs he takes," Jo says.

"Do you know anything about that?" I ask, turning to Janus.

"He's never shared much about what he does, Kate. I've had a go at him about it so many times, but he's always argued he doesn't want to put anyone else in danger."

"And he just ends up putting himself in danger," Jo grumbles.

Where might he go? I think about the prostitutes down by the river, that he was followed from parkour."Do you think, Darren … Oh! Hang on, he mentioned some guy at a shelter he knew, someone he got to know when Zach was alive. Maybe he could point us in the right direction."

"Do you remember a name?" Janus asks.

I screw up my face. "Sam? Simon? … No, Steve, I think."

Jo starts scrolling through his phone. "Ha! There's a contact called 'Steve (Shelter)' in his phone."

She hands me the phone, and I press the number with shaking fingers. The dial tone echoes into my ear as I wait for the call to connect.

"Hello, Steve Miller."

"Oh, hi, Steve, my name's Kate Thurman, and I'm a friend of Fabian Adramovich and …"

"Kate! How lovely to speak to you. Fabian's told me all about you."

He has?

"Bought you some fancy-ass bed when he messed up, he told me. Is everything okay?"

"Well, actually no. That's why I'm calling." I give him a rundown of his empty apartment, the fact that his phones are still here.

"Okay, okay," Steve says. "There are several places you can check where people go to buy stuff. There were a couple of places he used to hang out when he was looking for Zach. I think he got to know some of the squatters. But some guys have also come into the hostel this morning. Let me do a quick ask around and see if anyone's seen him. There're a few people here who know him. Last night, you say?" It's like he keeps an eye on people for a living, and maybe he does.

"Anytime between 3 a.m. and well, now really."

"Okay, give me ten minutes and I'll call you back."

But it doesn't take ten minutes. Five minutes later, Fabian's phone buzzes in my hand, and I put it on speaker and place it on the table.

"Steve?"

"Yeah, a guy here says he saw him last night, down in Greenpoint. There's an old factory building that squatters have been living in for years. He said they were having some kind of party. Said he was off his face, could hardly walk. It's near the old Budweiser factory on Huron Street."

It could still be bad but thank God he's not been kidnapped.

Janus nods. "We'll find it, and thanks, Steve."

"Hope you find him. That's not a great place. The guy who runs it is involved in all sorts of stuff. Let me know, yeah? I'm worried now. We've been friends a long time."

Another friend of his I've never heard about. He talks about preferring his own company, but he has so many friends in this city.

"The Uber is five minutes away," Janus says, and I grab my bag as we head down to the street.

# CHAPTER 39

## *Kate*

The cab drops us off in front of a wasteland by an overpass, and I stare at the wire fencing all the way around.

"You think this is it?" We got the cab guy to drive the whole area.

"There's nothing else," Janus says.

"It's all fenced off."

"We could go over the top," Janus says. He eyes the barbed wire at the top of the fence. "We need some wire cutters."

"Before we wreck their fence, let's just check it out," Jo says, rolling her eyes, and Janus grins, kissing her temple. "Mr. Impatient," she mutters.

But looking at the unbroken line of this fence I'm thinking Janus might be right: Cutting a hole could be the only way in here.

We split up going separate ways along the road, and I hurry along, birds wheeling overhead looking for scraps. Eventually, I spot a dirt path on the other side of the fence, and lo and behold a section has been cut so it lifts easily. I shout and wave toward where Janus and Jo are headed in the opposite direction, and they both turn and start trotting down the sidewalk toward me.

I head through the fence and across the dirt path on uneven ground.

It all seems so quiet in the early-morning air, two gulls swooping over the East River, sirens over the Manhattan skyscrapers a distant wail. The path weaves through piles of junk strewn across a grassy area, leading toward what looks like a derelict building. There's a noise, and I stop. Janus and Jo are not far behind me now. I start forward, but then I hear it again.

"Hello?"

Then unmistakably, a groan. Up ahead. And as I go past a pile of oil drums, there's a man on the ground and … my God, it looks like … oh my God, it's him!

"Kate?" Janus's voice drifts over from behind me.

"Over here!" I shout, going down on one knee to get a better look at Fabian. His face is grey, his lips turning blue.

"Call 911!" I shout. "Right now!"

I slide my hand to his neck, and his pulse is thready, weak, and I scan down his body, lifting his eyelids, and I'm surprised when his pupils look normal. What the fuck's happened to him?

"Oh my God!" Janus says, sliding onto his knees beside me. Jo's right behind him with her phone held to her head as she talks to the operator.

"What's happened?"

"I don't know, but he's not in good shape."

I lift my knee, and it's then I notice the blood on the ground and on my pants.

"Oh shit."

Janus and I roll him as best as we can, and I desperately wish I had some kit, anything. The blood's soaking out through his clothes from his side. I pull open his coat and yank up his T-shirt. Then I see it: There's a wound in his side, blood bubbling out of it.

"Oh my God," Janus says, going white.

I strip off my hoodie. "Hold that to the wound." I show Janus what to do, how to apply pressure.

"What's happened?" Jo says, still holding with the operator.

"Looks like a knife wound," I say. "How far out are they?"

Jo concentrates on the phone for a few seconds. "She says about five minutes. Do you want to talk to her? I take her phone and take the operator through the situation, listen to her talking to the ambulance crew as I examine the blood on the ground and try to work out how much he might have lost and how fast it's leaking. "One minute out," the operator says, and I suck in a deep breath. Thank God.

"Go back and direct them here," I say to Jo, handing her the phone, and she's off along the path, red hair flying. I put my hand back on his pulse, checking as Janus presses on the wound, face lined with worry.

"Who the hell did this? Fuck, this is my fault, I should have got him some security," he says. "I knew this was a problem; it's not like I can't afford …"

"What about me? I left him last night when he was out of it."

*Come on. Come on.* And just as I think it, Jo appears with two guys and a stretcher and, thank you, Lord, an IV drip. As they check his stats and fix up the IV, I tell them I work in the emergency department and what I've done so far, and soon we have him on the stretcher. The guys trot over the ground as we race along behind, manhandling him through the makeshift gate and into the back of the ambulance.

I climb in as Janus and Jo stare at me through the open back of the van. "We're going to the ER in Brooklyn. I'll see you there. Call Darren and Steve, and let them know we've found him."

# CHAPTER 40

## *Fabian*

For the first time, I'm not here because of something I've done to myself. But I also don't get it: Didn't I just die out on a wasteland right after an epiphany that my life wasn't like this anymore? Didn't I think that my visits to hospitals were a thing of the past? But the cold hard hit of relief inflates my chest. Unless this is some halfway house to the afterlife, I've not died just as I found something good in my life.

Someone squeezes my fingers, and my eyes fly down to my hands and then over to see Kate sitting there in scrubs, no less. I squeeze back and lift her fingers to my mouth.

"Do you think I'm going to spend the rest of my life in hospitals apologizing to you?"

This gets me a curl of her lips.

"What's my prognosis?"

"We've operated on you. They nicked a blood vessel and we had to go in to control the bleeding. You also had a nasty head wound, but we've stitched that up too, given you blood, and you're fine."

I close my eyes. "That sounds good. That's definitely very good." I kiss her fingers again, lips against her knuckles. "I really don't think this one was my fault, or at least not directly."

She chews her lip. "What do you remember about last night?" There's some expression on her face I don't quite understand.

I shake my head. "I remember waking up in a squat this morning. Last night, not so much. I remember staggering along the road." Lights flash through my head. "Cars. Meeting some people." I frown. "It's all mixed up with you somehow. Were you there?"

"I came home and found you spaced out in the apartment playing music at full volume." She looks away.

I frown at her, and she starts a step-by-step account of last night and everything that's happened since. As she runs through the story more and more flashbacks appear: Kate in my apartment in her lounge pants, a cup of coffee in her hand … dancing together … Kate bent over me on the floor. Then she tells me about what I said to her, and my whole body curls over, and I press my thumbs into the corner of my eyes.

"Please tell me I didn't say that." My throat tightens. "I'm so fucking sorry I said that to you. You have to know you're not like that at all, not under the surface; you're so full of life and strong, Kate, so sorted. I don't feel I'm like that, and I'm scared, scared of fucking everything up, and when Josh died I just … Every day I could see the pain in your face, and I didn't know how to help you."

"You could have just talked to me."

I look over at the hospital window. "It's not my first instinct to do that. But I swear I'll try harder in future. Forgive me?"

"I think we just deal with things in such very different ways and I …"

"We'll learn," I say, squeezing her fingers. "Learn how to adapt to each other. Yeah? That's if you forgive me, of course." I give her my best winning smile, and she laughs, nodding.

"I actually came back to the apartment this morning to sort things out with you, and then you were gone and I was worried. All your phones were there." She shakes her head. "Everything was where I left it, and you never go out without at least one phone. I called Janus and Jo, and we called Steve and he did some asking around. Darren too."

My God, these guys.

"I know I've said this to you before, and you've no reason to believe me more now than then, but I am so done with this, Kate. Just seeing all those people at the squat this morning—that's not my life. The experimenting wasn't really either, despite the relief it gave from the thoughts and the sheer barrage of bullshit in my head sometimes. I feel like I was trying to live Zach's life for him, to honor him and his choices in some fucked-up way. Deal with the guilt that I got away, and he didn't. I don't know. But whatever, it's not me now. Perhaps it never was. I'm going to get some counselling, see if I can't unpack it all a little."

She gives me a tired smile. "That sounds like a good decision. What happened on the wasteland this morning? Janus is beside himself. Me too actually if I'm honest for leaving you."

Oh God. I groan. "I don't know how I got there. I don't remember leaving the apartment, but I woke up there this morning. I hung around for a bit, had coffee with one of the old-timers there, and then …" The whole odd conversation burns through me. "One of the guys followed me when I left. Things were swimming in and out; I wonder if they put something in my coffee. But, Kate, he said, 'to mind my own business, to keep my nose out of South Africa.' It's something to do with the digging I've been doing on this job."

Her eyes go wide. She gets up and paces away from the bed. "You said that my father's company was involved in that. Please tell me this isn't something to do with my *father*?"

"I don't know. I uncovered a huge amount of information about bribes from Xeracorp going back decades. They've been paying off politicians there for years."

"I'm going to fucking kill him." Then her face suddenly falls and her hands flutter to her cheeks. "Oh my God, I told him you could hack into anything. This is my fault."

I frown at her. "When did you tell him that?"

"When I went to see him about Josh." Her voice comes out small. "Oh, what did I do?"

"No, no, no, Kate. *I* challenged him at the wedding. He knew I was looking into his company. I should never have exposed myself like that, but he and Javier were such assholes, I couldn't resist. I dug my own grave here." I blow out a long breath.

None of it adds up, though. Why would her father do that? "It's all odd to be honest. I don't think these guys at the squat knew who I was to start off with. The guy who stabbed me said, 'You're Fabian, aren't you?' I mean I'm sure he was checking he had the right guy, but your dad knows who I am; he could have tracked me down at any time I'm with you. Why would your father have me stabbed in some squat on an industrial park? It just doesn't make any sense."

But her face is devastated. "Kate." I reach up to squeeze her fingers. "Your dad might be an asshole, but do you really think he'd employ some young street kid with a knife?"

She chews her lip.

"The old-timer at the squat knew Zach," I say. "I think Zach told him I'd worked in a circus, the lunatic. We talked about parkour. There was nothing to link me to South Africa ... Oh God, someone asked Darren about me at parkour, that guy followed me from parkour. Maybe word was out on the street that they were looking for someone called Fabian who did parkour. Maybe I gave myself away."

"People really inform on other people like that?"

"If there's money involved, yeah. I need to report into Jeff what's happened. It's a significant escalation, and they'll want to know. I don't think I've got the whole picture here."

"Jeff? Who's they?"

"The FBI."

"You were employed by the FBI?"

I laugh. "Not directly."

# THREE MONTHS LATER

# EPILOGUE

## *Fabian*

For the first time in my life, I am settled. I don't know why I did all the crazy shit I did, what was missing from my life before, but Kate has filled that hole. With her clothes in my wardrobe and her bottles in my shower, the apartment feels like a home, safe and warm. I am cared for. And I'm doing a lot more of the boring stuff, and, somehow, it's okay. I have found the one person who will forgive all my missteps, who will sustain this despite everything. I am good enough for her.

Jeff fed back what happened to the FBI, and of course they wanted to talk to me. It meant me getting on their radar as a hacker, but once you've been knifed like that, things take on a new slant, and talking to them seemed like the least of my worries.

Apparently, Xeracorp have been trying to back out of this South Africa thing and cover their tracks ever since I warned Kate's dad, but it turns out there's all sorts of other parties involved. There's a bunch of thugs who don't want the gravy train to disappear, and the FBI suspect it was these guys who were following me, drugged and eventually stabbed me. They think these goons thought I was a Xeracorp guy because of the connection to Kate and her dad, and decided it was time to deliver a warning. If the assholes hadn't tried to kill me, I guess I would have found that funny.

My woman is a tiger too. She went to see her father, confronted him with what had happened to me, and although he didn't pull the trigger, he's the one who created the whole mess in the first place by doing these dodgy deals and paying a shit-ton of bribes to all these people, so in my mind he's fucking responsible. Of course, he just blustered, but the wheels of justice are grinding slowly, and the investigation is closing in, and her whole family is in uproar. I can't say I'm not hoping he sees a little jail time. There's no trace of the young guy who stabbed me, though, and the old-timer at the squat has disappeared too. I have a feeling they might find him at the bottom of the East River.

The front door shuts with a soft click, a scuffling noise of boots being toed off in the hall, and I stretch my arms over my head and check the time on my screen. 18.30. I've more work than I can deal with at the moment, turns out when you approach people and talk about what you can do, they bite your hand off.

This one I'm working on is a doozy, though. They're going to be delighted with the holes I've found in their system, or not, as the case may be. The chief executive was an asshole, and so convinced that his security was watertight, he let me build all sorts of performance bonuses into the contract. I'll make a ton of money on this; their systems are as leaky as shit. I've been tempted to take it all down for a laugh, so maybe the self-destruct button hasn't quite left me yet. They'd probably fire me. I guess I like things that make other people pay attention. Maybe I'll always like those things. And maybe I can sock this money away in case something else happens. That fear still niggles at the back of my mind.

All the shame I've been carrying around, my father telling me I'm a useless little shit, feeling the back of his hand whenever I messed up, has lessened its grip. Kate and I went to a dinner hosted by one of the doctors from the hospital a few weeks ago and when I came back from the john, I paused outside the kitchen hearing Kate's voice and my name.

"He's kind of a genius—all these other hackers look up to him. He's massively respected in his field."

I laughed quietly, but it still caught me in the back of my throat. My *field*? Hacking is a *profession*? What a doctor's way of describing things. But hearing it made me feel ten feet tall and flooded with a love so powerful it almost knocked me over. Several of the nurses at the dinner also came up and talked to me about all the romantic gifts I'd sent to Kate, and while I've not quite managed to throw off all the fuckups with her, I've grasped a branch and pulled myself out of the river.

Kate appears in the doorway, still in her scrubs. Her hair is clipped back, her face bare of makeup, even though I saw her apply it this morning as I sat on the toilet seat and she chatted about her patients. She crosses the floor and bends to press a kiss against my lips.

"Ugh, I need a shower," she says, but I slide a hand around her thigh before she can escape and she straightens, so I stick my face in her stomach and inhale, rubbing my nose from side to side across the blue fabric. "Mmm, antiseptic and handwash."

She laughs, pushing at me to move away, but I don't let go of my grip and smile up at her. "My favorite smell in the world, on my favorite girl."

She relaxes into my hold, smiling, and peers at my screen.

"How was your day?"

"Excellent. I did an insanely early parkour run. Came back and had amazing shower sex with this incredible woman I live with, then spent the day getting into various parts of Quixcomm's systems and was very tempted to take the whole thing down because their network is as leaky as shit and it wouldn't be hard to do it."

Kate runs her fingers through my hair. "I wanted to talk to you … They've said they want me to take a permanent role in the emergency room when I finish my residency."

My eyes widen. "Seriously? After everything? Are you pleased?"

She laughs. "It feels amazing given where I was nine months ago."

In my mind, she's been good enough ever since that first day she sorted me out in the ER. But she hums a little staring out the window. "They said I've demonstrated a great combination of compassion and good clinical judgment. I can't quite believe it to be honest, but it feels important to apply my knowledge this way."

"Are you going to do it?"

"What do you think?"

"I think I have an incredible woman who spends her days rescuing people. I think you're amazing, Kate. I've always thought that."

She laughs and taps my arm, and I pull her down into my lap and close my eyes so I can sink into her.

"We could try again?" It echoes through my head as she rests her chin on my hair.

*What*? Where did that come from? My eyes snap open again as an icy wind blows through my lungs.

"No."

She pulls back to look at me. "What? Why?"

I groan. "It was the wrong time for you, Kate. You need to finish your residency. There's no denying that it would have been difficult." I shake my head; there's no way I can do this right now. "I don't even want to be thinking a thought like that when he died. I keep imagining him as a toddler, teaching him to walk. That probably sounds totally insane."

"That's your subconscious filling in the gaps."

"Thanks, Dr. Kate."

"But maybe it's never the right time when you get pregnant."

"No, Kate. I'm not ready to go there yet. Not so soon."

"I want you to know I'm ready when you are," she says, and something sharp and sweet lifts my chest.

"You want to get pregnant again?"

She pulls herself off my knee and flops onto her back on the bed, and I stand and follow, falling down beside her and watching her face as she stares at the ceiling. When I look up, the sun is playing across the cracks and indents in the old plaster.

"Maybe, but I'm not sure it's for the right reasons. I miss the idea of where we'd be now. I missed meeting him." I watch her eyes pinch, my throat starts to tighten, and dammit, I want to stop the tears from leaking out.

"Okay." I prop myself up on my elbow. "I want kids." My hand tenses on her hip. "When I think about the mess I grew up in, I want to build something new and … children are part of that. But … not just yet."

She smiles up at me. "Okay."

She gives so much to me, every time. She's assuming that I won't mess up again, or if I do, we'll survive it. Her confidence in me, in our future, burns through me like a sparkling flame.

"Four," I say.

She grins. "That's actually the same number as my family."

"I don't actually care how many, I just … Not two, I guess." I squint at her. "With Zach and the fact I lost him, two wasn't enough." I lower my head and rub her nose with mine. "I love you."

She covers my mouth with her fingers. "I love you too."

She grasps my face in her hands, and I still. "What?"

"I want to give you everything. Everything you never had. I want to give you a family, me and, whenever we are ready to try again, kids. I'll go anywhere you want me to be, Fab, work anywhere. When you're in prison in Siberia, I'll be there too."

My laugh is rust, water, and relief, and it feels so good inside, like cotton wool and fire. Her eyes shine as she smiles.

And just like that, it's all settled.

THE END.

# THE TECHBOYS SERIES

THE REFUSAL

THE OUTCAST

All books available now, in paperback and for Kindle, from Amazon.

# REVIEWS AND MORE

I really hope you've enjoyed *The Outcast*, the second book in my *Techboys* series!

If you have, please consider leaving a review on either the book's Amazon page or any review sites that you frequent. Your feedback and support is greatly appreciated.

There are more books to come in the *Techboys* series and I'd be super-excited to share them with you. If you'd like to be the first to hear about the new releases, pre-orders, bonus chapters and special freebies, please join my VIP mailing list:

*evemriley.com/signup*

Thanks so much!

# ACKNOWLEDGMENTS

In the early days of *The Refusal*, I couldn't have imagined where the book would end up, especially as an inexperienced indie author. This last year has been a whirlwind, and after *The Refusal* won and was shortlisted for twenty-one awards, it created a huge pressure for book two, and, of course, a need for Fabian to live up to Janus.

But although Janus and Jo were book one, Fabian came to me first with all his drug-experimenting irreverence, and because he was my first love, this book needed a little extra tlc. And perhaps this is why the book has taken me so long. Or maybe I was just scared by the second-book-after-a-success thing.

Whatever. We are here! And I have *so many* people to thank.

I couldn't be more grateful to all the people who pushed me along and helped me get *The Outcast* into shape. To the lovely Sam Boyce, who was ruthless with me when I thought I was there with the first edit: I wasn't, and you helped me more than you know in nailing down what was wrong with the story. Your love for this series has helped immeasurably. To Robert Tuesley Anderson: Without your attention to detail and constant questioning, none of it would really add up. But also your little comments through the text like "nice line" or "great chapter" have made all the difference to my still-shaky confidence.

I am not a doctor, but I wanted the book to feel real. So I owe groveling thanks to all the medical people who beta-read *The Outcast* and checked all my medical scenes. Emily Day, Emily Hennah, Fiona Hussey and Terri Korenstein, I am very grateful for all your positive and thoughtful feedback. My apologies to you all if what I have written doesn't match up to the brilliant advice you gave. And also apologies to the person who said, "If only working in a hospital was this exciting." I feel your pain: I have always wanted my life to be as exciting as a romance novel.

Some of you know that this book was originally called *The Risk*, but with a number of other big titles in the romance space using this title, it was clear that I needed something else. I now have endless lists of "The *something*," to call on depending on how big the series gets. But thank you to Caroline Chitty, who eventually came up with *The Outcast*—the perfect description for Fabian.

To the villages that are BookTok and Bookstagram—thank you for your patience! The messages that you sent letting me know you were waiting were a real encouragement as well as a terrifying reminder! But the kindness you've shown to this newbie is more than I could ever have hoped for. Thank you for being a part of this journey. To all the bloggers, influencers, and book fanatics who helped me spread the word about *The Refusal*, thank you. Alyssa, Amanda, Anne, Ashley, Ayana, C.G., Chloe, Chrissie, Ciarrah, Clare, Courtney, Dodie, Emma, G.H., J.D., Jennie, Jessica, Kat, Lauren, Leigh, Lina, Linda, Lori, Taylor, Shay, and Vivien—I haven't forgotten what all of you did for my first book. And also to those who have come along with me for *The Outcast*: Andrea, Ann, Anna, Ashley, Bianca, Bobby, Byn, Carol, Catherine, Dana, Devon, Em, Emma, Erika, Fabi, Hannah, Jazmin, Jenna, Jessica, Kelly, Kerri, Kristina, Kym, Leigh, Lucid, Mac, Megan, Michaela, Nattie, Nicole, Patricia, Presley, Rudra, Sam, Sandie, Sionna, Susan, and Tammy.

To the lovely Nicky Melville, who keeps putting interesting writers, great ideas, and good writing in front of me. Thank you for being a great teacher, always being positive, even when the poetry was dire. To the girls of my writing group: Clare, Eimear, Jan, Jill, Kirsty, and Moira—we have a laugh every Friday, and I hope our sessions continue until none of us can make it up the stairs to each other's apartments anymore. I couldn't ask for a better group to hang out with.

To Mark Thomas, who produced a wonderful design which is coming ever more to life as we head through the series. I love it, and I love even more how it stands out as something different in romance. Thank you for all your hard work on the cover and the interior pages of this book, and for always turning things around so fast.

To my family, Rob, Grace, and Joe: thank you for always stepping in when I need your help and for your unfailing conviction that I am always writing a bestseller! Rob, who patiently read through every version of this manuscript: thanks for all your questioning and understanding of the male perspective. You have encouraged me at every point along the way, and I appreciate everything you do for me, every day.

To Grace, this book's for you. Having your help and support on *The Refusal* got me off the starting blocks and got the books that had been sitting on our computers at home for years out into the wild. Your work on all the marketing for this series has been nothing short of amazing: I couldn't have done it without you.

To everyone who reads this book or recommends it to a friend—thank you from the bottom of my heart. All books are important, and authors put years of effort into them. It means so much to me that you've enjoyed reading a story as much as I have enjoyed writing it! I'm looking forward to many more happy years of *The Techboys Series* and my lovely readers.

# ABOUT THE AUTHOR

I have worked for many years in the tech startup scene writing screeds of notes,* the results of which have inspired *The Techboys Series*. *The Outcast* is the second novel in this series, and in all eight books are planned.

I love helping people escape their daily lives for a short while with the help of some steamy romance, some fun, strong women, and gorgeous fictional boyfriends. *The Techboys Series* revolves around three young men, Janus, Fabian, and Adam, who by chance sit next to each other in their first computer science lecture at college. Their contrasting personalities result in them helping each other out, and, as they rescue one another from various scrapes, a deep bond develops. The books meet them years later in New York City as they struggle to get their lives on track.

I am a Scottish author living in Edinburgh with my husband and I have two grownup children. When I'm not reading or writing, I love running and can often be found in local cafés or out enjoying the beautiful wilderness of Scotland.

Thanks so much for buying this book. It's a joy when people reach out to me, so please feel free to contact me as follows:

Website: www.everiley.com

Instagram: @evemriley
TikTok: @evemrileyromance
Goodreads:www.goodreads.com/author/show/21475584.Eve_M_Riley

* Although I am surrounded by techies, I'm not, myself, a techie by background, which explains why all the tech references in the books are suitable for people whose level of understanding is plugging a wire into their phone to charge it up.

Manufactured by Amazon.ca
Acheson, AB

11247133R00164